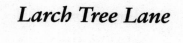

Larch Tree Lane

By Anna Jacobs

THE LARCH TREE LANE SERIES

Larch Tree Lane

THE PENNY LAKE SERIES

Changing Lara • Finding Cassie
Marrying Simone

THE PEPPERCORN SERIES

Peppercorn Street • Cinnamon Gardens
Saffron Lane • Bay Tree Cottage
Christmas in Peppercorn Street

THE HONEYFIELD SERIES

The Honeyfield Bequest • A Stranger in Honeyfield
Peace Comes to Honeyfield

THE HOPE TRILOGY

A Place of Hope • In Search of Hope
A Time for Hope

THE GREYLADIES SERIES

Heir to Greyladies • Mistress of Greyladies
Legacy of Greyladies

THE WILTSHIRE GIRLS SERIES

Cherry Tree Lane • Elm Tree Road
Yew Tree Gardens

THE WATERFRONT SERIES

Mara's Choice • Sarah's Gift

⁓

Winds of Change • Moving On
Change of Season • Tomorrow's Path • Chestnut Lane
In Focus • The Corrigan Legacy • A Very Special Christmas
Kirsty's Vineyard
The Cotton Lass and Other Stories
The Best Valentine's Day Ever and Other Stories

a&b

Larch Tree Lane

ANNA JACOBS

Allison & Busby Limited
11 Wardour Mews
London W1F 8AN
allisonandbusby.com

First published in Great Britain by Allison & Busby in 2022.

Copyright © 2022 by ANNA JACOBS

A CIP catalogue record for this book is available from
the British Library.

First Edition

ISBN 978-0-7490-2866-4

Typeset in 11/16 pt Sabon LT Pro by
Typo•glyphix, Burton-on-Trent DE14 3HE

Printed and bound by
CPI Group (UK) Ltd, Croydon, CR0 4YY

Chapter One

Wiltshire

When Lucia decided to leave her husband, take back her own name and become Ms Grey again, she found a unit to move out to and took all her things from their house before telling him she was going.

'*What?*' Howard's fury at her for daring to end their marriage was so fierce it echoed round the house.

'It's surely not a surprise. We haven't been getting on for a while now and you're sleeping in another room.'

'I was going to work it out.'

'It takes two to make a marriage, and I no longer want to work it out.'

'You're not leaving!'

When he raised his fist, she snatched up the nearest implement, a ghastly ornament he'd brought with him, and brandished it at him. 'Don't you dare touch me.'

She edged towards the door. She'd been right to get her things out before she took the final step.

As she stood by the door, she asked, 'Do you want to do this amicably and save money or are you going to pay a fortune to a lawyer?'

'It's not worth paying to keep you, but I'll make damned sure I get my fair share of the goods and chattels, believe me.'

From then on, he made every step of the process more difficult than necessary. He even appealed formally about the jewellery passed down from her grandmother being excluded from the financial settlement. But to her relief the appeal was dismissed because she'd inherited it on her twenty-first birthday, long before she met him.

Thank goodness she'd kept her finances separate! That had caused their first quarrel, but when you married at twenty-nine you were used to having your own money.

After the divorce was finalised, Lucia breathed a sigh of relief and prayed she'd never have to speak to him again.

That hope didn't last long. Howard stopped her in the street a few days later, smiling and speaking quietly so that no one could overhear what he was threatening.

'I'm not going to accept that financial settlement. You'll see. I'll be one step behind you till you sell that jewellery and give me my fair share of the money it brings. I know exactly how much it's worth because I had it valued too.'

'Go away and leave me alone. We're divorced now. It's over.'

'Not until I get my money. You'll find out, as others have, that no one *ever* gets away with cheating me or messing me about in any way.'

After that there were several nasty little incidents she was sure were down to him: a serious scratch along the side of her car, two flat tyres late at night when she was inside a restaurant with friends, the bedroom window of her rented unit smashed by a half brick hurled through it in the small hours of the morning, showering her dressing table with broken glass.

He walked past her several times in the street not saying anything but running one finger across his throat in a slashing gesture.

It was the stuff of nightmares. Would it ever stop?

Maggie was feeling old that morning, so she stared at herself in the mirror on the landing and stuck her tongue out. This usually made her laugh, it was such a silly thing to do. Today it failed because the mere thought of turning seventy next month was upsetting her more than she'd expected.

She sneaked another look in the mirror. Her hair looked pretty and like most of her family she had only a light frosting of grey. She'd been a bit plump all her life so she wasn't going to start starving herself now in what she knew would be a vain attempt to become slender. Been there, done that, total waste of time with the Hatherall genes.

No, she was doing OK for her age with regard to appearance. It was just the thought of being seventy that was getting to her.

She started walking down the stairs then ran down them instead. There! She was still able to do that with ease. 'You go get 'em, girl!' she told herself. But who or what was she going to 'get'? That was the problem. Her closest friends were starting to move away to live nearer to their children, a few of whom had settled in the valley, 'in case'. A couple of the older ones had died recently and another one was ill.

When they said growing old was not for the faint-hearted, they were right.

Don't get maudlin, she told herself firmly. *You're physically fine and you've still got things to do.*

Her main concern at the moment was to find a way to ensure that this house would still be cared for after she was gone. It had been in the family for over two centuries and she didn't want to be the one who let it slip into other hands. It was such a warm, lovely place to live, a comfortable little manor house, not a stately home or anything.

But she couldn't seem to figure out which of her relatives to leave it to. Which one, if any, would keep it safe? The men of her branch of the family hadn't done well with their lives. Her older brother had never married and had died ten years ago, leaving her as the last of this branch of the family.

The only relative who still lived reasonably close was a cousin ten years younger whose company Maggie didn't really enjoy. It had especially annoyed her when Sheila had hinted more than once that she would love to have the old house 'to love and care for' when the sad time for that came.

As if! Sheila would sell it to a developer as fast as she could. In fact, one of her closest friends *was* a developer. And whoever bought it would certainly find a way to persuade the local council to change the zoning, then would build small identikit houses on the land, with gardens not much bigger than tablecloths, even if they were forced to keep the listed family home intact.

And why was she standing here going over the same old ground? 'Get on with your day, Maggie Hatherall. What will be, will be.' Oh dear! She was talking to herself aloud again, something she'd vowed to stop doing. That's what happened when you lived alone.

She saw that the clouds had passed. Good. She'd go out for a walk and enjoy the bluebells. She tried to walk most days because exercise was good for you. She only used the lower part of the semi-circular drive these days to drive in and out of the grounds, so she'd finish her walk along the upper part of the drive. It was overgrown with gates that no longer closed properly but she liked to keep an eye on it.

From mid-April to early May it was no chore to walk there because the beauty of the bluebell woods filled her soul, making her feel relaxed and happy. And they were an English variety, too, growing naturally here and smelling beautiful, not the showy foreign invaders which were almost scent-free.

Locking the house doors and slipping the key in her jacket pocket, she strode briskly towards the patch of natural woodland between the two parts of the drive, slowing down when she reached it to revel in the sea of soft blue.

Ten minutes later, she caught sight of a greater spotted woodpecker and looked round eagerly, hoping it was nesting nearby. Such attractive, cheerful-looking birds.

Did that hollow in a nearby tree contain a woodpecker nest? She took another step to one side to get a better view and next thing she knew her foot twisted awkwardly as she trod in a concealed hollow and tumbled helplessly sideways. Pain shot through her head as she landed.

When she managed to pull herself together, she realised she was lying on the ground in among the bluebells. She wiggled her arms about and they seemed all right. She moved her left leg and that was OK, but when she tried to move her right leg, pain stabbed through her ankle and she couldn't hold back a whimper. She must have twisted it as she fell. Or broken it. *Oh, please, don't let it be broken!*

She pushed herself into a sitting position but couldn't stand up because she couldn't bear to put any weight on the foot and there was nothing nearby to hold on to.

What the hell was she going to do? She hadn't brought her mobile phone with her, never did when walking round her own grounds. Her cousin had told her more than once that was stupid when you lived alone and she'd been proved right.

'You're a fool, Maggie Hatherall,' she muttered.

She decided to try crawling but that hurt too. She'd have to do it, though, couldn't lie here because people rarely used the upper drive these days, even though it was part of an ancient right of way through the grounds of Larch House.

Tears came into her eyes involuntarily at the pain of moving, but she blinked them away. 'No good crying,' she said aloud and took a few deep breaths. 'You've no choice but to do it, my girl.'

She had to stop talking to herself or people would think she was losing her wits. That was the trouble with being old: some people assumed you were automatically becoming more stupid and forgetful by the year. She wasn't. At least, she didn't think she was.

'Just do it!' she said aloud.

And even though it hurt, she continued crawling towards the road.

*   * . *

On her thirty-first birthday, a sudden attack of appendicitis sent Lucia to hospital for an emergency operation. Howard sent her a get-well card afterwards, which proved he was still watching her every move, damn him.

When she got back, she realised he'd broken into her unit and gone through every single drawer and cupboard, leaving them messy enough to show that they'd been touched but not taking anything. The police said nothing could be proved and at least she hadn't been robbed.

As if that wasn't bad enough, to her dismay, two days after she returned to work, she was made redundant.

She signed up with a temping agency for any sort of office work, something she'd done years ago as a student, because she wasn't sure yet exactly where she wanted to live, only that she wanted to move as far away as possible from Howard. His actions were, she admitted to herself, getting her down, as well as making her worry that they might escalate into something physically dangerous.

To top it all, a few days later her landlord offered her a rent-free week and full refund of her bond money, no questions asked about damage, if she'd move out at the end of that free week. He had a niece looking for a flat to rent and, well, blood was thicker than water, wasn't it? He didn't meet her eyes as he said that.

It seemed like a sign, a good hard nudge from fate to admit defeat and move away from Bristol and Howard. She decided to look for somewhere safe and quiet in the country, and try to stay off his radar. Surely he would leave her alone if he felt he'd driven her away?

Or was he serious about getting more money out of her? She drew the line there!

Their house had recently sold so she had just about enough money for a deposit on a smaller house or unit, but she probably wouldn't be able to buy one till she got another permanent job so that the bank would give her a mortgage.

The trouble was, she didn't want to move too far away because her parents lived in Bristol and when they returned from their holiday in Australia she'd want to visit them regularly – more often than she had during her marriage, for sure. They had never got on with Howard and hadn't been fooled by his initial efforts to charm them.

She planned her departure from the flat carefully, had her furniture and most of her possessions taken away in an unmarked vehicle during the time of Howard's weekly staff meeting, which she knew he never missed. She put them into storage and camped out in the flat for two days till she'd finished this temping job, sleeping on the cushions from the seat in the bay window, praying Howard wouldn't find out she was leaving.

And all the time she felt furious. Why should she have to go to these lengths to sneak away without him knowing?

It wasn't a free country for people as long as ex-partners could get away with doing that to you.

She packed the car in the middle of the final night, glad there was an underground car park at the block of units, which would hide what she was doing. And even so, she was jumpy as she moved in and out of the big, echoing space, slinging bags and boxes into the car boot any old how, till the flat was empty. She drove out of the basement car park before dawn, not switching on the car lights till she was a few streets away.

She stopped at a motorway services after about an hour and parked near the entry road for a full ten minutes to make sure he wasn't following her, getting angry all over again at the need she felt to do this.

When she continued her journey, however, she felt much better about the future. She'd done it, got away.

She turned off the M4 at Royal Wootton Bassett, simply because she liked the name. She'd never actually been to the small town before. She stopped there for a coffee and toilet break, then headed off into the nearby countryside, driving more slowly now. After a while she turned left at a minor road on a whim, because it looked so pretty, and drove even more slowly, stopping occasionally to enjoy the lush green scenery.

She didn't bother to plot a course, turning down roads simply because they looked attractive. She hadn't relaxed this much for ages.

When the car started to jerk, slowing down briefly then moving smoothly forward for a hundred metres or so, before slowing down again, she let out a yelp of dismay and studied the various dials, desperate to figure out what was happening.

It didn't take her long. The petrol gauge was showing that the tank was empty. Oh, no! She'd meant to fill the car up once she'd left Bristol, but she'd been so desperate to get away undetected, so happy when she thought she'd done it that the need for petrol had slipped her mind.

Staring round now, she saw only a narrow road and had no idea where it led. There were no signs of houses and in fact, it looked more like a lane than a road, only one car wide with occasional passing places. Burgeoning hedgerows further reduced visibility and a bend completely hid whatever lay ahead.

When had she last seen any other vehicles? Not for ages. She hadn't a clue how far she was from a village with a petrol station. All she knew was that she was somewhere in Wiltshire. And she didn't have a satnav program any longer because Howard had played a few nasty little tricks and had wiped a few programs from her car's system, doing something to stop her reinstating them. She'd get them fixed, should have done it before now. The break-up had affected her life in so many small and uncomfortable ways.

He was good with digital stuff, damn him. And she wasn't. She shook her head. *Stop that. Forget about Howard and just get on with building a new life.*

Her car's next slow-down and jerking about lasted slightly longer and she began to worry that she'd have no choice about stopping. The car seemed likely to decide that for her – and soon.

Then the road widened slightly to show a proper road. It had a sign which showed that it was called Larch Tree Lane, and there was another sign below the name directing people to turn left to the Marrakin Hiking Trail, whatever that was.

She turned the other way therefore, praying that this would take her to the nearest village. Her car must have found another spoonful of petrol in the tank because it started functioning normally, though she didn't try to drive faster.

Unfortunately, after about a couple of hundred metres the engine gave a feeble cough and cut out completely.

There was just enough downward slope for her to guide the car off the road onto the verge before it stopped. Beyond the verge was a pair of tall, ornate double gates, which must have been open for a long time, judging by the unkempt grass and vegetation growing in front of them. Behind them were huge trees, one on either side with another pair of the same trees further along the weed-filled drive.

Did the drive lead to a house or was it just the remnants of a former country residence?

She closed her eyes for a few seconds and managed not to burst into tears. 'You need to do something,' she said aloud, so got out of the car and stood listening.

There were no sounds of humanity at all, not even a hum of distant traffic, only the sounds of nature: birds, the faint buzz of an insect passing busily by and a breeze rustling the bright, spring-green leaves of the huge trees. Mother Nature might be beautiful here but Lucia would rather have found a village and petrol station for stranded travellers.

Make that stranded idiots. She definitely considered herself to have been an idiot today. That's what stress did to you, she supposed.

She had her phone with her but without her satnav had no idea where she was and anyway, there wasn't much of a signal here. She should have got a new satnav program installed. If she'd needed one sooner, she'd have got it all sorted out, of course she would, but there had been so much to deal with and she hadn't planned to go anywhere new – until today.

She shot a worried glance at her car. The possessions she felt she might need, including some of the things she valued most in the world, like her family photos, were crammed into it. She didn't like to leave it here in the middle of nowhere, but she had no choice.

'Oh, just do it,' she muttered, locked the car and set off walking along the overgrown drive, praying it would lead to some sort of habitation.

Chapter Two

Maggie managed to crawl awkwardly through the bluebells and took a short rest before tackling the short distance towards the drive. 'Come on!' she told herself. She didn't care now that she was crushing the flowers, only that she was managing to move along, albeit slowly and painfully.

After a while she had to stop for another rest and it was a struggle to hold back sobs of pain.

When a young woman walked round the bend towards her, she thought for a moment she was hallucinating then realised the woman was real and called, 'Help!' before bursting into ugly sobs of utter relief.

The stranger hurried towards her. 'What's wrong? Can I help?'

'I had a fall and – and I think I've sprained my ankle. I can't bear to walk on it. Only, people don't often come this way, so I've been trying to crawl to the road and that isn't much used either at this top end. Thank goodness you're here!'

'Oh, poor you! Shall I help you up?'

'I daren't try to put any weight on that ankle. I'm praying I haven't broken it.' She looked down the drive. 'Don't you have a car?'

The stranger flushed and looked embarrassed. 'I do, but it ran out of petrol just before I got to some big gates. Life has been, um, rather difficult lately and I was in such a hurry to get away today I forgot to fill up the car.'

Maggie stared at her in dismay. 'Oh dear. What are we going to do?'

'Don't you have a car nearby?'

'I don't live far away and I came out for a walk. My car is still at home, a couple of hundred metres away. What a pair we are! Do you have a mobile phone?'

'Yes. But the signal is very weak round here and my phone hasn't got a satnav program on it at the moment. It, um, got wiped off. I don't even know whereabouts in Wiltshire I am.'

'If you'll let me use your phone, I can try to call Ted at the garage in the village and get him to come and help me – and he can bring some petrol for you at the same time.'

She did that but Ted apologised for not being able to come immediately because he was at a delicate stage in a bodywork repair and it'd ruin the whole thing if he stopped now. He'd be there in about three-quarters of an hour, sooner if he could.

'Thanks, Ted. I'll send our visitor to fetch my car and if she can get me to the house in it, we'll both be a lot more comfortable while we wait. Try the house first. You can pick her up and take her to deal with her car.'

The phone began fading in and out and a message popped up. *Battery low.*

Maggie gave a wry smile. 'Phew! I just got through in time, didn't I? Did you hear what we said? He'll be here as soon as he can. I can't thank you enough. You're getting me out of what could have been really serious trouble.'

'You're getting me out of trouble too.'

'Well, there you are. I'm Maggie, by the way, Maggie Hatherall.'

'Lucia Grey, late of Bristol, currently of nowhere at all.'

'Are you on your way somewhere?'

'Not really. I was just driving round the countryside, trying to find a new place to live.'

Maggie stared at her as an idea popped into her mind. 'You don't sound to be doing that in any particular hurry. Don't you have a job to go to?'

'Not at the moment. I've been made redundant and at the same time I was asked to vacate my flat, so I'm just trying to get myself together again.'

'Are you on your way to stay with your family?'

'No. My parents are in Australia at the moment and they've swapped houses with an Australian family so I can't stay at their place. And, well, I'm recently divorced.'

'Must be a real turning point in your life. I've seen friends go through that. Not easy, is it?'

'No. Not easy at all. And my ex is being . . . difficult.'

'All my friends came good eventually, and you'll probably do the same, especially if you can get away from him. I'm just wondering whether you'd like a temporary job for a few days.'

The silence went on for so long that Maggie braced herself for a refusal, then realised she was being subjected to a very thorough scrutiny.

'Really?'

'Yes.' She gestured to her ankle. 'I'll need help getting to the doctor, or even to an A&E if necessary, to find out what's wrong with my ankle. And the way it's hurting when I move it, I'll need help in the house for a while till I can walk comfortably again. I don't have any close family to turn to, you see, and most of my friends are quite elderly and have enough trouble managing their own bodies. I can pay you to help me and give you a bedroom.'

They stared at one another again, neither saying a word till Lucia asked suddenly, 'What made you ask me? I'm a complete stranger.'

'It was a sudden impulse,' Maggie admitted. 'But you have an honest face and in case you're worrying, I promise you I'm honest too.'

Lucia smiled. 'You don't look crazy and I think you're definitely going to need help, so all right, I'd be happy to accept your offer. It's a godsend, actually. I'll be right off the grid here.'

Maggie closed her eyes as relief skittered along her veins. 'How about we say you help me for about four days to start off with, which will take us past the weekend, then we'll see how I'm managing to move around?'

'Sounds like a plan. How much are you paying?'

'I haven't the faintest idea. Think about it and tell me what you'd be happy with, given that I'm providing accommodation and I'll pay for the food though you'll have to cook it.'

'I'll do that. I promise not to overcharge you. And I won't let you down, I promise.'

Maggie shrugged. 'Sometimes you have to take a risk. I'm not usually wrong about people, though. After seventy years in this world, I've had a lot of practice.'

'Goodness, you don't look seventy.'

She chuckled. 'Now I know I like you. I must admit I'm vain enough to think I'm wearing quite well.'

Lucia put her phone away, happy that she'd have somewhere to sleep tonight which wouldn't cost her a penny.

It was more than that, though. She didn't want to be on her own at the moment; she felt so disoriented about where life was taking her and there was still a faint worry about Howard, she didn't know why, even though she'd checked that he hadn't been following her.

No, surely she'd be free of him now and he'd find something else to focus his nastiness on. Unfortunately, once she was settled somewhere, she'd better not give her new address to any of their mutual friends. How unfair that all was!

She realised Maggie had spoken. 'Sorry. I was thinking about something.'

'Not something pleasant from the look on your face.'

'My ex.'

'Ah. Understandable. I wonder if you could fetch my car now, please? It's parked behind the house, which is the only one at the end of this drive. If you'll get me home in it we can have a cup of coffee while we wait for Ted.'

'If you'll trust me to drive it.'

Maggie chuckled. 'It's not a new vehicle.'

'Keys?'

'It isn't locked and the keys are under the floor mat at the passenger's side.'

'Goodness, you're trusting.'

Maggie shrugged. 'It's pretty safe round here.'

'Sounds like the sort of place where I need to live, then.'

'He's really frightened you, hasn't he?'

'Yes. Anyway, forget about him. How about I help you across to lean your back against that tree trunk before I go? You look so uncomfortable, half-lying like that, and the tree is next to the drive so I can stop your car next to it.'

'Good idea. Thanks.' It was a painful transition, but they got there and as Maggie leaned back, she let out a long sigh of relief. 'Yes, that feels much more comfortable.'

'What sort of tree are these? They look attractive in pairs on either side of the gates like that.'

'Larch trees. They've been there for over two hundred years, ever since the house was built.'

'And the road I came along was called Larch Tree Lane.'

'Yes. And my house is Larch House. We don't have much imagination round here, do we? This is the top end of the drive and it isn't much used these days. There's a minor walking trail at the top end of Larch Tree Lane, not far away from here. And the lane is the major road in the district, if you can call it major. It only carries local traffic down to our village, Essington St Mary. There are various clumps of houses strung out along the sides of the lane, as we call it, and the village is right at the lower end. Even the village is a bit of a backwater, really, since no main roads pass through it.'

'Sounds more and more like the sort of place I'd like to live in. But what am I doing chatting like this when we need to get you home and comfortable? Sorry.'

'That's all right. I'm rather proud of the area I live in and I'd show you round if I were in a better state.'

From her new position, Maggie watched the younger woman stride off along the drive, then allowed another couple of tears of sheer relief to trickle out.

What would she have done if Lucia hadn't come along? It didn't bear thinking of. Her ankle was throbbing painfully even after moving only twenty or so extra metres to this tree. The whole incident was a reminder of how your life can change in a few seconds. Was it only an hour since she'd run confidently down the main stairs? She couldn't even crawl confidently now.

She hoped she was right about Lucia being trustworthy. She thought she was. The young woman was tallish, with a striking face, beautiful auburn hair and a very pleasant smile. Well, she wasn't all that young really, about thirty at a guess. But that seemed young to someone who was almost seventy.

If Lucia hadn't come along, there might have been no one passing along the upper part of the lane for a day or two because the hiking season was only just beginning.

When she crested a rise and saw what must be Maggie's home, Lucia stopped dead in amazement. Goodness! This wasn't an ordinary house but a country manor, early Georgian in style she'd guess. Not huge but what she'd heard called a 'gentleman's residence'.

She studied it with interest because she loved houses with historical character and this one had a beautiful symmetry to it. There were two windows on either side of the front door and matching windows not quite as tall on the storey above, then what must be attics above judging by the dormer windows jutting out of the roof.

Wow! This would give a fair number of rooms inside the house. And she'd be staying there. Double wow!

There were no other dwellings in sight, just some lower buildings which looked like stables or outhouses partly concealed behind the house at the right-hand side. As there were no other houses nearby, all this land probably belonged to the house as well.

She walked round to the rear as instructed and found an old Renault, faded silver in colour, small and very upright, parked to one side of a gravelled area.

She found the key and got into the car, surprised at how comfortable it was to sit in such an upright position. It started first time and purred its way happily round the house. It didn't take long to get to where Maggie was leaning back against the tree, looking white and strained, poor thing.

Lucia parked with the passenger seat as close as possible to the injured woman and helped her into the vehicle. She winced in sympathy when the poor thing banged her foot and let out an involuntary whimper.

'Thanks.'

'I'll close the car door.'

As she turned the vehicle round and set off back along the drive, she asked, 'Do I park in front or behind this time?'

'I always park behind. As close to the kitchen door as you can this time, please.'

Once she'd parked, Lucia had an idea. 'You don't happen to have an office chair on castors, do you?'

Maggie nodded. Why hadn't she thought of that? 'What a good idea, and yes, we do have an office chair. Maybe I could use that to get around downstairs at first. Most of the floors are wood or tile, so it should roll along OK. And we have a pair of crutches somewhere as well, I think.'

'Good idea. Tell me where to find the chair first. We can look for the crutches later.'

Lucia felt like an intruder as she walked through the spacious rooms to the library, which was at the far end of the building from the kitchen. The office chair was old but rattled along easily and though it couldn't be moved over the gravel outside, she put it ready just inside the kitchen doorway.

She helped Maggie to hop across and sit on it, then pushed the chair further into the kitchen. 'We should probably stay in here, don't you think? We still have to go and see your doctor.'

'Yes. I'll phone Tom first and explain what's happened. He's been my doctor for years and I know him socially. Could you pass me the phone? It's over by the window.'

While Maggie was speaking to whoever had answered her call, there was the sound of a vehicle approaching and a van with *Ted's Garage* written on the sides drew up outside. A sturdy, grey-haired man got out, striding across to the kitchen door.

Lucia went out to greet him. 'Maggie's on the phone speaking to the doctor. I don't think she'll be long.'

'You're the lady who needs petrol?'

'Yes, please. I'm Lucia Grey. I stupidly forgot to fill my car before I set off today.'

'I've got my grandson with me.' He pointed to a young

man in the van, fiddling with a mobile phone. 'If you tell me where exactly your car's parked, we can fill it up and bring it back to you while you continue to keep an eye on Maggie.'

'Thank you so much. I can pay by credit card, if that's all right.'

'That'll be fine.'

She didn't hesitate to hand over her car key because he was another person with an immediately likeable face and a warm, genuine smile. She watched the two men drive away, by which time Maggie had finished her call.

'Tom's coming round to check the ankle first. If it's only sprained, he can bind it up and save me a trip to hospital.'

'Can he be sure without an X-ray?'

'He says if there's any doubt, you can drive me to the hospital and the A&E people will check it. But it's over twenty miles away on the other side of Swindon, so I'd be glad not to have to drive there and no doubt hang around for hours. I'm feeling a bit washed out, I must admit.'

'I'm not surprised. Shock and pain can do that to you. Your friend Ted has brought his grandson and they've gone to fill my car and bring it back here.'

'How about making us all a cup of coffee? Ted never says no to one.'

By the time they'd drunk the coffee and Ted had taken her payment details then driven off again, the doctor had arrived.

He checked the ankle and said, 'I fairly certain it's not broken, Maggie, though it's a bad sprain. It'll feel a lot better if you can get the swelling down. Icing it at regular intervals should help.'

'You're sure?'

'You couldn't have done some of those movements with a broken bone.'

'Thank goodness.' Maggie sagged back in her chair and closed her eyes.

'What do I need to do to look after her?' Lucia asked.

'Ice it at regular intervals for a while, and apart from that only time and rest are needed. She's a tough old bird, should be OK in a few days. Better not let her climb the stairs yet, even on her backside. If you'll make up a bed downstairs for her, you could perhaps sleep nearby in case she needs anything during the night. There is a cloakroom down here, if I remember correctly.'

'I can do that.'

'I'll call in on my way to the surgery first thing tomorrow morning to check that she's all right. If you have any worries about her condition before then, don't hesitate to give me a call.' He handed over a business card.

When he'd gone, Lucia could tell that Maggie was ready for a nap and wheeled her to the cloakroom just off the entrance hall. After that Maggie said she'd sleep quite well on the big sofa in the library. When Lucia saw it, she wasn't surprised. It was huge, made of burgundy-coloured leather in an old-fashioned buttoned style, and would tempt anyone to take a seat.

Once again, following the older woman's directions had Lucia going into uncharted territory, this time upstairs, to get her a quilt and a blanket to go under her. What a big house it was!

She found the linen cupboard easily enough, at the end of a big gallery landing but was astonished at how big it was, more like a room than a cupboard. It was far bigger than her bathroom had been at the rented flat. It felt strange to be rummaging through someone else's possessions, but she found what she wanted quickly: a pillow, quilt, blanket and sheets.

Maggie smiled at the sight of the quilt. 'I used to have this on my bed when I was a child.'

When a bed was made, she snuggled down and closed her eyes.

Lucia stood watching her for a moment or two. The house was quiet except for the faint ticking of a grandfather clock in the hall. She'd hear Maggie calling if she was needed, but just to be sure she put a hand bell she'd found on a low table next to the sofa.

She brought everything inside from her car, just in case Howard found her and took or damaged things out of spite. Surely she'd got away from him now? She hoped and prayed so.

She'd brought her microwave oven, camping stove and kettle, thinking she might need them if she found somewhere unfurnished to rent. She could make do on those three for cooking if she had to.

She looked round and found a second pantry that was completely empty. There was plenty of room to stack all her things in it. She'd check with Maggie, but she felt sure there would be no problem about using that space. She couldn't imagine the older woman being unreasonable about anything. She added the leftover bits and pieces of food to the supplies in the fridge.

And all the time she worked, she had a strong sense of welcome from her surroundings. Some houses were like that.

Suddenly she was ravenously hungry and after a brief hesitation she decided to fry the last of her bacon, together with an overripe tomato she'd not liked to throw away because she hated waste of any sort. She took one of the eggs from the fridge because there were plenty, as well as bread to make some toast. Again, she was sure Maggie wouldn't mind.

When she'd finished eating, she tiptoed into the library to check on the invalid but found her still fast asleep.

It was wonderfully peaceful so she sat down to rest in a huge old armchair near the unlit kitchen fire, just for a few minutes.

Chapter Three

Australia

It was a shock when the phone call from England turned out to be the family lawyer, telling Corin in a hushed voice that his father had died suddenly of a heart attack.

'I think you should come home at once, Mr Drayton, and . . . well, I'll explain it all when I see you. I've taken the liberty of booking you on a flight tomorrow. I'm afraid the only one left was economy class and you'll have to change at Dubai.'

He didn't let himself sigh aloud, but he'd spent a lot of hours at Dubai between flights and at the moment he wanted more than ever to get home to his brother, who would be bearing the brunt of things with their mother.

'All right. Give me the details and I'll be on it.' Corin scribbled them down. 'Got that.'

'I'll have a car waiting for you at Heathrow Airport.'

'That's very kind of you.'

'I wonder if you could call in to see me on your way home?'

'Can't that wait?'

'Not really. You see, you're the main heir.'

'What?'

'I'll explain in more detail how things have been arranged when I see you, then I'll try to answer any questions.'

Corin put the phone down and stared into space, wondering why on earth his father had left the family brewery to him. He'd refused to do as expected and make a career there, partly because he didn't like the smell of the place. He'd studied architecture at university instead, a subject he was passionate about.

So why was he the heir? He certainly hadn't been close to his father. Well, none of them had. Charles Drayton hadn't been a family man by any stretch of the imagination. Or even a very sociable person. Which had always seemed strange for someone who ran a business focusing mainly on hospitality.

Corin hadn't been back in England for more than an occasional few weeks' holiday for nearly a decade and even then hadn't spent much of them at his family home. The only person he cared about there was his younger brother, Pete.

He'd loved working for a housing charity in a series of developing countries, using his training and experience to help people. He'd learned so much about what worked and what didn't, because he had the freedom to design homes that suited the climates and the various groups' needs – well, freedom within their financial constraints. He'd even won a minor award for one innovative design.

Oh well, he'd been near the end of this project and had been thinking it might be time to move back into the commercial world. He could leave the wind-up of the project in the capable hands of a colleague. She was an architectural star of the future, he was sure.

The flights seemed to go on for ever, partly because he was too tall to sit comfortably in an economy class seat and couldn't easily fall asleep, and partly because his mind seemed unwilling to switch off its speculation about why his father had done this.

To his relief he passed smoothly through customs and found a limousine waiting for him.

In Swindon, the car deposited him at Mr Minchington's rooms and the driver said he'd been told to wait in the rear car park but he'd get a cup of tea for himself first if Mr Drayton didn't mind.

'Go for it.'

Corin looked up at the tall, narrow building and sighed, already feeling hemmed in. He'd never be a city dweller by choice.

He was shown into Mr Minchington's office and offered a comfortable armchair.

'I'll get straight to the point, Mr Drayton. You've inherited a major share in the family business.'

'So you said. Why me and not Pete? He's the one who works there. It ought to go to him.'

'Only your father could tell you that. He never conversed much when he conducted legal business with me.'

'He didn't converse much, period! How major a share?'

'Fifty-one per cent. Your mother has the income from ten per cent for as long as she remains unmarried and those shares are to be divided equally between you and your brother when she passes away or remarries. Your brother has the rest of the brewery shares.'

'That seems grossly unfair. I've never been near the place since I worked in it during school and university holidays. I only did that because I needed to earn money. I haven't a clue how things are organised there nowadays. Why on earth would my father do that?'

'Mine not to reason why, Mr Drayton.'

'Is there anything to stop me transferring some of my shares to Pete?'

The lawyer looked surprised. 'I suppose not. But I'd advise you to look at your own situation in this country before you do anything drastic. I'm sure your brother will be able to help you settle in and you can run the brewery together.'

Corin wasn't settling into it, wasn't even going to try. No way. He didn't even like to drink beer, let alone have the expertise to make it. His brother had not only worked at Drayton's since he left school but was reputed to be a connoisseur of beer.

When he got to the brewery, he was greeted by a receptionist new to him. 'Mr Drayton is busy today, I'm afraid, sir. Would you care to leave a message?'

'I'm Corin Drayton and I'm quite sure my brother will see me without an appointment.'

She gaped at him for a moment. 'Oh, I'm so sorry, sir. I'll go and tell him straight away.'

When he was shown into Pete's office, he was greeted by a dark scowl.

'Come to gloat, have you? How did you persuade him to leave the major share to you? Well, I shan't linger here to get in your way once I've handed over, believe me, and if you don't buy me out I'll sell it to someone else.'

'You'd better linger if you want the business to continue operating. I wouldn't have a clue what to do with it.'

'You must have shown some interest for our dear papa to leave it to you. And I'm *not* working under someone who doesn't have the skill to operate it efficiently, let alone to develop new products and—' He snapped his mouth shut abruptly.

'I showed no interest whatsoever. He and I rarely communicated even when I was visiting them. I didn't have the slightest idea that he'd ever leave it to me, nor did I express any wish to run it.'

There was dead silence for a few minutes as if Pete was digesting this. Some of the hostility faded from his expression but he still looked puzzled. 'If he hadn't left me to run it and dealt only with the financial side of things, I'd have found another job years ago. I . . . really care about it.'

'I know, Pete. We can do something to remedy the situation, surely?'

'Ha! Like you're going to give away all your share of the business to me?'

'I'll donate some of it to you, for sure. Not all.'

'I can't afford to buy your shares.'

'I said "donate", not sell.'

Pete opened and shut his mouth. 'Really? Won't you want to remain the majority shareholder?'

'Hell, no. Unless you need new premises designing, I'll stay out of things. I'm an architect, not a brewer, Pete. That hasn't changed, except that I love what I do even more than I'd expected when I chose to train in those skills.'

'Hmm. Fine words. Let's see how you carry through.' He looked at his watch. 'Anyway, you look exhausted so you'd better get home and let Ma weep all over you, then get some rest.'

'She's bound to be upset.'

Pete opened his mouth as if to comment, then snapped it shut again.

'What?'

'They were never a close couple and that only changed for the worse, especially during the past year or two. They'd hardly spent any time together lately. She's enjoying being centre stage as the grieving widow at the moment and is planning a huge funeral, but she's not really upset.'

'She enjoys the social whirl. He never did.'

'She enjoys the masculine attention part of it, not so much the women.'

'You mean—'

'Judge that for yourself. Anyhow, you'd better slow her down a bit on the funeral expenses. There isn't a lot of money to spare. In fact, if we don't do something drastic, the company will go down the gurgler. I hadn't realised till Pa died and I got hold of the books what a mess he'd made of things.'

'How did things get to be that bad?'

'Times and tastes have changed but Father wouldn't finance me to do much about keeping up with trends in boutique brewing, so Drayton's will go bust if I don't do something about the situation quick smart. All he ever did was tick along and force me to do the same, producing the same beer as always. It's still a good beer, mind, but customers like more variety these days.'

'His love was always reserved for Roman remains and sites. He knew Hadrian's Wall better than the centre of

Swindon. Anyway, I'd better get going.'

Pete glanced at his watch. 'I'll cancel the rest of my appointments and finish for the day, then follow you home. It'll be interesting to see if you have any better success at reining in Ma than I've had.'

Corin's mother hadn't changed at all. She was as exquisitely dressed as ever, with no signs of puffiness about the eyes. She flung herself at him and wept delicately and tearlessly against his chest, managing not to disturb her hair and make-up.

'My dear boy, I knew you'd come home as soon as you heard.'

A car door slammed outside and Pete came in to join them, whistling in that tuneless way he had when he was feeling tense. Some things never changed.

She scowled at her younger son. 'You're home early, Peter. I would have thought you'd be more busy than usual, given that my dear Charles isn't there to manage things. Still, Corin is back now. He can sort the finances out and let you get back to your brewing.'

There were undercurrents pulsing between them that were far more hostile than Corin had expected.

Before he could say anything, his mother grabbed his arm. 'Come and sit down, darling. I have a lot to talk to you about. I've been looking into funeral arrangements and we need to make some decisions quickly. People in our position can't neglect the observances, you know.'

He shot her a puzzled look. *In our position?* They were the owners of a small brewery, for heaven's sake, not members of the nobility. 'We can talk about that later.

How about a cup of tea and a quick snack? I didn't have any lunch. I also need to shower and change my clothes after such a long flight.'

But she didn't listen, didn't even wait for the tea to arrive to start telling him about her plans. She was clearly intending the funeral to be a massive production. He glanced sideways at his brother and gestured to him to take over.

'I've already told you, Ma: we can't afford a showy funeral.'

Corin followed that lead. 'And if Pete says there isn't a lot of money to spare, then we will have to be careful. Funerals can be ridiculously expensive.'

As Pete opened his mouth, their mother said savagely, 'Your brother's got to you already, hasn't he, Corin? He's been very mean about money since Charles died. Well, I intend to give your father the respect he deserves.'

'We can discuss the specifics tomorrow, surely?' he said soothingly.

'We can discuss them now because we need to settle on which firm is to conduct the funeral as a matter of urgency. I'm starting my widowhood as I mean to go on. I helped your father in the early days. I'm *entitled* to some say in what we do with the family fortune now, even if your father has left things in that dreadful sexist way.'

'Then you'll get a say in how we deal with nothing. We don't have enough money to pay the costs of a fancy funeral,' Pete stated slowly and loudly. 'I've told you several times already that the brewery isn't doing well. Father was too cautious about running it. The money just isn't there, Ma. The company's bank account is in overdraft, not profit.'

Corin ignored his mother's mutterings and looked across at his brother. 'Is it really that bad?'

'If we don't do something, we'll be in real trouble but with care, I'm hoping to avoid us going bankrupt.'

Their mother's voice rose to a shrillness that echoed round the room. 'You're lying! We should have christened you Scrooge! Your father told me there was plenty of money for my needs only a couple of weeks before he died. He never stinted on anything I needed and I won't stint on burying him now.'

She glared at them both. 'Things will be better with Corin in charge. You are a beer maker, not a businessman, Peter.'

Corin shoved the rest of his biscuit in his mouth, drank his tea and stood up. 'We can discuss it over a meal, Ma. As I already said, I'm in desperate need of a shower.'

He strode out rapidly without giving her a chance to say anything else. Her hostility towards his brother upset him. Apart from anything else, he knew Pete cared deeply about the family business, was the only one who did. Their father never had.

When he went up to his old bedroom, he found it had been completely redecorated, and recently too by the untouched look. It was exquisite, if you liked that sort of fussiness, which he didn't. How the hell much had that cost? And why had she done it when he didn't live permanently at home?

Pete knocked on the half-open door and came in. 'Beautiful, isn't it? She did the whole house last year, used up all the brewery's development money.'

'The whole house?'

'Yes. How long are you staying this time? Three days?
A week? Or has Father trapped you here at last?'

'No, he damned well hasn't. I'll stay till we've sorted
the business out but then I'm getting on with my life and
leaving Drayton's to you.'

'If you can afford it.'

'I have money of my own. I don't take after our mother
in that way and I've never lived extravagantly. We'll talk
to her again after dinner and try to slow her down. There
are a lot of things I need to ask you about, but maybe
without her there. I need to know the full financial details
of our inheritance for a start.'

Pete stared at him. 'You really didn't know, did you?
That he'd made you the heir, I mean?'

'No. And I won't take the job. I haven't a clue about
where brewing's at these days.'

'She'll find a way to trap you.' With a sniff of scornful
laughter, Pete ambled out of the bedroom again, pausing
in the doorway to give him another puzzled look.

Corin went down to fetch up the rest of his luggage,
then locked the bedroom door on his family.

He felt like Alice falling down a rabbit hole into a
lunatic universe.

Dinner was served in style by a maid dressed in black with
a fancy white apron. He glanced at Pete for enlightenment.
They'd never had live-in staff before.

Another of those shrugs.

His mother intercepted the exchange. 'I'm not as young
as I was so your father said I could hire some proper
full-time help.'

After that she led the conversation lightly into catching him up on what their neighbours and acquaintances were doing. He was only half paying attention, so it was a while before he realised she was preparing the ground and sure enough, as they were finishing the dessert, she said, 'Now that you're about to settle down, Corin dear, we must introduce you to some new people and see about getting you settled.'

He thought he'd nipped her matchmaking in the bud on his last visit. 'I am *not* ready to settle down, Ma, either into the family business or into matrimony. You know I don't enjoy formal socialising.'

'But you're nearly thirty-four. Surely you want a family? And how else are you going to meet suitable people if you don't join in the local social life? There aren't many eligible women left at your age.'

Pete sniggered audibly.

'When I do want to settle down, I'll find my own partner, as I told you last time I was home.'

She burst into tears, one of her favourite ploys, but he didn't rush to comfort her. Instead he stood up. 'You'll have to excuse me, I'm utterly exhausted. I've been on the go for nearly two days. I need to catch up on some sleep.'

There was still an edge to her tone. 'You'll become as anti-social as your father if you don't watch out, but at least he didn't disapprove of my having a decent social life, which I still intend to continue. Widows don't sit around draped in black and weeping non-stop these days, you know.'

'I'm sure you've got plenty of friends you can call on for sympathy and drinkies.'

She raised her hands in a theatrical gesture and addressed her remarks to the ceiling. 'I don't know what's wrong with my sons. Both of you in your thirties and not a sign of either of you settling down and starting families. Where did Charles and I go wrong?'

She then clapped one hand to her bosom and added in throbbing, dramatic tones, 'Just *tell me* if you're gay, for heaven's sake, Corin.'

'I'm not gay. And I told you that last time. I'd not be ashamed of it if I was, believe me. I just haven't met a woman I want to spend the rest of my life with. End of.'

He hurried up to his bedroom, intending to unpack a few of his things, but finding himself standing staring into space. He'd only been home a few hours and the nagging had already started. He wasn't interested in the brewery, never had been. Or in a lavish social life and least of all in making what his mother considered a *suitable* marriage.

This settled one thing: he definitely wasn't going to move back into this house. His mother would drive him mad in no time flat.

Which made him frown. Who did the house belong to now, anyway? He'd have to ask the lawyer to give him the details again. Jetlag played havoc with you mentally as well as physically.

He hadn't a clue exactly what he was going to do with his life now, except that he would be working in the field of commercial architecture. He was *not* going to run that damned brewery or dance to his mother's tune.

She'd asked if he was gay last time as well. Why did she go on about that? Just because one of his friends was gay. She'd always disliked Tim.

Who cared about other people's sexual orientation? Not him. All he cared for was whether they were kind and interesting, which Tim was.

There was a knock on his bedroom door.

'It's only me, safe to open up.'

He unlocked the door and found Pete standing on the landing holding a couple of glasses and a bottle of cognac, and without that nasty sneering expression on his face, thank goodness.

'Come in quick.' He locked the door again and took the proffered glass, letting Pete pour him a small cognac. He gestured to a chair and sat on the bed before taking a sip and enjoying the soothing taste of it. 'That's a good cognac.'

'My favourite. Thought you might need a little strengthener, Corin my lad. She's been even more difficult than usual since Father died; I can't figure out why. She'll do her best to manage what you do with your inheritance if you don't watch out.'

'Well, you can run the damned brewery, whatever she says or does. And with my blessing.'

'Thanks. I would actually love to run it without Father holding the financial reins. I have a lot of ideas to improve things. But I'm only taking over if I get full control. Did you mean what you said?'

'Yep.' Corin raised his glass in a salute and took another sip. 'Never mind that now. Tell me about the people I do like. Do you still have that crazy friend with the equally crazy dog?'

They chatted for a while but Corin found himself nodding off.

Pete stood up and took the half-empty glass from him. 'We'll discuss business in the morning. You're not in a fit state to take anything in.'

'No, I'm not.' He clapped Pete on the back as he walked him to the door. 'Thanks for this visit. I'd hate to be estranged from you. And I *will* transfer some shares and hand control over to you, I promise.'

Pete gave him one of those solemn looks. 'I'll make sure you don't regret that long-term, I promise you.'

'I'm sure I won't. I've proved good at choosing my investments.'

'You're OK financially, even without the brewery?'

'Very OK.'

'Good to hear.'

Chapter Four

Breakfast was served in style in the dining room, but there were only two places set. His mother was standing staring out of the window, but came across the room to meet him. 'I'm glad you got up late, Corin darling. I thought you and I could have a nice leisurely breakfast and a cosy chat.'

'What about Pete?'

'Oh, he'll be at the office by now. He just about lives there.'

She linked her arm in his and was tugging him towards the table when Pete came in. He looked at the table settings and went out again without a word.

Oh, hell! Was his brother going to leave him to deal with their mother on his own?

To his relief, Pete returned a couple of minutes later. 'I've told Maria to cook me some bacon and eggs.' He took some more cutlery and a place mat out of the sideboard drawer, poured himself a cup of coffee and sat down opposite his brother with their mother at the head of the table between them.

She breathed deeply and turned her attention to Corin.

'We really do need to sort out the funeral arrangements before we do anything else, dear.'

Pete answered for him. 'It won't take all that much organising. I've told you several times, Ma: we can't afford to spend lavishly. Or perhaps you'd enjoy dealing with a bankruptcy afterwards?'

She scowled at him. 'I've already told you I don't *believe* it's that bad. Your father would have said something.'

'Said something to you? Father has never ever discussed business with you and he spoiled you rotten. He even forbade me to tell you how bad things really were. Only, didn't you even wonder why he and I had been working longer hours lately?'

She shrugged.

'He didn't tell you, but I will now. Pethick's have been trying to buy us out, not to mention playing a few dirty tricks on the business, trying to tip us over the brink into insolvency so they can pay as little as possible, I'd guess.'

She frowned at him. 'Pethick's? No, you must be mistaken. They're some of our best friends.'

'What's the saying: with friends like that, who needs enemies?' He looked at Corin. 'I'm not mistaken. Fortunately we've still got some loyal customers left but we'll need to make changes quickly if we're to keep Pethick's from putting us out of business.'

Corin frowned. He'd never liked their generation of that particular family. Frank, the oldest son and only a year older than him, had been a bully from an early age but fortunately Corin had been big for his age, so had nearly always managed to hold his own physically – and had occasionally had to protect Pete as well, because his brother had been late growing into his man's body. You didn't forget things like that.

Pete nudged him to get his attention. 'Unless you *want* to sell the brewery to them at the knock-down price they're offering, bro? You have the majority share, after all.'

'Of course I don't want to sell. My only plans at the moment are to try to understand what's going on and to leave you in charge while I find a job for myself.' Corin poured himself a glass of water. 'Give us a summary of the financial situation now and keep it simple so that Ma can understand.'

Their mother listened to the broad figures and percentages, and it was all too obvious from the couple of questions she asked that she understood it perfectly well.

'I don't believe it,' she said in a whispery voice when he'd finished.

'Care to see the account books?' Pete asked. 'And the letter from the bank, saying this will be the last time they'll extend our overdraft?'

She gasped, clutched her forehead and fell forward, knocking her cup over.

She usually fainted more gracefully than that, Corin thought as he moved her arm out of the spilled tea and let Pete support her body. Was this collapse a genuine one or did she have a health problem?

'She's done this for real a couple of times recently but insists there's nothing wrong with her,' Pete whispered. 'I'll carry her up to her bedroom. Come and open the doors for me.'

By the time they got her to bed, she'd recovered enough to tell them crossly to go away and leave her to recover in peace, for heaven's sake.

When they were back in the dining room, they found that the maid had cleared up the spilled coffee and tidied up, setting out the warm dishes on the heater at the side. They helped themselves then sat down.

Pete picked up his knife and fork. 'Maria's a good maid, but unless Ma starts paying her wages, she'll have to go.'

'Well, I certainly don't need waiting on.'

'Me neither. If it's all right with you, I'll organise the funeral. Unless you want to do it?'

Corin waved one hand in a permissive gesture. 'Be my guest. I wouldn't know where to begin.'

Pete's words came out muffled by a mouthful of food. 'I've already made preliminary inquiries and settled on a company.'

'Thank goodness for that. How are you going to stop Ma interfering, though?'

'I'll tell them frankly that I won't pay for any changes she tries to make to the arrangements and they're to deal only with me. Money usually talks.'

Two days later, Corin decided to nip up to London to settle a few details about leaving his employment with the charity. Before he went, he asked Mr Minchington to arrange to transfer some of his shares to Pete.

The lawyer was horrified, but since his client insisted on doing it, he agreed to do as he was asked, muttering, 'I just hope you don't regret it.'

After he got back, Corin checked that the transfer of shares had gone through, then went into the office at the brewery.

'Everything OK?' Pete asked.

'Everything's fine. Here, read this.' He tossed the lawyer's letter to his brother.

Pete read it and gulped, bending his head but failing to hide the tears brimming in his eyes. 'Thanks,' he said huskily. 'I'll try my best to get Drayton's on a level keel again. I think I can do it.'

'You're the one with the best chance of succeeding.'

'Yes, I am. And have been planning for it in case I got the chance. The first thing will be getting our new non-alcoholic drink on the market. Come and see the sample labels for the cans and bottles. I'm torn between two of them.'

They studied the drawings and eventually both agreed on a cheerful cover with a glass showing a selection of fruits inside it.

'I'd drink that myself,' Corin said. 'I don't always want alcohol.'

Pete grinned. 'Why not have a try? I happen to have a sample locked in the big bottom drawer of my desk.'

Corin sipped, not expecting to care one way or the other, then looked at his brother in surprise and took another mouthful. 'This is great! Just the right amount of tang.'

'And it comes out nicely in a diet version, too.'

'Well done!'

'Finish it all or pour it away. I don't leave any lying round for sneaks to take to our competitors. And that includes our mother.'

'*What?* Surely she wouldn't?'

'She's very good friends with Lionel Pethick, whose wife died a couple of years ago.'

Corin closed his eyes for a moment at the implications of that, then changed the subject. 'Is there anything I should look at to familiarise myself with how we're doing?'

Pete took him through account books and records till his head was spinning and he raised his arms in a sign of surrender. 'My brain can't take in any more details.'

'I think I've told you enough to show the general picture.'

'You have. And I think you've done well to keep things going. Look, if you need some money, I can let you have a hundred thousand or so.'

Pete stilled. 'Just like that?'

'Yes. I told you: I'm good at investments and I think you'd make an excellent one, long term.'

He went into the office again before the funeral, determined to have a better idea of where Drayton's stood with regard to premises. He insisted on Pete continuing to use their father's office and took an empty office nearby for himself. What he found was not good.

He went in to see Pete later and tapped one page on the old-fashioned account book his father had insisted on.

'A surprising amount has been paid regularly to Mother as an allowance. That can't continue. Why does she need this much? She has no household expenses.'

'She likes to live in style, dine in expensive restaurants and buy designer clothes.'

'Well, it definitely can't go on.'

Pete gave a wry smile. 'I've already stopped payment of the allowance. I'll tell her after the funeral. She'll create a fuss, but the money simply isn't there.'

'I don't envy you staying here,' Corin said later as they again shared a few moments over small glasses of cognac just before bed. 'I am definitely leaving as soon as the funeral is over.'

'Back to another developing country?'

'No. I meant what I said. I'm settling down in England from now on, and working on the commercial side of things, though I have no idea where or exactly what I'll be doing.'

The funeral was to be held as soon as it could be arranged. There was no need to wait for an autopsy because it turned out their father had been seeing a specialist and his doctor regularly for a heart problem.

Corin went to see Dr Stewart, who told him their father had been aware that his health was not promising, but had refused any procedures to prolong his life because the specialist couldn't guarantee anything and had felt duty-bound to inform him that depending on what they found, an operation might even make matters worse.

Their mother seemed indifferent to that information rather than upset and in any case was still not speaking to them unless she had to.

'Do you think she ever really cared about him?' Corin wondered aloud as the two brothers shared what had become their nightly ritual glass.

Pete shook his head. 'No. It's my guess he was the best prospect for marriage financially and socially, because the brewery was doing quite well under Grandfather. Her side of the family are much more modest folk.'

'By the time I realised she was deliberately staying away from her relatives, it was too late to get to know them better. Some of them had moved to Australia and her parents had gone up to live with her brother in Newcastle. And *he* wanted nothing to do with our mother. I don't know why, but they fell out big time.'

Pete scowled down at his glass. 'I reckon the main thing our father wanted from her was an heir. And he got that, at least.'

'I'm never going to marry for such a reason. If I don't care about a person, why would I want to spend my life with them?'

'Why do you think I haven't married?' Pete asked. 'I've got friends who are happily together, whether married or not, and I watch them in envy. If I can't find something similar, I'll stay single.'

'I'm with you on that.'

They clinked glasses.

'I've been thinking about Father making you the heir. He wouldn't change anything and he grew more rigid in his ideas as he grew older. The inheritance goes to the oldest son and all that sort of stuff. During the past couple of years we disagreed so often I nearly left Drayton's a couple of times. If he hadn't left me to run the practical side, I would have done. I've had tempting offers.'

'Well, I'm glad you can continue here. I have confidence that you'll succeed.'

His mother dressed all in black on the day of the funeral, wearing a hat with a veil that obscured her face. She was uncharacteristically quiet at the service and sat between her sons at the front of the church. There were more people than Corin had expected, split into two distinct halves, and he asked his brother what was going on.

'The ones near the front are invited; the others have just turned up. I've told the ushers to seat them in different areas.'

'What a load of silly fussing there is in funerals!'

Towards the end of the relatively brief service, their mother muttered scornfully that it had been 'a mean little affair', though not loudly enough for anyone other than her sons to hear.

Corin found the service tedious and couldn't wait for it to end.

But he and Pete had to lead the way out, walking behind the coffin. He'd expected his mother to link arms with one of them but she waved them to go ahead of her and followed them out of the church on the arm of a man of her own age, who fussed over her as if he were part of the family.

'Who's the guy she's clutching?' Corin whispered.

Pete rolled his eyes. 'Lionel Pethick.'

'*What?* The Pethicks were invited to the funeral?'

'Only him. He's her special friend.'

'You mean—'

A shrug was his only answer.

'Is he involved in trying to cheat us?'

'Not sure. He doesn't seem part of their business team. In fact, he doesn't seem to work at all. More of a playboy really but without the finances to do things in style.'

At the house there seemed to be a surprising number of people, more than there had been in the church, so the brothers couldn't escape playing host.

'I thought there were only going to be thirty people max coming to the house,' Corin whispered as he and Pete lingered by the door, even though the guests seemed all to have arrived.

'She told me as we arrived that she'd invited "a few more" people to the house. She hadn't told me till then,' Pete murmured. 'It was too late to stop it, so I told Cook not to bother with trying to provide more food, just to serve the cheap wine I'd bought specially and the few nibblies we'd decided on.'

He saw his mother's outraged expression as the refreshments were served almost immediately to the guests and no further platters of food offered to them. There was only one brief speech from Pete, mainly thanking the guests for their attendance today, after which no one was encouraged to linger.

Once the guests had all left, Corin insisted on a business conference.

'Surely this can wait till tomorrow?' their mother asked wearily, sipping a fresh glass of wine.

'We need to discuss the new arrangements, Ma.' He moved to block the way out because she'd been avoiding doing this for days. 'Come and sit down.'

She flung herself into an armchair. 'What new arrangements? Have you come to your senses about the brewery, Corin?'

'If by that you mean am I going to run it, Ma, no. Apart from my ignorance about what to do for the best in these difficult times, you must surely remember that the smells associated with brewing made me feel nauseous when I worked there for a holiday job – and they still do. I don't even like the taste of beer, so what use would I be at producing it, even if I wanted to get involved?'

'Surely you've grown out of that!'

'Nope.' He took a deep breath. He'd been dreading telling her this. 'So you need to know that I've passed over some shares, twelve per cent of the total actually, to Pete. That was finalised yesterday and will make him the majority shareholder now.'

She let out a little scream. 'You fool! He'll plough the money back into the business and lose it.'

'Thank you for your confidence in me, Ma.' Pete turned to his brother. 'I can't thank you enough and I won't let you down.'

Corin smiled. 'I know. In the meantime I'll back you up on whatever needs doing to sort out this trouble with the Pethick family.'

'None of them ought to be invited to the house again,' Pete said sternly to his mother.

'Lionel comes because he's a special friend of mine, and to give me his support. Why would the rest of them want to come here when you two are such skinflints about entertaining people?'

'Whose side are you on?'

'My own.'

Corin gave up. 'Let's move on to something else now. As soon as the business arrangements have been sorted out, I'm going to move on and start working on my own future.'

'Which is what exactly?' his mother asked acidly. 'You might have come back to the UK a big hero, but have you even the faintest idea what you're going to do with your life?'

He shrugged. 'Not yet. But I won't find anything if I hang around here. I'll know it when I see it. Not another charity, but I don't have a lavish lifestyle to support so I can take my time and find something I'll truly enjoy doing.'

'The real world isn't like that. You need money to face the future.'

'Some money, not a billion pounds. What I care most about is finding an interesting and worthwhile project where I'm not hamstrung by company rules and regulations. And I don't want somewhere I have to fight to climb the corporate ladders.'

'You sound like a schoolboy. "Play up! Play up! And play the game!"'

He ignored that. He had never liked Sir Henry Newbolt's poem or playing the game in that sense. 'I've packed all the things I want and if you don't mind me leaving them here, I'll have them put into the attic with my other things when they arrive from overseas.'

Corin saw the thoughtful look his mother gave him and was glad he'd put padlocks on the trunks and suitcases he was leaving behind. He'd mention that to Pete. It made him feel sad not to trust his own mother.

'I'll see to that, bro,' Pete said.

'Thanks. Unless I can find somewhere to live very quickly, that is. You can turn what was my room into a guest bedroom.'

'For what guests?' Pete mocked. 'I have no time to entertain and the maid will be leaving soon.'

Their mother sat bolt upright. 'Who organised that?'

'I did,' Pete said. 'We can't afford fancy staff or entertaining.'

'You should have told me.'

'I have just done so.'

'You'll regret doing that. I'll make sure of it.' She turned to Corin. 'Have you got any sort of a job lined up?'

'No. I'm going to have a bit of a holiday first.'

'How on earth are you going to live after you've given so many of your shares away? They don't offer high dividends, you know.'

'I've got some money saved, enough to see me through for a while.'

He hadn't told either of them exactly how well off he was, though he'd hinted at it to Pete. He'd found he was good at analysing some types of business trends and had played the stock market in that area for years, usually to his own benefit.

Pete joined in again. 'One final thing. Given the financial situation, I'm afraid we won't be able to pay you any allowance for a while, Ma, though of course we'll pay any reasonable running costs for this place.'

'*What?*' His mother glared at them both. 'You can't mean that.'

When neither of them answered, she banged a clenched fist on the table again. 'What am I expected to live on, then?'

'You have the money you inherited from that old uncle of yours,' Peter said.

Corin stared at him in surprise then looked back at his mother. 'What money?'

'Didn't she tell you? She was Uncle Martin's sole heir. She never mentions it and certainly hasn't offered to invest any of the money in the company, but it must have been a juicy amount because she didn't stop smiling for a week after she found out. And he left her that big old house, which she sold very quickly. It was advertised for a couple of million.'

His mother gave him a dirty look. 'It's none of your business how much I inherited or what I got for my uncle's property. I was married to your father for over thirty years and put up with a lot in the name of business, so I deserve my share of the income from Drayton's. I earned it. He wasn't easy to live with, you know.'

'As I said, there won't be any income at all for a while,' Pete said.

'I'll sue you for maintenance if you arrange it like that!'

'You won't have a leg to stand on,' he tossed back at her. 'I haven't arranged anything: that's how Father left the business – with empty coffers and a big overdraft.'

Corin intervened before they could start quarrelling again. 'Well, I won't be costing you anything, Pete. And I'm sure you'll be all right with Drayton's long-term, Ma. My brother is more than capable of turning the business round.'

'You should sell it now while it's still got some worth. Pethick's made you a very fair offer.'

'It was a rubbish offer,' Pete snapped. 'Anyway, I'm not giving my heritage away. I happen to *like* running a brewery.'

His mother ignored him and turned back to Corin. 'Why are you leaving so hastily? There's no need for you to move out of your home till you have somewhere to go, surely?'

'It's not my home, hasn't been for years. Anyway, you'll be living here.'

Pete smiled. 'She only has a lifetime occupancy of the house, with rates and such paid. If she remarries, the house will come to you and me. And she isn't allowed to move a lover in or she'll lose the tenancy. Father was obviously more aware of what you'd been doing behind his back than you realised, Ma.'

'Just because he lived like a eunuch didn't mean I had to live unnaturally.'

Corin didn't say it, but she'd definitely given him to understand that she now owned the house and needed help financially to run it. He was beginning to realise how greedy she was for money, something Pete had hinted at more than once during their chats. He really should have paid more attention to the financial details the lawyer had bombarded him with when he first arrived.

He must have been far more jetlagged than he'd realised.

Why hadn't she corrected him about that? How many other lies had she told him or allowed him to believe, which amounted to the same thing?

He should have paid more attention to the fine print of the will as well, but there had been so many quarrels between his mother and brother about it over the past couple of weeks that he'd zoned out half the time.

'I'm moving out of here, too,' Pete said. 'There's a small flat at the brewery. I shall be working very hard from now on and it'll be easier if I'm living on site. So you won't need more than a cook-housekeeper and a cleaner – unless you pay for other staff yourself, of course.'

'You're both unnatural!' his mother flung at him. 'And you're as bad as your grandfather was, Pete, in love with that stupid brewery.'

Corin didn't comment but he suspected that was the simple truth. Unfortunately, it sounded to him as if it was going to take all the love his brother could summon up to save Drayton's.

He envied Pete even so, wished he had something or someone to fall in love with. He'd never admit it to his mother, but he did want a home and family now.

Only, he'd been telling the truth when he said he hadn't met anyone he wanted to spend the rest of his life with. And it wasn't that he hadn't looked.

Was there something wrong with him? What did people call it? Fear of commitment?

Chapter Five

Two weeks after the important discussion with his brother and mother, Corin drove along a country lane, enjoying the mild sunshine and the lush green foliage. It was over. He was free now from squabbles with his mother and from that damned brewery.

He suddenly shouted 'Hurrah!' at the top of his voice, then grinned at himself for being so daft. Well, the outlook was bright now, or at least brighter.

It was great that Pete was now the owner of a majority share in the brewery, which was what his brother had always wanted. He'd concocted another new non-alcoholic drink, a mocktail instead of a cocktail, provisionally titled Gaudy Lady

If the subtle taste was anything to go by, not to mention the delightful tang that lingered in the mouth afterwards, Pete had a real talent for creating drinks and Corin was beginning to believe that he might be able not just to save the brewery but to see it flourish.

Their mother had been sulking and refusing to talk to either of her sons in more than monosyllables ever since their financial discussion after the funeral. She'd gone out a lot, staying away late sometimes and if Corin was any judge, driving under the influence of more alcohol than the law allowed.

Ach, to hell with all that! 'I'm not my mother's keeper,' he muttered. This was his first taste of total freedom from responsibility for many years and he should concentrate on enjoying it. The work he'd done overseas had put moral shackles on him and it had been a hard slog at times, demanding but so worthwhile. And last year's events had been . . . challenging, to say the least.

Now he needed to do something for himself that didn't suck away all his mental and physical energy. It might be a cliché but what he needed at this stage in his life was something he felt passionate about on a personal level, but not too stressful.

He'd bought a car with Pete's help, a medium-sized SUV with good safety features, two years old, and was enjoying driving it. Why waste money on a new car when its value went down by a huge chunk the minute you put it on the road? He wasn't into fast driving or showy vehicles anyway.

His brother had taken over their father's old Rover and was using his own former vehicle as a company car, lending it to a young guy who had recently started working at the brewery. Dylan was apparently a whiz kid with machinery and theirs was quite old.

Corin spent the first night away from his family in a comfortable hotel, enjoying the solitude and excellent service. He felt to have been swamped by people for years.

This morning he'd made a leisurely start, with no

particular goal in mind. The countryside in Wiltshire was so beautiful, he stopped once simply to enjoy a fine vista. No wonder Blake's poem was so often quoted. England really was a 'green and pleasant land'. The contrast to most of the places he'd lived in over the past few years was striking.

Just before lunch, he stopped for a second time at a place where there was parking on the verge and a glorious view to refresh the spirit.

He got out, breathing in deeply and moving about to stretch his legs. Then he noticed a nearby drystone wall and walked up the slight slope from the verge parking area to study it more closely. Its skilful construction and honest beauty greatly appealed to him. Who knew how many years it had been standing there defying wind and weather? Talk about 'fit for purpose'!

When he could see over the top better, he was surprised to find a group of tumbledown old houses scattered about like a child's abandoned toys on the other side, where there was a fairly level area before the land began sloping again. It looked as if it had once been a pretty little hamlet but was deserted now. Indeed, the houses looked as if they hadn't been occupied for many years but most appeared sound and weatherproof, another thing that was unexpected. Who had been maintaining them?

They were from several different eras, but the latest must have been built in the early twentieth century. He still remembered his studies into the history of British house-building with great pleasure and clarity. He loved designing good family homes for people.

There was a turning off the main road quite close by,

and a gateway. It wasn't worth driving that short distance to park a hundred metres closer, so he locked his car and strolled along by the side of the road, hoping to get inside and see the houses better.

The gateway proved to be partly concealed from the road, as if to discourage people from visiting. From it he could see that the houses were set out as if they had once formed a street. There was long grass around them now rather than proper paths, and it was studded with a glory of wildflowers that took his breath away.

The padlock on the gate was new and solid but it looked as if a few cars had driven into the area recently, though not enough of them to wear a proper track or destroy the wildflowers, just to leave indentations in the grass.

There looked to have been some sort of sign to one side of the entrance. It had been placed a little further back but had fallen down. He couldn't resist it, was dying to find out what this place was. *In for a penny, in for a pound*, he thought and climbed over the gate, laughing at himself again as he jumped down on the other side. He hadn't trespassed anywhere in staid old England for years.

He turned the sign over with some difficulty because it was the size of his outstretched arms and too unwieldy for one man to handle easily. The words *FOR SALE* were blazoned across the top in huge red letters. Beneath it was the terse statement: *Several period cottages and surrounding land*. There was only a long-distance photo of the area, no detailed images of the nearby houses.

Across the bottom it gave the name of an estate agent

in some village called Essington St Mary and said simply *Apply for details*. Someone had painted out what might have been a phone number, not scribbled over it but painted carefully and completely over it to prevent it being seen. Strange, that. Surely they wanted people to phone about the land?

He got out the small notebook that went with him everywhere and wrote down the name of the estate agent. He hadn't acquired the mobile phone addiction of most of his contemporaries because he'd spent a lot of time in places without mobile phone coverage. Then he went back to studying the houses, most of which looked very solidly built, old now but clearly well maintained and weatherproof.

He saw another piece of rusted metal lying under a tree, almost completely hidden by the long grass. It looked much older than the big sign and was only about half the size but felt just as heavy and awkward when he turned it over.

This one read *Keep Out: Property of the War Office*.

The sign made him wonder whether this was one of those places he'd read about in history books, whole hamlets or farms requisitioned during the Second World War for secret government use. He knew that some of them had been kept in official hands for decades even after the war and, indeed, he had a vague idea that the government still hadn't given them all up to private use again.

If these houses fell in that category, that must be why they'd been kept in reasonable order. The older sign made him even more keen to get a better look at them.

He loved history, especially that of the everyday life of ordinary people.

He went towards the front door of the nearest house. The grass growing between the crazy paving stones on the footpath hadn't been crushed or disturbed so whoever had visited this place recently mustn't have gone inside this one. He turned to look round and sure enough, the paths to the nearby houses were similarly untouched.

What had they come here to look at, then? The answer seemed fairly obvious: the land. You could fit many more of the modern style in houses on this patch of ground than the group of old dwellings, especially if you crammed them together as closely as local building regulations allowed.

He peered through the one window at the rear of the first house whose curtain hadn't been fully drawn and saw to his surprise that there were a few pieces of furniture inside it, old-fashioned, the wooden surfaces of the table and sideboard thick with dust. When was the last time anyone had bothered to go inside?

The situation just got stranger! And more intriguing. He couldn't resist trying the door and though it was locked, to his surprise when he felt along the lintel above it he found an old-fashioned key.

Should he? Dare he?

He looked round and saw no one, heard no noises that would signal people or other habitations nearby. What the hell! Why not do it? He could simply say the house was unlocked when he got here, if anyone asked.

He opened the door and found the air inside the house stuffy as if it hadn't been opened for a long time. His feet left faint tracks across the dusty wooden floor, the only tracks there were. The building was larger inside than he'd realised because it stretched further back. It could be made into a desirable modern residence with very little trouble, but perhaps with a larger garden than the pocket-handkerchief-sized areas usually provided these days.

If developers bought the land, they'd only knock this building down, which would be a real shame because it was so typical of its time and, from his initial viewing, very soundly built.

The bathroom was extremely old-fashioned, though the claw-footed bathtub was popular again in some quarters. A modern house this size would have at least one ensuite bathroom as well, but that could easily be fixed. He smiled at himself. He couldn't help thinking like an architect, could he?

He let himself out and locked up again, putting the key back on the lintel, then continuing to wander round.

Only one other house had a key sitting conveniently above the door and again, it was larger than it looked from outside, with several pleasant rooms on both floors and three smaller rooms in the attic.

He had to rely on peeping through the uncurtained windows or simply guessing what the other houses might be like inside if judged by where the windows were located.

Most of the houses were in a reasonable state externally except for the one at the far end, which had sagged into a dangerous ruin and been left where it fell. Strange, that. Two other dwellings also looked to be in need of urgent remedial care. Their gutters and roof in particular needed serious attention, with long trails of damp down the outer walls at a couple of points.

There was a large mound of roughly head height to the right of the group of houses. It was clearly an artificial construction and it seemed fairly obvious that something lay buried beneath it. A few low shrubs and plants had started to grow on it, but nothing of any size. When he studied it more closely, there seemed once to have been access to it from the road.

All in all, he had a wonderful time looking round and no one came to disturb him. He hoped someone would bring this place back to life in a sympathetic way rather than knock everything down.

By the time he'd finished exploring the site it was late afternoon, nearing closing time for shops, and he'd missed his lunch completely. He hesitated. Should he? Oh, why not? He'd risk driving back to the village specified on the for sale board: Essington St Mary, the one he'd driven through as he went up the hill. It wouldn't hurt to find out the price of the parcel of land, just out of curiosity.

He stopped to look at the window displays of properties at the estate agency and it surprised him that the land he'd been looking at wasn't there. You'd have thought it'd attract clients easily and they'd be geared up for a rapid sale.

He went inside to where a young woman had been sitting yawning over her desk.

She straightened up as he approached and fixed a bright, artificial smile to her face. 'How may I help you, sir?'

'I saw a piece of land with some old cottages on it which said to apply here for details. It was near the top end of Larch Tree Lane.'

She frowned for a moment, then snapped her fingers. 'Oh, yes. The old Marrakin estate.'

'Is the place still for sale?'

'Yes. Would you like to look at the details?'

He hesitated then nodded. 'I would, please.'

She went across to a filing cabinet and pulled a folder out, spreading its contents on a high desk nearby. 'There you are, sir.'

He looked at the price and hoped he'd hidden his delight. It was more than reasonable; it was an absolute bargain. He went through some of the papers and there was enough of a summary for him to see that there wasn't likely to be a problem building on the land, unless the local council was unusually strict about older properties. There was a good site map, too.

After that he took a deep breath and did something very unlike himself. 'I'd like to buy it.'

She gaped at him.

He waited.

She gulped and said, 'Mr Begworth is handling that particular property but he's just gone away for a month's holiday in Spain.'

'Well, surely there's someone else who can deal with it?'

'Ms Perry might be able to.'

She sounded doubtful. Why? A potential buyer was good news, wasn't it? 'I know it's late but could you give her a call and see if she'll come and talk to me about it now? I don't live in this area, you see.'

'Of course, sir. Could I have your name, please?' She noted it down and went across to make a call from a partitioned-off space that formed a tiny office, speaking in hushed tones. After a couple of minutes she poked her head out and called, 'Ms Perry can be here in twenty minutes if you don't mind waiting, sir?'

'I don't mind at all. I can study the details of the property while I wait.'

'That's fine.' She spoke on the phone again and when she put it down she asked, 'Would you like a cup of tea or coffee?'

'I'd kill for a coffee.'

This time her smile was genuine. 'How do you take it?'

'I'll drink it as it comes, but I'd prefer no milk or sugar.'

'Black it is, then.'

By the time he sat down, reaction had set in and he was wondering what on earth had got into him. He never made financial investments impulsively. It was one of his golden rules.

But the group of houses seemed to have been waiting for him. It had even felt as if the dwellings had welcomed him as the new owner.

Oh, he was being stupid.

But he might as well read the details in the folder while he waited.

And if this agent could take him to look inside the other buildings there, so much the better.

Ms Perry arrived in just under fifteen minutes and stopped near the door to study him, as if checking whether he was to be taken seriously. She looked about his own age, perhaps a little older, and was dressed in a very severe navy-blue trouser suit.

After a moment or two she moved forward, hand outstretched. 'Mr Drayton?'

'Yes. My first name's Corin, which I prefer.'

'I'm Nina. Pleased to meet you.'

While they were shaking hands, the receptionist began putting on her outdoor clothes.

Nina turned round. 'Thanks for holding the fort, Angie. I owe you one.'

After the younger woman had left, Nina turned back to him, all business now. 'If you were wanting a brochure, I'm afraid they didn't make any. But I can probably tell you what you want to know about that particular property.'

'I had a good look at the buildings from the outside, but is it possible to see the interiors? There's still an hour or two of daylight left.'

'You're serious about buying it, then?' She sounded surprised.

'Very serious.'

She continued to look at him, head on one side. 'Are you any relation to the Draytons who own a brewery? You have a look of Pete.'

'You know my brother?'

'Slightly. He went out with a friend of mine for a time.'

'It's a small world.'

She looked a little more relaxed and he guessed that the relationship would have shown her that he might be able to afford to buy the houses, since the brewery's poor financial state wasn't known. Well, he hoped it wasn't, for Pete's sake.

'Do you want me to drive you there, Corin, then I can point out the nearby local amenities as we go?'

'Good idea.'

'Angie said you asked to *buy* the property, not just look at it. Am I right?'

'Yes, I did. I'm not usually so impulsive, but it's just what I'm looking for. I'm an architect, have just finished one project overseas and I'm looking for another back in Britain, one of my own this time.'

'Sounds good. Let's go, then.'

When they stopped at what she said locals called simply 'the Marrakin', she produced a set of keys then came with him into the first two houses. She didn't seem much interested in what they were like and, after that, said she'd wait in the car while he looked his fill, if he didn't mind.

Gradually dusk started to settle in and he stopped looking, had seen enough to convince him that most of the houses would make excellent restoration projects and could be made to ooze the period character which buyers talked about longingly on the TV property shows he'd watched a few times since he came back.

He got into the car and said it before he could lose his courage. 'I'm sure now that I'd like to put in an offer. Could we do that tonight, do you think?'

'Yes. Well, I suppose we can. It's one of Don Begworth's acquisitions and since things have been rather quiet lately and his wife wanted to go on holiday, he said he'd be out of touch for a few weeks. I don't suppose he'll mind me selling it for him, though.'

Back at the office they filled in the forms, he did a deposit by bank transfer and then asked if an accelerated completion was possible.

Nina stared at him in surprise. 'My goodness! You're certainly an impulsive guy.'

'Not usually. But this feels just right for me and I'd like to get started.'

'Well, I'll contact the seller and see what I can do. It may be possible to speed things up.'

'Thanks. Is that all?'

'For now. I'll be in touch.'

'Is there somewhere nearby that I can find a place for the night, a hotel or B&B, doesn't matter which.'

'There's a pub in the village that has rooms to let. They're clean but very basic. They'll probably find you something to eat, too, if you beg nicely. I drive past it on my way home, so if you follow me, I'll stop and toot my horn when we get to it.'

'Does it have a name?'

'It's had several names over the years, but it's like those cottages of yours, in the process of being sold, so the ratty old sign that was blown down in a storm hasn't been replaced. And I doubt whether a new buyer would want to call it the Negger's Arms after the owner who passed away recently.'

'It's not the most appealing of names.'

He found the landlady very helpful, was given a room, then served pie and chips at a small table in the corner, even though it was after hours for a meal by then. He finished up by indulging in a glass of brandy to celebrate.

He missed sharing what was usually his one drink of the day with Pete and would have liked to clink glasses with his brother tonight and drink to the success of his new venture.

Had he really been so impulsive? That was so unlike him where financial matters were concerned. But there was something about the Marrakin that called to him.

Nina drove home slowly, feeling absolutely delighted at the prospect of this large sale and eventual commission. She'd phone Don Begworth tomorrow and let him know.

She frowned as she stopped the car outside her home. Or should she just go ahead and put the sale through?

Yes, she would do exactly that. Don had acted strangely about this property right from the beginning, with minimal advertising and a surprisingly low price. She suspected he had an arrangement with someone to sell it cheaply and they might be waiting for finance to come through or doing nothing to prove a point about it not being sellable.

Why should she give up her chance of a good commission?

She had suspected him of doing that sort of thing before in the two years she'd been working here. It didn't feel right to her to cheat sellers that way but she felt helpless to stop him. She'd have looked for a new job only she'd rashly bought a house in the village, a fixer-upper at a bargain price, with great potential. She didn't want to leave it, had put a lot of effort into it and still had some work to do before selling it.

However, she had recently begun looking for a job

elsewhere because she wasn't happy working with Don for other reasons as well. He was extremely sexist, for a start, and his private manners reflected that, even though he had the wit to moderate his language with clients. He didn't always moderate it with her and though he'd never touched her, he sometimes stared at her breasts as if hungry for a meal. Ugh! She hated that sort of look.

She received a phone call before she left for work the following morning to say that she'd got the job in a nearby town that she'd had an interview for two days previously.

After she'd put her phone away, she danced around the kitchen. She wouldn't even have to sell her little house because her new territory would partly overlap the valley.

That decided it for Corin Drayton's sale as well. She was going to push the transaction through so that she could confront Don with a fait accompli when he returned. And serve him right if what she suspected was true.

Corin seemed a decent guy and she'd hate to see him cheated out of buying the land at the last minute by Don. Well, gazumping had always seemed unfair to her. If you made an offer to buy a house and it was accepted, that should be it. She'd worked in Australia for a year or two and there, offers were legally firm the minute both parties had signed the offer and acceptance form.

This sale would be her parting gift to Don and she intended to tell him bluntly what she thought of the way he stared at women and talked about them before she left.

When she got to work, she contacted the government

official whose name was on the file as handling the sale for the Ministry of Defence and was fortunate to catch him free to speak. When she explained that she had a firm cash offer for the Marrakin, Jeff Lister was delighted.

'That's great! The other guy at your place thought it might take a while and we might have to drop the price. He said he hadn't even had anyone showing signs of interest.'

Which just went to show she'd been right in her suspicions. 'Well, you never know when a buyer will turn up out of the blue. A guy looked round it yesterday and fell in love with it. He's a cash buyer too, so it couldn't be better. Don Begworth is away on holiday at the moment, so I'll be handling all the paperwork. Will that be all right with you, Jeff?'

'Perfectly fine. It doesn't matter who I deal with, I just want to get it off our books. My predecessor loved the place and had far more maintenance done than was strictly necessary, so your buyer will be getting a bargain.'

'Even better. You'll find it easiest to contact me on my mobile phone, rather than via the office. There's only an inexperienced receptionist here at the moment.'

'Give me your number.' Jeff repeated it after her then said, 'Great.'

'The thing is, my client wants to expedite matters. He's in a hurry to start. Would you mind doing that?'

'Not at all. In fact, the sooner the better, as far as I'm concerned, because I've booked a holiday next month. Um, he knows the electrics and so on aren't connected or viable? Well, the water can be connected but not the other utilities.'

'He understands all that. He's an architect. He's going to rent in the neighbourhood and personally manage the restoration and development work.'

'I thought whoever bought it would be knocking everything down.'

'Not this guy. He says there's a good market for sympathetic restorations and there are clients desperately looking for period character and larger gardens, who'll pay a premium price.'

'Good for him. I don't like to see history wiped out completely, I must admit. That makes me even more keen to push this sale through quickly.'

'Oh, good.'

'I'll start at once and be in touch very soon.'

When the call ended, she smiled and dialled Corin's number.

Chapter Six

Lucia heard a noise and went to check on Maggie, finding her in the middle of transferring to the office chair. 'Are you all right?'

'Yes. Just need to use the bathroom. I think I can manage to get there on my own. This office chair was a brilliant idea.' She started to scoot along using her good foot, moved into the hall, then stopped and looked round. 'If you could get me a glass of water, I'd be grateful. I'm not at all hungry but I'm really thirsty and even with the chair, I struggle to reach a clean glass, not to mention being afraid to fill it up in case I spill it.'

When she was settled on the couch again with the glass of water within easy reach, Maggie said sleepily, 'I forgot to tell you to bring down a single mattress and bedding, and put them on the kitchen floor. Just in case I need help with anything during the night, as the doctor suggested. Would you mind? I hate feeling so helpless.'

'I was intending to sleep in an armchair so I don't mind at all.'

'How kind of you! I'm sure a mattress would be much

more comfortable than a chair, though, and the stairs are wide enough to get one down fairly easily. There are several single beds, both hard and soft.' She laughed and added, 'And an antique flock mattress, which I don't recommend. Take whichever one you think is most likely to suit. They're none of them new, I'm afraid.'

'I brought in my things from the car and put them in what looked like an empty second pantry. Is that all right?'

'Perfect.'

Within ten minutes, Lucia had dragged a mattress down and taken a selection of bedding from the huge linen cupboard. She draped the latter on chairs to one side of the kitchen fire to air, and stood the mattress at the other side.

Later on, she made up a bed, tested it out and found it surprisingly comfortable, even without a proper base. Or perhaps she was so tired anything would feel good.

A sudden thought made her get up again to check all the doors and windows she could find downstairs, just in case any were unlocked. She should have asked Maggie about them earlier but her hostess was now sound asleep again. However, as her companion seemed to have a rather casual attitude towards security, Lucia would rather be sure she was behind locked doors and windows at night.

She went round the ground floor, doing the best she could on her own to check everything. To her relief she found all the doors and windows properly secured and didn't think she'd missed any.

Feeling she'd made everything as safe as she could, she left one light on in the entrance hall, in case Maggie needed help during the night, and went back to her makeshift nest in the kitchen. As an afterthought, she took the poker from the fireplace stand and placed it right next to her before she lay down, just in case.

If she was being a 'nervous ninny', to use one of her grandma's terms, too bad. That poker being nearby made her feel safer.

Damn Howard for doing this to her! If she could ever pay him back, she would, not out of revenge but to teach him a lesson about bullying.

Some time later, Lucia woke with a start and didn't know where she was at first. Then her eyes began to adjust to the dim light in the kitchen and she remembered what had happened the previous day.

She listened carefully. There were no sounds coming from Maggie in the library.

What had woken her, then? Something had, she was quite sure. A shout, maybe. She had become a light sleeper since she broke up with Howard.

She sat up and listened even more carefully. From outside came the sounds of what she thought – hoped! – were night animals or tree branches rustling. Then she thought she heard someone yell. She thought it had sounded more human than animal, but the sound wasn't repeated so maybe she was wrong.

Well, if anyone was prowling around, they hadn't tried to come inside. She reached down to pat the poker. Who was there to prowl anyway? There were no houses nearby, no main roads to bring burglars easily to this district and she'd checked that Howard wasn't following her.

She told herself she was getting paranoid and shouldn't let the thought of her ex get her down. He couldn't possibly have followed her here. And since she hadn't even known this little valley existed, she couldn't have mentioned it to him.

Even so, she didn't get to sleep again for a while, kept listening with all her senses on alert. She felt vulnerable, partly because he was bigger than her and partly because he was so sneaky. She might be reasonably tall but she wasn't strong in the way he was. He used to joke that he had muscles on his muscles and prided himself on keeping fit, using the gym to offset the hours he spent sitting at a computer.

Would she ever be free of worrying about him?

That was such an upsetting thought.

The man standing outside near what had been the stables cursed the rubbish bin he'd knocked over. Some idiot had placed it in the deepest shadows and he'd bumped into it because he'd been studying the house.

There was no sign of movement inside the place, no lights being switched on and off, so no one could have noticed the noise he'd made.

He moved forward carefully towards the house then forgot about the bin and stopped to smile. Yes, that was her car, parked to the other side of a large older vehicle. So the tracking program he'd downloaded onto her phone was still working. She must be in the house, but why had she come here? And who else lived there?

He made a fist of triumph sign in the air with his right hand, then went to stand in the doorway of a musty old outhouse, checking what was inside it as well as he could by moonlight. No living creatures were kept here and there were no signs of recent human usage, only a few old boxes lying around in one corner. He noted the place for his next visit, and watched the house for a while from inside its shadowy interior, trying to figure out the layout of the big house.

This wasn't at all the sort of place where he'd have expected to find Lucia. Who did his ex know in a posh house like this? She'd never visited whoever it was while they were married, nor had she kept in touch with them. He'd have known because he had a bug in her phone.

Which just showed how stupid she was not even to consider such a possibility after they broke up. Even if the owner of such a large house wasn't well off, anyone who lived here would know useful people who had money. It was a good job she hadn't worked in sales. She'd have been pitiful at sussing out potential buyers.

He frowned and mentally went through the people she knew again, just to be sure, then got out his phone and went through her online contacts. Nope. No one lived anywhere near this district. He'd have to check out the person who owned this house but he'd do that from home later. He'd need to find out what the property was called first, though.

Ideally, he'd have loved to wake Lucia up with a start, just to let her know he was staying on her tail till he got his share of the jewellery. He'd had it secretly valued when they were first married, but had stupidly let her deposit the collection in the bank herself, and she'd done that in her own name only.

No, however tempting it was to wake her up, it'd be rash to cause trouble until he knew exactly who else lived here.

The owners might have friends or relatives in positions of authority, or even be important in their own right.

And besides, he didn't know yet where her bedroom was or whether she'd be moving on tomorrow. This might be a fancy B&B for all he knew. She'd have needed to find somewhere to sleep and you didn't get much choice out here in woop-woop. He smiled at that term, which he'd picked up from an Australian client. It summed up the countryside nicely.

It was annoying to have that stupid company workshop taking place for the whole of this coming week. There was no way he'd be able to get even a half day's leave, not if he wanted to stay in the manager's good books. The new owners must have rocks in their heads to waste staff time like that but he'd show up and behave like an eager beaver, as he always did.

Well, he could always catch up with Lucia again, wherever she went. Thank goodness for digital technology.

A yawn took him by surprise. He'd better get back now. He could still grab an hour or two of sleep before he had to go to work.

He started trekking back through that damned wood, annoyed that the moon kept getting hidden by clouds or the foliage of big trees. In one period of darkness he tripped over a half-concealed log and let out an involuntary yell, only saving himself from a bad fall by grabbing some sort of smaller flowering tree that made him want to sneeze.

He moved more cautiously after that, not wanting to use his torch to light the way till he was completely out of sight of the house. You never knew who was looking out of a window.

Note to self: buy some night vision goggles for future forays.

As he stumbled along, he remembered a soppy poem he'd had to learn at school about the beauty of woods, and cursed Wordsworth and all the other literary idiots he'd been forced to waste his time studying.

They'd raved on ad nauseam about the beauties of the countryside but he'd never understood that obsession. Stupid people could keep Mother Nature, for all he cared. The people who mattered these days were urban creatures, important for their brains and ability to develop and use computers and other new technologies, not for mucking out pigsties and digging up plants.

He grunted in relief as he came to the edge of the woods, then cursed again under his breath when he had trouble finding his car because he'd come out of the woods at a different point to where he'd entered. Those bloody trees all looked alike after dark – well, the big ones did.

In the morning Maggie woke early, so it was a good thing Lucia was an early riser too and was able to help her get washed and dressed, fetching and carrying and passing things.

The doctor arrived at a quarter to eight, examined the ankle and pronounced it to be definitely a sprain.

'I think so too,' Maggie said calmly. 'It's much less swollen now than it was last night, Tom.'

'That doesn't mean you should walk around on it, my girl. It needs rest to help it recover.'

She flourished one hand towards Lucia. 'Hence my handmaiden. I've hired my young friend for a few days.'

He looked across the room 'Are you a nurse?'

Lucia shook her head. 'No. I did a first aid course at one place where I worked, but that's my total experience.'

'Well, try to stop her moving around too much. Sit on her, if necessary.'

'She'd not be very comfortable to sit on. Too thin.'

They all chuckled and Lucia waited for the laughter to die down before she continued. 'Seriously, though, it'll be all right if she moves round the house on the office chair, won't it?'

'Yes, of course. As long as she doesn't try to break the speed limit.'

He started to leave then frowned. 'I nearly forgot. Have you been having any trouble with trespassers lately, Maggie?'

'Not that I know of. Why?'

'Well, you might like to check your outhouses and grounds once your ankle is better. That laburnum you planted a few years ago has been damaged and the broken branches need trimming. It looks as if someone trampled all over it recently and then went off through the woods.'

Lucia's breath caught in her throat. 'I thought I heard noises during the night. It could have been an intruder.'

The doctor frowned. 'Come with me and have a look at it, Lucia. I think there were some footprints and if they're at all clear, we'll take photos of them.'

A cry escaped her before she could prevent it. 'Oh, no!'

They both stared at her and she blurted out, 'My ex has been stalking me. But how could he possibly have found out where I was? I left my rented place before daylight yesterday and checked really carefully at a motorway services to make sure he wasn't following me by car.'

There was silence while they digested this idea, then Tom said, 'He could have put a tracking app on your phone and/or your car. One of my patients found out her ex had been doing that. Do you think yours is capable of such behaviour?'

Dead silence followed and she stared from one to the other, her heart suddenly pounding with fear. 'Yes. Definitely. Only, how do I find out? I'm not wonderful with the fancier aspects of technology. My ex is, though.'

'You'd need to hire someone to find out if anything's been tampered with on your phone and if so, ask them to get rid of the problem for you. Maybe Maggie and I can ask around. Between us, we know a lot of people round here. There must be someone in Essington St Mary who's tech savvy enough to check your devices.'

'I'll definitely look into that. And I'll come and look at the laburnum with you now.'

She got into his car and after a hundred metres or so he stopped and they walked across to a mangled tree.

'Careful how you tread, Lucia. We don't want to destroy any evidence. The poor tree has been bashed around a bit, and recently too, but I think we can still save its life. I was here a few days ago and it looked lovely. Ah! There's a partial footprint here.' Tom put out one arm to bar the way and pointed. 'And aren't those a couple more further on?'

'Yes.' She took a photo of both tree and footprints, then he drove off and she walked back to the house, feeling jumpy on her own. Howard couldn't still be here, could he? No. It was a working day and he boasted about never missing a day, from illness or anything else.

Maggie looked at her sympathetically as she made

herself a cup of coffee and stirred it round and round till her hostess put a hand on hers to stop her. 'If you stir that any more, it'll evaporate.'

She stared at her mug and put the spoon down.

'Do you need to get away, Lucia? If so, I'll understand and find someone else to help me.'

'Well, actually, I'd rather stay here, if you don't mind, Maggie. Howard can't get lost in crowds in a small village, can he? And if he's planted something to track me, it'll still be there wherever I go so I need to sort that out before I do anything. Or does this make you want me to leave?'

'No, of course not. He'll not get lost among the inhabitants of our valley, I promise you. We've got some very nosey people round here and they'd notice an outsider who hangs about for no obvious reason.'

'Do you call it a valley? It doesn't seem a pronounced enough geological formation for that.'

'To us it's a valley. There is a long but admittedly shallow declivity worn away by the River Esse on its way down to Essington St Mary. It's barely big enough to be called a river, but it's more than just a stream.'

Lucia smiled and nodded, which her companion took as a sign to continue.

'Unfortunately, the district has been losing population steadily for the past decade or more, so I'm not sure you'll find anyone to help you locally. We used to have several small businesses owned by residents, but some of them have been taken over by big companies and others put out of business by the new supermarket. Their former shops are just standing empty. It upsets me to see them. Whole families have moved away, have had to in order to earn a living, sadly.' Maggie paused to sigh and stare into space.

Lucia started thinking about the possible existence of a tracking device or program on her phone. That would explain why Howard had kept turning up nearby, even after their divorce. How stupid of her not to think of that herself! But you didn't start a marriage by suspecting the husband who seemed to love you of being sneaky, did you? And she'd assumed that his attentions would stop once the divorce went through.

She looked up and saw Maggie watching her with a sympathetic expression. 'Sorry. I was just wondering how long he's been tracking me for. Shall I make you something to eat now? Do you like a proper cooked breakfast or just a snack?'

'I'm a morning eater. I usually have fruit, something protein with egg or ham or whatever, followed by toast with jam. Will you join me?'

'If you don't mind. There's more of me to support than most young women carry around.'

'Who wants to look like a gaunt scarecrow? You're not at all fat; in fact, you have a lovely figure.'

'Oh. Well, thank you.'

She tried to chat cheerfully as she cooked the food, but underneath it all she felt a leaden sickness. What was she going to do if it was Howard and he could track her down anywhere? He'd probably installed a program on her phone but she didn't want to spend money on a new one unless it was absolutely necessary. Only, she hadn't the faintest idea how to check it for spyware, or whatever you called it.

Knowing him, she'd guess he'd have put something in her car too. He had always boasted that complete control of every detail of a project was why he was so successful at his job. And he was successful, damn him, earned a really good living. That attention to detail was what he had wanted to do to her: control every aspect of her life.

And why was she sitting here lost in thought, like an idiot at a fair with her breakfast going cold? She had to do something about Howard.

'I've got a friend in the village,' Maggie said abruptly as Lucia began to clear away. 'How about I contact Liz? She went to some computer classes last year. She isn't very well but I could ask her if she knows anyone who'd be able to check your phone and car?'

'Would you mind? I'd be really grateful. The mere thought of him knowing my every move gives me the shivers.'

'It'd upset anyone. He's clearly what an American friend of mine calls a fruit loop.'

Maggie rang her friend while Lucia was clearing up and when she put the phone down, she stared at it sadly.

'Liz is about to go into a hospice. I knew she had cancer but I hadn't realised things had got so bad. She doesn't know anyone near here who's skilled enough to help you, but she's letting her nephew stay in her house for a few weeks and he's coming tomorrow. He's into technical stuff so she'll leave a note asking him to give us a call if he can recommend anyone. He's stayed here a few times so knows the area.'

'That's so kind of her. And at a time like this.'

'Yes. She's a lovely person. I'm going to miss her. Most people round here are kind, given half a chance. It's why I like living here, even though I rattle around in this house on my own these days.'

'Have you ever thought of turning it into a B&B, or making a couple of flats or bedsitters to rent out? Or even taking in lodgers, if you have the energy to look after them?'

Maggie blinked and stared at her. 'No, I haven't, well, not seriously. I'll have to do something soon, though. Larch House needs quite a few major repairs that I've been putting off because I'm not exactly rolling in money.'

When she'd cleared up the kitchen, Lucia caught sight of the sun outside and asked, 'Would you mind if I went for a short walk? I did a lot of sitting in the car yesterday and I feel a bit twitchy.'

'Go for your life. Now that you've fed me, I'll be all right for an hour or two with my trusty steed.' She rattled the office chair, which was 'stabled' nearby.

'I shan't be that long, maybe half an hour.'

'There are paths through my woods that you might enjoy. Go right to the end of the one that starts to the right of those outbuildings.' She pointed out of the window. 'When you get to the wire fence, which is the boundary with the Marrakin, turn right, not left, and it'll take you along by a drystone wall to the bluebell wood, which is where you found me yesterday.'

She sighed and added, 'Watch your footing there, though, and this time you may be able to enjoy the flowers. They're such a beautiful shade of blue. Only, if you see signs of any other trespassers, please take note of it.'

Lucia set off along the path Maggie had pointed out, breathing in deeply, enjoying the fresh air and lack of traffic noise. As her new friend had said, it led to a skimpy wire fence that was more of a marker than a barrier, so she turned right there, looking forward to seeing the bluebell wood.

When she reached the drystone wall, she stopped to admire it as well, then looked over the top. Was that a group of houses further along, slightly downhill from where she was? She carried on, stopping to look over it again about a hundred metres further on. Yes, they were houses and included some really old ones. None of them looked occupied and the gardens were more like hayfields. One house looked to have fallen down but the others seemed to have been cared for and most were, or could have been, very attractive.

She walked along the wall and more houses came into view. What a lovely spot to live! She wondered what would become of them. Probably get knocked down by developers. Pity, though, if that happened to these.

Then she saw a flash of blue through the trees and wound her way to the bluebells. How beautiful they were!

By the time she got back to the house, she felt refreshed by the walk and was thinking that she might try to find somewhere in the country to live, perhaps even near here if there were any jobs available – then she could keep in touch with Maggie.

Chapter Seven

Corin woke in the middle of the night worrying about what he'd done. Dived head first into unknown waters, that's what.

Too late to back out now. And anyway, he didn't want to back out. Not exactly. But he did wish he'd exercised due care and diligence before buying that block of land, if only to stop himself worrying about what might go wrong.

It was a while before he got to sleep again so he woke later than he'd intended. He lingered over breakfast in the dining area to one side of the bar, reading a newspaper they'd kindly provided. Should he stay another night and do some poking around? Why not? His time was his own now. He hadn't got used to that sort of freedom yet.

He went to find the landlady and ask if his room was free for another night.

She beamed at him. 'It certainly is, Mr Drayton. And will you want an evening meal?'

'I'm not sure. I'll try to get back before you stop serving them if I do. Oh, and is there a bookshop in the village?'

'Sort of.'

He was puzzled by that response and it must have shown.

'There's a second-hand bookshop which orders in some bestsellers when they're new and also books by authors that their regular customers love. Were you wanting something in particular or just a book to read?'

'I'm looking for a map book that shows the valley and surrounding districts in detail.'

'Oh, Petra always stocks those, because we get quite a few tourists passing through in the warmer months, especially hikers going up the valley to the Marrakin Trail. It's a relatively gentle walk that takes in a few historical sites and monuments and is quite popular. It regularly gives me customers, that trail does, so I contribute to its maintenance.'

'And the bookshop is where?' he prompted.

'In the centre of the village. The shops are spread out round our lovely old church. You can't miss that. The bookshop is opposite the lychgate. You may enjoy looking round the church too. It's open from ten to four each day.'

Armed with this information, he strolled out into the village, happy to see the sun shining today, easily finding his way.

He spent over an hour in the bookshop, which had an amazing range of books for such a small place. In the end he bought two backlist novels by an excellent author he'd discovered recently and a history of the district as well as the map book he'd gone in for. It was lovely not having to order books from the UK or US and then wait a couple of months for them to be shipped out to him as he'd had to do when working overseas. He'd so enjoyed being able to browse today and find unexpected treasures.

He flipped through the map book, gradually getting the gist of how the village and surrounding hamlets were laid out. Satnavs were all very well if you wanted to get somewhere by the most direct route, but if you wanted to learn about a region, flipping between 'views' on a screen could be irritating. Well, it was to him anyway.

He bought a sandwich and chocolate éclair together with a can of lemonade for lunch and consumed them sitting on a bench in a sunny corner of the churchyard, watching butterflies and small birds flitter around. After that he decided to drive round the nearby countryside during the afternoon and get to know the locality.

As he was coming out of the churchyard, a car screeched to a halt just ahead of him and when he looked at the man getting out of it, he beamed. What a happy coincidence!

The driver came back to join him. 'You only get uglier as you get older, Corin my lad.'

'And you're as handsome as you ever were, Nate Logan.'

They hugged briefly and thumped each other on the back, then stared, taking in the slight changes that a few years apart had made to each of them.

'Seriously, you're looking well,' Nate said. 'What the hell are you doing in this neck of the woods? I didn't even know you'd come back to England. You're not the world's best at keeping in touch.'

'My return was rather sudden. My father died recently, you see.'

'Oh, no! I'm so sorry. Didn't mean to touch a sensitive spot.'

'You didn't. He and I were never close, and I'd hardly spent any time with him during the past ten years. Look, the village pub will be open. I don't like drinking alcohol in the middle of the day but they do very nice coffee.'

'I have an even better idea: I've just arrived here and am on my way to house-sit for my aunt. Why don't you come there with me, then we can have a catch-up in absolute privacy? Unless you're on your way somewhere?'

'No. I was just having a look round the village and getting to know the area but I can do that another time. I'll follow you. I don't think I'll lose you on these busy roads.'

'It'd be hard to do that. They're never what you'd call really busy, even Larch Tree Lane, the main thoroughfare.'

A single car drove past slowly as if to emphasise the lack of traffic and Corin chuckled. 'What a road hog!'

Smiling, they both got into their vehicles.

Nate led the way, turning off to the right onto the second street outside the village proper. He stopped fifty metres along it outside a picture-book pretty cottage. He led the way to the front door. 'Auntie Liz said she'd leave a key under the doormat for me. Ah yes, here it is.'

'Trusting soul.'

'I've told her that she should be more careful but she said if anyone was so desperate they needed to steal her well-worn clothes and rickety old furniture, they'd be welcome to them.'

They found the cottage neat and tidy, with a fruit cake sitting in a transparent container on the table and a scrap of paper with the word 'Enjoy!' sticking out from the edge of the top.

'Has she gone on holiday?'

'No. Sadly she went into a hospice this morning but I had arranged to give a breakfast talk and I couldn't let them down. Besides, what do you say to someone who's going away to die? I'm gutted about that happening to such a lovely person.'

He looked at the cake and ran his fingers round the edge of the container, staring blindly down at it and blinking hard. 'Cancer. She's not got long to go. And as my mother said, she's only seventy-three, far too young and lively to leave us.'

They were quiet for a moment, then Nate shrugged and said, 'Anyway, what can't be cured must be endured. Liz has been so brave and practical, I must follow her example. Let's have a cup of coffee and a piece of cake while you tell me what you're doing here.'

As he went to fill the kettle, he found a further note weighted down by it, scrawled as if dashed off in a hurry.

PS: my friend Maggie has someone staying with her who's being stalked by her ex-husband and they think her phone must have something on it to keep track of her. Do you know enough about technology to sort it out for her? If not, would you see if you can find someone to help her?

Nate grimaced and showed the note to his friend. 'I pity the poor woman but sadly, though I'm a dab hand at word processing for my writing, I'm not much good at fiddling with that sort of thing.' He looked at Corin thoughtfully. 'On the other hand, you're pretty tech savvy. Would you be able to do anything about it?'

'I suppose I could have a look at it. I hate to think of someone being hounded like that. Will this woman want a complete stranger fiddling with her phone?'

'I should think she'd welcome help from anyone if she's being stalked. I don't understand why people do that sort of thing.'

'There are some folk who don't seem to belong to the same species as the rest of us, from the way they behave. Subhumans, with no morals.' Corin picked up the note and shrugged. 'I'm happy to have a go. I'll phone that number after our chat.'

'Phone now while I'm making our coffee.' He began to hunt through the contents of the nearby wall cupboard. 'It gives me the shivers to think of a man doing that. And if his ex is staying with my aunt's friend, this woman must be a decent person because Maggie's as shrewd as they come.'

Someone picked up the phone after only two rings. 'Larch House.'

'I'm trying to contact Lucia Grey.'

The voice became suddenly wary. 'May I ask why?'

'Maggie Hatherall left a message asking whether my friend's aunt, Liz Barker, knew someone who understands computers. My name is Corin Drayton and I'm a friend of Liz's nephew. I have some skill with computers but whether it's enough to help this woman with her problem I don't know. I'd be happy to try, if that's any use.'

'Oh, thank you. Actually, I'm Lucia. Sorry to be so cagey but I have to be careful in case it's my ex phoning.'

'Must be difficult. Do you want to bring your phone here or shall I come to you?'

'Are you in Essington St Mary?'

'Yes.'

'Then it'd be better if you came here, if you don't mind. I'm helping Maggie, who's sprained her ankle, you see, and I don't want to leave her alone for too long. I'm at a place called Larch House.'

'OK. Let me ask my friend how long it'll take to get there.' He explained the situation quickly to Nate.

'Tell her we'll be there in about an hour, which will give us time to enjoy our snack. I know where that house is and it's only a few minutes away from here.'

Corin nodded and told Lucia, 'We'll be there in about an hour. We're just sitting down to a snack.'

'Thank you so much.'

'That's all right. See you soon.'

He ended the call and gave Nate a wry look. 'Do you mind coming with me? Or if you're busy, give me instructions and I'll go on my own.'

'I'm happy to come and catch up with Maggie. Sounds like this Lucia – lovely name, by the way, and I like it to be pronounced Loo-chee-ah – badly needs help. Trust Auntie Liz to spare time to try to help someone, even now.' His voice came out choked.

'Very kind indeed. Ugh, I loathe the thought of people being stalked. Now, I'll give you a quick summary of what I'm doing here while we enjoy our snack.'

When he'd finished his tale, Nate looked at him and shook his head. 'I never thought my staid and careful old friend would turn into such a risk-taker. I don't think I could spend that much money so quickly, even if I had it.' He snapped his fingers. 'And if I remember correctly, we pass the place you're interested in on our way to Larch House, so I can stop and have a quick peek over the wall.'

'I'd welcome your opinion. I don't usually take financial risks but it seemed so right.'

'Let's hope this one pans out for you, Corin, my lad. It looks like we'll both be moving to Essington if everything goes according to plan. Sadly, I'm my aunt's beneficiary.'

'Yeah. Seems a nice place.'

'I've always liked visiting the valley. Um, you won't have had time yet to find somewhere to live, will you?'

'No.'

'So why don't you come and stay with me for a while till you can find a place of your own?'

'Will you be staying long?'

Nate went a bit pink. 'Quite a while, I hope. I've, er, had a novel accepted for publication so I'm not doing any major contract work for a while. I'm very grateful that my aunt has given me free use of this place. I shall be deep into writing the sequel, mind, so I can't promise to be an attentive host.'

'Nate Logan, bestselling author!'

'One can only hope.'

'Are you sure you wouldn't mind me coming to stay with you? I must admit, it'd be a lot more pleasant than the hotel, which is a bit noisy for my taste, even though they're clean and kind there. I don't want to rent anywhere long-term yet in case the sale falls through.'

'I'd be happy to have you here. I may welcome some company . . . especially later, after my aunt . . . goes.' His voice wobbled and he stopped to breathe deeply.

Corin patted Nate on the shoulders and changed the subject. 'Tell me about this novel.'

'I'll bore you with the details later. If we finish our snack quickly, we can call in at the pub and pick up your things, then keep our appointment with your Ms Grey.'

'She's not exactly *my* Ms Grey. I've never met the woman.'

The landlady at the pub was very kind about Corin changing his mind and leaving, and refused payment. Everyone here seemed so nice and easy-going.

Partway up the hill, he told Nate to stop the car by the side of the road.

'This is the place I'm hoping to buy.'

They both got out and went to peer over the wall.

'Looks like a lot of work,' Nate commented, 'but it's a nice location.'

'My sort of work. I love designing homes that work properly for families.'

Nate shot a surprised glance at his friend. 'Can you afford the development costs?'

'I think so.'

'You must have done well with your investments.'

'Yes. Quite well.'

'It's right next to the grounds of Larch House.'

'Yes, and I hope that it's a listed property, then my houses won't have their rural vistas spoiled.'

'I don't know about being listed but I doubt that land is likely to be built on while Maggie's living there, which amounts to the same thing and won't do your sales any harm. My aunt said her friend had already refused offers to buy it.'

Corin glanced at his watch. 'We'd better move on.' He forced himself to turn away though he was itching to have another look round. 'I hope we can help this Ms Grey.'

* * *

Lucia worried to Maggie about the stranger who'd rung up. 'I *think* he's genuine. I hope you don't mind me asking him to come here to look at my phone but I didn't want to leave you on your own again and, well, I didn't want to be on my own with a complete stranger.'

'Of course I don't mind. If we don't like the looks of him, I'll pretend to faint and that'll drive him away.' She patted Lucia's arm. 'Only joking. If he's an acquaintance of Liz's nephew he'll be OK, I'm sure.' She couldn't help sighing.

'Is something wrong? You're suddenly looking so sad.'

'Liz has just left the village for good. She's told most of her family she's going into hospital for an operation, but actually, she's got cancer, poor love, well into stage four, and has been taken to a hospice because she can't cope on her own any longer and the pain is getting her down.'

'Oh, heavens! I'm so sorry.'

She shrugged. 'Liz is very stoic about it. I can't tell you how much I admire her. She says she's had a good life and reached her three score years and ten, so she can't complain.'

'But you're going to miss her.'

'Yes, dreadfully. I said I'd go to the hospice to visit her, but she said—' She broke off with another gulp of emotion.

'I can drive you there and we'll hire a wheelchair if you're still having trouble walking.'

'It's not that. She says she doesn't want visitors, just emails to keep in touch. She'd rather make the final journey on her own, especially now that she looks so gaunt. I can understand that, sort of.' She fumbled for a tissue and blew her nose. 'Sorry.'

Lucia risked giving her a hug and Maggie clung to her for a minute or two, then moved away. 'Thanks. Hugs are useful things sometimes, when you don't have words to ease the pain. Anyway, enough of that. What time is your man coming?'

'He's not exactly *my* man. I've not even met him. He said he'd be here in about an hour. And he's bringing your friend's nephew to help him find his way.'

'Nate Logan. I've met him a couple of times. Nice young guy. You can talk to them in here.'

'Will you stay with me, Maggie? I'm a bit nervous about meeting strange men, given what's happened to me lately.'

'Yes, of course I will.' She grinned. 'I was hoping you'd say that. I'm dying to see what this man finds on your phone.'

When they heard a car drive into the parking area outside the kitchen, Lucia went to peep out of the window.

'Give me a running commentary since I can't easily join you,' Maggie ordered.

'Two men are getting out. They look about my age. I'm so glad they're not young.'

'You all seem quite young to me. Go on.'

'They're both rather nice looking. Not handsome or anything like that, just . . . nice.'

She moved quickly away from the window. 'I don't want them to see me gaping at them.'

'Open the door. Why wait for them to knock? It's obvious we'll have heard them drive up.'

Lucia did as ordered, feeling a little apprehensive as she waited for them to join her. 'Hi. I'm Lucia.'

'I'm Corin Drayton and this is Nate Logan.'

'Do come in. This is Maggie.'

'Nice to meet you again, Maggie. It's been a while. Sorry about the ankle.' Nate moved across to shake her hand. 'Are you still painting?'

Lucia saw Maggie flush a little.

'She's a talented water colourist,' Nate explained.

Lucia hadn't expected Maggie to be an artist. There were no signs of painting materials let alone a studio in the parts of the house she'd seen. She suddenly realised she'd have to play hostess. 'Do sit down. Can I offer you a tea or coffee?'

'We've just had one.' Corin could see that Lucia was somewhat embarrassed so said calmly, 'I don't know if I'm good enough to help you but let's have a try. Why don't you get your phone out?'

She pointed to the table. 'It's there.' She didn't even want to touch it now she knew it was bugged.

'Do I need a password to get into it?'

'Yes.' She wrote it down, staring at it and shaking her head. 'I never bothered keeping the password secret until just before my ex and I split up because he used to help me with technical stuff sometimes. I know now why he said that I couldn't hide anything from him. I'm not the world's best at computers and digital stuff, but I have at least changed my password.'

Nate sat down near Maggie and started chatting to her in a low voice.

Lucia sat quietly while Corin began to fiddle with her phone, muttering to himself and asking her the occasional question.

'Ah! I think I've found something,' he said after a few minutes, then began to fiddle again.

It took him about half an hour and a few muttered curses to make any real progress, then he suddenly exclaimed, 'Got you, you sod!'

After that he went back to the programs and as far as she could see, he seemed to be checking through a list he'd got up on the Internet on his own phone.

In the end a full hour had passed before he sat back and beamed at her. 'I've removed your intruder. There were a couple of problems, not just one. I'm pretty sure I've got rid of him but you should change your password yet again, and do it straight away.' He held her phone out.

She let out her breath in a whoosh and did as he suggested. 'I can't thank you enough.'

'What about your car? Has he done something to that as well, do you think?'

'Probably. He always makes double sure about the details of a project, used to boast about it.'

'I'm not good enough with the various programs they use on cars to help you with that, I'm afraid.'

Maggie had stopped chatting to Nate to listen to them. 'We could take your car to Ted at the local garage. He'll be surprised to see us again so soon, won't he? He isn't full-on with digital stuff, but his grandson is supposed to be good at that sort of thing. Young Eddie fixed my car's antique computer system quite easily when it started playing up.'

She chuckled. 'It didn't take him long and he said it was primitive. It'd be worth asking him to try, don't you think?'

'I'll do anything to get my ex completely out of my life,' Lucia said fervently.

'Are you fully divorced now?' Corin asked.

'Oh, yes. Have been for a few months. But that hasn't

stopped Howard harassing me, sometimes quite openly. Which is why I moved away from Bristol.'

'We'll call Ted and see when his grandson will be free to look at the car.' Maggie looked at the clock. 'How about a glass of wine as a thank you?'

'That'd be nice.' Corin's eyes lingered for a moment on Lucia. She was rather attractive, he thought, as well as reasonably tall. At six foot four, he found short women less appealing. Unfortunately, this wasn't the time to see how well the two of them got on. She was too upset about her ex and probably wouldn't be ready to give another man a chance for a while.

Well, at least he'd cleared up one problem for her, so he'd won a few brownie points if he wanted to try chatting her up another time. If she stayed around, that was.

Anyway, this wasn't a good time for him to start a new relationship, either, not with the purchase of the property next door pending. Pity. Meeting someone you fancied was a chance happening, could strike at any time – or not strike. And the good prospects you encountered were as rare as hen's teeth at his age. Or at least, he'd found it so.

Something occurred to him and he turned to her again. 'Why don't you let me know when you're going to see this guy at the garage? You might need a lift back, and anyway, I'd be interested to see if they find any problems.'

He'd noticed that Nate hadn't mentioned to Maggie that his novel had been accepted, was just chatting lightly as the four of them shared a bottle of wine. So he didn't mention it either. But he was very proud of his friend, who'd been trying to write a publishable novel for a few years now.

Writing always sounded a bit chancy to Corin as a way of earning a living – but then, what he might be doing if the sale went through would be rather chancy too. And expensive.

Chapter Eight

The following morning, Lucia drove into the village to leave her car at the garage, stopping on the way outside Nate's house to toot her horn at Corin so that he could follow her to the garage, as arranged. He was right behind her when she arrived.

Ted greeted them with his lovely wide smile.

His grandson came across to them, looking at her car with what could only be described as a hungry expression and laying one hand on it possessively. 'Can you leave it with me for an hour or so, maybe an hour and a half, just to be sure? I'll know by then whether I can help you or not.'

'There's a nice little café behind the church,' Ted said when Eddie had taken the car away.

'Thanks.' She turned to Corin. 'I'd rather have a walk round first if you don't mind. I'd like to get to know the village better.'

'I'll leave my car here and come with you if that's OK? Apart from the fact that you may need a lift back to Larch House after this, I'd like to get to know the village better too, since I'm hoping to make it my permanent home.'

She wondered if she'd ever feel safe enough to settle somewhere openly. It hadn't happened since the divorce, that was sure. She spoke the simple truth: 'It'd be nice to have company.'

As they walked along, he said quietly, 'It's good that we're both reasonably tall, isn't it? Our steps match quite well. I sometimes have to slow down to allow friends to keep up with me.'

'So do I.' She had to slow her brain down as well, sometimes, when chatting to people who had little interest in the wider world. Not with this man, though. He had an attractive mind as well as body.

Most of the people they passed nodded a greeting or said hello, an old-fashioned courtesy, which they both commented on.

'They're strangers, yet behaving in such a friendly way,' he said at one stage. 'I love that. I do hope nothing goes wrong with my purchase of the land here.'

She nodded, but knew she was being a bit quiet today, because she simply couldn't settle, was on edge to hear whether Eddie had found anything in her car. She was glad when the time was up and they turned in unspoken agreement to walk back to the garage.

They found Eddie standing by the car, scowling down at it. He looked up and said apologetically, 'I found one or two places where tiny physical tracers had been attached then painted to look like part of the standard framework. If I hadn't been looking for something, I'd never have noticed them. Even though I've got rid of those, I'm not confident that I've found everything, I'm afraid, because whoever did this is very skilful.'

'Oh dear! What am I going to do now?'

Ted moved forward to join in. 'Are you particularly attached to this car, Ms Grey?'

'No. I only use cars to get around in. I just need something reliable.'

'Then I suggest you sell it.'

'But Howard will still be able to follow the trail of sales when I buy a new one, won't he? He's boasted to me that he can hack most government websites.'

Ted snorted in disgust. 'You're well shut of that chap. As it happens, I can send you to an acquaintance of mine, who buys cars for use in demolition derbies. He's already agreed in principle to buy yours and has offered as reasonable a price as you can expect. You should buy another car privately elsewhere, which will be harder to trace. You won't get as good a price for yours from Jack as from a regular dealer, but you'll surely puzzle your ex because this car will be smashed beyond repair after a few races.'

'I'd never have thought of doing that.'

'Well, here's another thing to think of. If you sell it to Jack quickly, you can give your old address on the sales documents. You only moved out a few days ago, after all, and I doubt anyone will take much interest in the details of a car that's going to be destroyed.'

'I didn't realise they still held that sort of race,' Corin said.

'Oh, yes. Very popular in some parts of the country, demolition derbies are.'

'Where is this friend of yours located?'

'Jack's main base is in Leicester. You'll have to drop the car off to him there then get back here under your own steam. He doesn't collect vehicles from people or give them a ride home, I'm afraid.'

'I can follow you there and bring you back, Lucia,' Corin said.

His generous offer took her breath away for a moment and all she could manage to say was, 'I can't ask you to do that.'

'I'm waiting for settlement on my contract so I've got too much time on my hands till that's sorted out.'

'Oh. Right. Well, thank you. But you must let me pay for the petrol.'

'Whatever.'

'I'm extremely grateful.' She turned to Ted and his grandson. 'How much do I owe you?'

'Two hours' labour,' Ted said.

'I ought to pay you. I really enjoyed the challenge,' Eddie said. 'Sorry I couldn't do more.'

When she'd paid, she waited while Ted phoned his friend and told him she'd agreed to sell her car, then she noted down the details of where to take it in Leicester. That done, she went outside and found Corin waiting for her, even though she didn't need a lift back.

'We didn't arrange the details of our trip tomorrow, Lucia.'

'Would setting off first thing in the morning be too early for you?' Before he could answer, she'd had a sudden thought. 'Oh dear, how can I leave Maggie for so long? It'll take us most of the day to get to and from Leicester and sort out the car sale.'

'I'm sure she can get a friend to come in and help her, or perhaps Nate can take his laptop and work from her house.'

'It's mainly to get her cups of tea or coffee, because she spills it as she limps – and I don't tell her this, but I worry in case anything goes wrong when she's on her own. She is almost seventy, after all. I can leave them some sandwiches for lunch. Would he mind, do you think?'

'I doubt it. He's a really nice guy and he's on your side.'

'So are you and it's amazing how you seem to have answers to all my problems.'

He smiled. 'Not all of them, I'm sure, but I like to help people as I go along. Let's have a coffee now and plan our outing.'

'I'd love to but I've been away for longer than I intended and I'd better get back to Maggie. I still have to nip to the shop and buy her a few groceries. I could have done that while I was waiting to hear about my car, but I forgot. I was too nervous about what my ex might have done to it.'

'I'll phone you later, then, after I've checked the road map so that we can make the final arrangements.'

'Will you ask Nate for me whether he can spend tomorrow at Larch House while we're away?'

'I won't forget. I'm sure he'll be happy to take his laptop and work there. He's not worried about what's going on around him when he's writing, so it won't matter too much where he's doing it.'

Which was stretching the truth a little about his friend's writing habits but Nate wouldn't mind.

Lucia did the shopping quickly, still marvelling at how helpful Corin had been as she drove home. What a great guy he was! She'd better be careful. It'd be all too easy to be attracted to him.

She sucked her breath in suddenly on that thought. Correction! She was already attracted to him. Oh dear. But she wasn't going to act on it, didn't intend to go out with any guy till she'd got rid of Howard once and for all, and had set her new life in order.

Maggie greeted her with obvious pleasure when she got back. 'How did it go? I was starting to worry about you.'

'We made some progress. Sorry to be so late. It all took longer than expected but unfortunately, Ted's grandson still isn't sure he's found every problem in my car.'

'Oh dear! Look, if you don't mind, I'd like a coffee now, then you can tell me all the details as I drink it. Nate was just going to get me one but when you rang to say you were coming back, he said he wanted to finish writing a scene and went home. I'm still nervous of carrying hot drinks around. I'm not nearly steady on my feet yet and I'm afraid of the ankle giving way.'

'I'm sorry to have left you for so long.'

'Your need was far more important than mine. Did you get some drinking chocolate? I've run out.'

'Oh, yes. I got everything you wanted at that village shop you told me about. It stocks a surprisingly wide range of products. Now, this is what Ted suggested I do . . .'

Maggie was fascinated by her tale but became rather thoughtful after it ended.

'Is something wrong?'

'I was wondering whether your ex will come back here if he suddenly can't trace your car. After all, he's been here once, it seems.'

Lucia looked at her in dismay. 'Surely even he won't go on harassing me for ever?'

'You didn't say that as if you were convinced.'

'You're right. It'll take a lot to convince me that I've got rid of Howard. He's very tenacious and he's brilliant at gathering information online. Perhaps I'd better move on, for your sake.'

'No, no! Don't do that. I'm not his target anyway, so there's no need to worry about me. And actually, I'm really enjoying your company.' She began fiddling with the edge of her top before adding, 'It gets a bit lonely at times rattling around this big house on my own, especially as I lose long-time friends one by one, as I'm about to lose Liz. That's one of the big downsides of growing older, the loss of people you care about. I enjoy having a head full of experiences and information, but I'd like more company, so you're welcome to stay as long as you like.'

'It must be awful to lose the people you love one by one. I've never really thought through old age doing that to people.'

'Well, you can't change the way life is, only your attitude towards it. It's you I'm more concerned about at the moment. What does your ex think he'll gain from all this harassment? Or is he just unstable mentally?'

'I think he's definitely unstable but from what he's said, the main thing he's fixated on is for me to sell my family jewels and give him a half share in the proceeds.

He's furiously angry at the mediator for not adding them to the joint possessions, though why Howard seems to be convinced that the jewels are worth a lot more than I've been told, I have no idea.'

'Perhaps he got them valued sneakily?'

'If so, I never noticed they were gone.' She frowned. 'But come to think about it, he suddenly insisted they should be stored in a bank security box one day, so perhaps you're right. I did have enough sense to do that in my name only. He was furious when he got home one day and I told him I'd been to the bank in my lunch hour.'

'Could he be right about their value?'

'I doubt it. My family were never rich and the jewels aren't even pretty. I never wear them, just keep them as a financial fallback.'

'What were you told they were worth?'

'About four or five thousand pounds.' She shrugged. 'Anyway, I'll worry about them later. They're quite safe in the bank. My priority now is to get rid of that car.'

Maggie gave her a sly grin. 'And you can enjoy some more time with Corin while you do that. He's a very attractive man, isn't he?'

And heaven help her, Lucia couldn't stop herself from blushing. Especially when her phone rang just then and it was Corin, ready to sort out the details of their trip.

They went on to chat for a while, but when she put her phone away and rejoined Maggie, her friend winked at her.

'Easy to talk to, isn't he? You've been on the phone for over twenty minutes.'

Lucia could feel herself blushing all over again. 'You'll

find him just as easy to talk to when you get to know him better, I'm sure.'

'I doubt it. I've seen the way he looks at you. He'll never look at an old woman like me in that way.'

Later that afternoon, Corin received a call from the real estate agent, Nina Perry.

'How are things going?' he asked at once.

'They're going well, far better than I'd expected, actually.'

He could hear the satisfaction in her voice as she replied so he expected good news even before she brought him up to date on the details.

'I think we're going to be able to sort it all out in just over two weeks, which is amazingly fast. I shall need you to sign some more papers tomorrow morning and to be around during the afternoon because we're hoping to get another stage of the process ready to go and I'll need a proper signature on that, too.'

'Do you think you'll get to that or is it just a possibility?'

'I actually think there's a very good chance we'll get that far.'

'Can't I just, you know, give you carte blanche to sign things on my behalf? Or do it online.'

'Not this time. It's a government contract and sale, and the guy who's handling it seems to want all the details done according to the book, and a very old-fashioned book it is, too. We can email signed documents but he'll want the originals sending on to him by post. You have to give this guy his due, though, he's prepared to act far more quickly than usual.'

'Oh, dear!'

'Is there some problem?'

'I'd made arrangements for tomorrow, but it's all right, I can change them. The property sale is much more important and I'm sure my friend will understand. Will I be safe to re-arrange our outing for the day after, or should I leave that free as well?'

'You'll be OK to fit in your outing then. It's getting things underway that matters at the moment. There won't be any action after tomorrow for a few days, then it'll go quickly at the end. You'd better have your payment ready, though, or that could slow things down.'

'OK. What time shall I come in to see you?'

'Um, I'd rather not do this at the office. Such a depressing place! How about I come to you?'

'OK.' He gave her his address at Nate's then phoned Lucia again and postponed their trip to Leicester for a day.

'Are you sure you should go away at this crucial time, Corin? I can always get a train home or even a taxi. Some of them will do fixed-price journeys that cost little more than the ridiculous fares the railways can charge for train journeys if you haven't booked in advance.'

'I was looking forward to our day out, so let's postpone it – unless you're desperate to get rid of the car tomorrow? It's only one more day to wait.'

'OK. I can hang on for a day during the week easily enough. It's weekends I worry about more. My ex is a workaholic so he's less likely to pester me in person on working days in case he misses something important at his office. He boasts about never taking time off work.

Though he might come to harass me during the night, I suppose.'

She hadn't told anyone, but she kept waking up, thinking she heard something outside. But she'd walked round the house and outbuildings in the early morning, carrying her trusty poker, just in case, and had seen no sign of any footprints or anything else that might show someone had been prowling around.

When he switched off his phone, Corin was amazed to find that they'd been talking for over half an hour, even though they'd already chatted earlier. They shared quite a few common interests in world events so they'd had some lively discussions about points of disagreement. In fact, he'd thoroughly enjoyed chatting to such an intelligent woman.

He felt pleased that things were gradually being sorted out for her. How long would it take to deal with her ex? The more time he spent time with her, the more Corin wanted to get to know her and perhaps go further before any other guys came along and asked her out. In fact, let's face it, he was determined to be first in the queue when she started dating again.

He was a bit old to fall head over heels in love, he thought, then suddenly realised that's what had happened. And impossibly quickly, too. Who'd have thought that might happen? Not he, that's for sure.

He smiled. He didn't mind at all, though.

Two mornings later, Lucia got up really early and was on the road before eight o'clock, hoping to get to Leicester before eleven. Corin would be setting off at about the same time and meeting her at the address she'd been given, but she saw no sign of him on the way.

She wasn't the fastest driver on the planet, she knew, one reason being that she always tried to drive safely, which she considered to be far more important. Howard had mocked her driving skills many times during the latter part of their marriage. To her annoyance, the memory of his unkind words still lingered and made her feel nervous whenever she got behind the wheel.

At the dealer's she found Corin already there, sitting in the office chatting and drinking a cup of tea. Her heart did a happy little skip at the sight of him.

Oh dear! It shouldn't be doing that.

But it gave another happy little skip when he stood up and gave her a glowing smile when the secretary took them in to see Jack.

As the three of them chatted, she had to admit that she'd only ever glimpsed demolition derbies on TV and Jack at once offered them free tickets. She declined without even consulting Corin, saying she was too busy at the moment looking for a job and a new home. In reality, she hated the thought of watching things being destroyed. That wasn't her idea of fun.

As they got into his car, Corin asked, 'Would you fancy stopping somewhere for lunch? I'm hungry even if you aren't.'

'I'm ravenous. You must let me treat you, as a thank you for driving me home.'

'Sorry, but I suggested lunch first, so I pay. You can pay next time, though. I've checked online for places to eat at along our route and have found one whose menu looks reasonably healthy. Eating there will also save me having to cook tea tonight. It's no good expecting Nate to do that at the moment. He's lost in his story – talk about absent-minded.'

She'd noticed before how Corin talked about food, working out how healthy something was and wrinkling his nose in disgust at the thought of eating certain popular junk foods. She felt the same after years of seeing Howard eat sugary rubbish and avoid vegetables and salads as if they were poisonous.

At one of the later stages in their marriage, her ex had thrown a bowl of salad she'd made for tea into the rubbish bin, not even allowing her the chance to eat it and claiming it was bird food and a waste of good money. 'You'd better not serve that sort of thing to me again, you stupid woman.'

She'd pulled it out of the rubbish bin and thrown it at his head as he left the kitchen, covering him with bits of food and gobs of dressing. She'd always been a good shot and it was worth cleaning the floor afterwards to see his face.

He'd raised a clenched fist so she'd grabbed a frying pan and brandished it at him. 'Just try it!'

'You'd drive a saint to drink, you bitch!'

'You're no saint.'

He hadn't done that sort of thing again, but then, she hadn't prepared meals for him again. And she still remembered that incident clearly as the final straw where she was concerned.

Why on earth had she put up with him for so long, even? Perhaps out of shame at how rapidly their marriage had fallen apart.

When she and Corin stopped at a large pub that had a car park half filled with luxury cars, she couldn't help commenting, 'This looks expensive. We should find somewhere cheap and cheerful and just grab a quick meal.'

'Who said it had to be quick? Nate's keeping an eye on Maggie again so I hope you'll humour me today. I missed places like this while I was working overseas. There's nothing quite like a well-run pub for wrapping happy warmth around you as well as providing good, hearty food.'

He parked the car and they walked inside, where she watched as the wait staff responded to his easy charm.

'What's so amusing?' he asked when they were seated and about to study the menus they'd been handed.

'You had those people happily fussing over you without even trying to charm them.'

'Did I? Well, I definitely wasn't trying to do that. The only one here that I want to charm is you.'

She froze and blurted out, 'I can't do that sort of thing,' then found herself adding involuntarily, 'not yet, anyway.'

'No, I can tell that, so I'm trying desperately to hold back my almost overwhelming passion for you.'

'You spoiled the effect of that statement by the way your eyes crinkled at the corners after you'd said it,' she pointed out, relaxing again.

'Drat.' He chuckled then his smile faded and he said gently, 'But your fear of giving in to your feelings won't last for ever, I hope, and I'll be waiting. Your ex did a real job on you, didn't he, destroying your self-confidence among other things? But real men are nothing like him, any more than real passion is like my jokes.'

She could feel herself flushing. He'd read her emotions so well. 'I'm improving gradually, pulling myself together. I'm only too aware of what being with him did to me, I assure you.'

'Good. You've got a lot to be proud of as a person. I really enjoy your company and your lively conversation.' His voice grew suddenly tighter as he added, 'I'd like to punch him to kingdom come, though, for the way he's hounding you now. And maybe one day I'll have that pleasure.'

'He's not worth it. And he claims to be good at fighting, says he had to be, growing up in a rough area. I'd not like you or anyone else to get hurt on my behalf.'

'I'm quite good at fighting too, because sometimes we had to be able to defend ourselves literally when I was working in less developed countries. I was glad of that in my last posting, because we had an incident. Luckily we managed to work it out.'

'Did you really? What sort of incident?'

'Rebels trying to steal our supplies and not minding who got hurt in the process, then trapping some people inside the compound.'

'How terrible to do that when you were there to help people!'

'They wanted to keep people afraid of them and therefore subservient.'

'Howard only helped people when he wanted something from them.'

'He sounds totally worthless, but I'd still like to

express my feelings about him physically. Sadly, some people only understand brute force.'

He saw her expression and clicked his tongue in annoyance at himself. 'Sorry to be so personal. We had to be more direct about our feelings and interactions where I've been working. I'm not quite back into a tame British mode yet.'

'Do you find it tame here?'

'Beautifully tame at times, tediously long-winded at others. But I'm meeting some very nice people, making long-term friends, I hope, and renewing old friendships, like the one with Nate.'

His gaze said he included her among them and she couldn't help saying, 'I'm sure you are and I'd be happy to be numbered among your new friends.'

'Well, that's a start, anyway.'

The meal was served just then and it was a good thing, she thought, because they were tiptoeing along paths she didn't dare follow anyone along yet.

They began their meal but after a couple of mouthfuls, Corin stopped eating suddenly with a piece of steak suspended on his fork halfway to his mouth. 'Oh drat! I nearly forgot to tell you something important.'

'Oh?'

'When he heard about the trouble you were having with your car, Nate asked his aunt Liz whether you could borrow hers while you were living in the valley, promising that you'd pay her the costs. Sadly, she won't need it again and it's just sitting there. She sent an email back saying she thought it was a great idea, only she'd prefer to give you the car outright.'

'I can't accept a present like that!'

'Why not? It's at least ten years old and I doubt it's worth much, but it's low mileage and she's looked after it, so it's not likely to let you down. We found the service record among her papers when we were clearing out the desk. She's asked Nate to clear up the mess she leaves behind her, as she phrases it, you see.'

'What a wonderful woman she must be. That gift will be so helpful. I wish I could meet her and thank her in person.'

'She doesn't want anyone to see how ravaged she's looking now. Nate says she was a good-looking woman for most of her life. But you could email her care of Nate and thank her. I'm sure she'd like that.'

'I will. And that'll not only save me buying another car; Howard won't be able to trace it as easily.'

'He won't be able to trace it at all if you don't transfer it into your name till you've truly got rid of him. How about we put it in my name? He doesn't know me from Adam! And I hope you can trust me.'

'You are so kind. And of course I trust you. I'd not trouble you but I'm desperate so I accept. Thank you so much, Corin.'

They continued to chat and once again the minutes flew by.

By the time they got back to Essington, Lucia was tired but she wanted the car as soon as possible in order to stay independent, 'just in case', so suggested they go and look at it straight away. 'I'll need to take down the details and I'll pay for the insurance and so on, even though it's in your name.'

He hesitated, then said slowly, 'He'll probably still manage to trace your financial transactions, if he's as skilful online as Eddie says. Let me put it all in my name early tomorrow and bring the car round to you afterwards. I'll simply take out insurance that allows anyone to drive it and you can pay me back later.'

'As long as you do let me reimburse you.'

'Of course. But it'll be safer to do that later.' He shot a quick glance sideways and saw that sad expression settle on her face again. 'It'll all come right in the end, Lucia, you have to believe that. Just keep plodding on. One step at a time gets you there in the end, as they say.'

Tears came into her eyes and she didn't bother to hide that, just nodded and blew her nose a couple of times. 'I've never met such kindness as I have in this valley. And a lot of it from strangers.'

'You can pass the kindness on to someone in need once you've sorted your own life out.'

'Yes. I can do that, can't I? And I will.' She brightened visibly, nodding as if to emphasise the vow.

Chapter Nine

Corin sorted out the paperwork for the car, though why they still called it 'paperwork' he had to wonder since so much was now done online. He then took the vehicle up the hill to Larch House, where he found Maggie moving around more freely.

That worried him. What if it meant Lucia would be leaving soon? Would she even let them know where she was if she had to leave in a hurry? She probably wouldn't know where she was going anyway.

'Lucia won't be long,' Maggie told him. 'She's just nipped up for a quick shower. She's been watering my kitchen herb garden and pulling up a few weeds for me.'

'Do you know how long she's staying with you?'

'No.' She glanced upstairs and lowered her voice. 'I'm worried that if she leaves us, that horrible man will go after her again and she'll have no one to help her.'

'I'm worried about that too.'

She smiled at him. 'I think you're also worrying because you're getting quite fond of her and don't want to lose her. Am I right?'

He hesitated then admitted it. 'Yes, you are. More than quite fond, very fond.'

'That's great. You two are really suited to one another. Anyone can see that.'

He didn't even try to pretend. 'Yes. And I'd very much like to pursue it. But whether the relationship works out or not, we'll have to find her somewhere to live nearby so that we can keep an eye on her. She's so alone in the world, and besides, she really fits into the valley, don't you think?'

'Both of you are our sort of people. I was wondering . . .' She added in a low voice, 'Do you think she'd like to stay on here at Larch House for a while? There are enough rooms for her to have the equivalent of a flat. I could charge her a modest rent and maybe she could find a job in the village. She's apparently done all sorts of office work over the years.'

'I think she'd love to live here with you. She's already told me how much she enjoys your company.'

'Has she really?'

'Yes.'

Maggie beamed at him. 'I'll ask her later then. I'll need to check rental prices round here. They're probably much lower than they'd be in a town.' She winked at him. 'Mine would be, anyway.'

'Corin's dealing with a really nice estate agent in the village. She's called Nina Perry. I'm sure she'll be able to tell you about prices.'

'Good idea. I'll contact her. I haven't actually spoken to her, but I think I've seen her in the shops.'

When Lucia came down, she was wearing jeans and a tee shirt. She had a great figure, Corin thought, and always looked nicely turned out. Her eyes betrayed her tiredness, though, as if she wasn't sleeping well. She was undoubtedly worrying about her ex.

He pushed back his anger at that sod and tried to speak cheerfully. 'I've brought your car, Lucia. It's licensed in my name and insured for any driver I approve of. You can drive it legally from now on, because I definitely approve of you.'

'You'll have to tell me how much I owe you.'

'We can discuss that as you drive me back. We don't want to bore poor Maggie to tears, do we?'

'No, of course not. Will you be all right while I'm out, Maggie?'

'I'll be fine. I can limp brilliantly now.'

As they set off along the rather bumpy drive, he had an idea. 'Could we stop at the place I'm buying? If you're not in a hurry, that is. I want to do a rough plan of where the houses are situated, so that I can start thinking how best to develop the whole place. And I'd love to show it all to someone. Do you enjoy looking at houses?'

'Very much. A home is such an important part of your life.'

As they turned left onto the main road, he said, 'The entrance isn't far down Larch Tree Lane.'

'I guessed that because the land's right next to Maggie's grounds. I peeped over the wall when I went walking in her woods but there were trees here and there, and I was too far away to see the houses clearly. I'd love to get a proper look at them. Some of them seemed quite old.'

'Some have serious historical value and most of them have been well maintained. You'd better slow down because the turn-off isn't much further. The gate is half-hidden so it's easy to drive past. It has a big new padlock on it, so we'll have to clamber over.'

They stopped the car and got out, leaning on the gate to study the group of houses before they went any further.

'They look as if they're nestling cosily together there,' she said after a few moments.

'That's what I thought! Talk about great minds. I want to keep that cosy homely look, if I can, even if I build new houses.'

'Have you got any ideas about what you might do with the property yet? Presumably you'll have an overall plan?'

'I've been trying not to get too specific till the sale has gone through. I have to admit that I'll be gutted if something goes wrong.' He banished that thought and gestured to the gate. 'Come on. Let's trespass. Do you need help climbing over?'

She proved she didn't by clambering over easily before he did, then standing smiling at him from the other side. 'No, thank you. Perhaps it's you who needs help, slowcoach.'

So of course he had to leap over the gate – only just managed it, though.

He took her hand and led her straight towards the first house. He held his breath for a few seconds as he kept hold of her but to his delight she didn't pull away.

They stopped to look at the house and she stared beyond it as well. 'What's that big mound over there?'

'I don't know yet. Still to be investigated. I can hardly start digging into it till I own the place, but I must admit I'm curious. I suspect this place was used for secret government purposes during World War Two and is only just being returned to public use.'

'Really? How exciting! I've read about that sort of thing, never thought I'd see it for myself.'

'Luckily, someone left a key to this first house so we can go inside it.'

'Fantastic!'

The key was still there and he guessed the estate agent didn't even know it existed. He opened the door and flourished a bow. 'Will you walk into my parlour, *madame*?'

'*Oui, s'il vous plaît, monsieur.*'

'*S'il te plaît*, surely?'

She nodded, accepting the more intimate '*te*' form instead of '*vous*' for 'you'.

He'd switched into French more easily than she had but she knew enough to keep up a brief conversation in the language, and she continued to use '*tu*'. That hinted at how she might feel about him if things worked out, surely?

'Is there no end to your talents?' he asked after they'd switched back into English.

'Of course there is. I'm not very good at swimming because I can't bear to put my head under water. Makes me panic. What about your weaknesses? I've not seen any so far. Howard was terrible at foreign languages and had no ear for music. I bet you can sing, given what a lovely deep voice you have.'

'Well, yes. I'm good enough to be in a choir, though not to be a soloist. I love singing and as you have guessed, I'm a bass. We all used to sing together sometimes in some of my placements. Music can be a good way of bringing people together and some of the people we were working with made wonderful harmonies, just instinctively it seemed to me.'

Without thinking, he added, 'I think your ex has no understanding of how to treat women with respect, either. That's a very serious weakness in my book.'

He saw the wary look come into her eyes again and abandoned that topic, annoyed with himself for making her tense up again. He pushed the front door wide open. 'Come on or I'll think you don't want to see inside.'

As they walked round the house, he explained what he might be able to change without destroying the historical integrity of the building and how a garden room would brighten the whole ground floor. She listened intently, asking sensible questions and even coming up with one idea for the kitchen that he might actually use here.

He answered his own earlier question about her capabilities silently. No, there was no end to her talents and attractions, not that he'd found anyway.

On an impulse, after they'd come out and he'd locked the door, he slipped the key into his pocket rather than putting it back on the lintel. He didn't want anyone else walking round his houses. She watched him do it, raised her eyebrows in a question but said nothing when he only shrugged in response.

They went into the other house to which the key was available and he took the key to that away with him, too, after their tour. They could only look round the outsides of the rest of the buildings, after which she said regretfully, 'We'd better leave now. There's Maggie to think of.'

As they set off again, he tried to plant a seed or two to encourage her to rent rooms at Larch House. 'I like Maggie, but she's rather lonely, isn't she? Older people often are.'

'Yes. Maggie tries to hide it but I can tell she is,' she said softly and let the words lie quietly between them for a while, looking thoughtful.

He knew why: because she was lonely too.

Lucia dropped him at Nate's place then drove straight back to Larch House, going over their conversations and gentle jokes in her mind and smiling all over again.

He was such a lovely man! So easy to talk to.

She found the car a pleasure to drive with good brakes and comfortable seats. She didn't need or like fancy show-off cars. How lucky she was to have found such kind people! She didn't want to leave them. And why should she?

Maggie greeted her with, 'Have you a minute to discuss something?'

'Of course.'

'Let's sit down. Might as well be comfy. I've been thinking about what you'll do after I stop needing help, which will be in another couple of days, I should think.'

'I've been wondering about that as well.'

'Why don't you rent a couple of rooms here and try living in the valley? Our recent discussion made me think seriously about renting out some rooms because I do need money for ongoing repairs. I could make a start with you if you're planning to stay round here. In fact, I'd like it very much.' She paused, head on one side, waiting for an answer.

Lucia loved the idea of staying as well, but had to get something clear first. 'Are you doing this for real or out of pity for me?'

'For real. To be frank, I'd welcome the company and the money both.'

It was just as Corin had said: she was lonely. Well, Lucia had been lonely recently too and would love to live here. 'Which room were you thinking of?'

'I thought you could have a couple of rooms, to use as a bedroom and a sitting room. Which ones you take would have to tie in with the bathrooms. There are three of them and they work OK but they're dreadfully old-fashioned, as you must have noticed, and while I'm at it, thank you for cleaning the one you've been using so thoroughly.'

'It was no trouble.'

'There's another spare bathroom as well up in the attic. It was put in for the servants. It's in need of a good cleaning plus a few minor repairs. I have never used that one. I could start off as a landlady with you and one other person, then modernise the bathrooms later on.'

'The bathroom being old-fashioned doesn't matter to me, Maggie, as long as it has hot and cold running water and the necessary other amenities. How much are you thinking of charging?'

'I'll have to find out the going rate then reduce it a little to compensate for everything being rather old-fashioned.'

'Done.' They shook hands.

'There's something else I've thought of that might help you, Lucia. There's a small employment bureau in the village. It's been there for years and is run by the daughter of a friend of mine now that her mother's retired. They do most of their business online these days, of course, but they do still have a small office near the church. If you're looking for work round here, Jennica may be able to help you.'

'That'd be wonderful.' On a sudden impulse, she gave Maggie a hug and for a moment or two the older woman clung to her and Lucia wondered when had been the last time someone had hugged her regularly. She made a mental note to hug her companion often. It'd work both ways. She could use a few hugs herself. She'd heard a nurse call it 'skin hunger' once and could see why.

'Can I go up and look at the available bedrooms and bathrooms, see which ones I like best?'

'Let's both go up, though I'll probably have to do it on my backside. Stairs still seem to bring out the worst protests from my stupid ankle. I intend to sleep in my own bedroom tonight by the way, so don't try to stop me. This will be a good test of whether I can manage to get up there without too much pain.'

Maggie went up the stairs slowly but got there without too much trouble. 'Thank goodness!' She beamed at Lucia then pointed. 'Try that bedroom first. It's the one I think is best and it's right next to the bathroom you're using.'

The bedroom was old-fashioned and Lucia remembered peeping into it when she'd been hunting for a mattress. It was a pleasant room but had far too much furniture in it – well, all of them did. Had the Hatheralls never thrown anything away?

After glancing into the other rooms, she agreed with Maggie about the first one she'd looked at being the best. It looked out to the front of the house and had a large bay window with an armchair in it. She could imagine sitting there reading or just daydreaming.

She studied the view, loving the way the house was surrounded by greenery on all sides, but that it wasn't too close to the house, so didn't make you feel hemmed in. There was something about the lighter green of the spring foliage at this time of year that lifted your spirits.

'I agree with you. This is a lovely room. Could I please rent it from you?'

'Of course.'

'Would it be all right if I removed some of the furniture? It feels a bit crowded for my taste.'

'Yes, of course. We'll ask Corin to help you carry it up to the attic. There's plenty of room to store it there. I think you should use the room next door rather than this one for a bedroom and this room as a sitting room where you can bring your friends.'

'I don't have many friends yet.'

'You will have. We're friendly folk in the valley. See – there's a connecting door hidden behind the wardrobe at present. Corin can help you move that as well. We could get you a small microwave and a kettle so you could make a cuppa or grab a quick snack without coming down to the kitchen.'

'I already have a small microwave and kettle among the stuff from my unit that I dumped in your second pantry, so I can provide my own. But I will do that, if you don't mind.'

'Oh yes. I'd forgotten about those things of yours.'

'And what about an internet connection?'

'I'm not that out of date. I do have one and you can have access to my system as long as you don't download too much.'

'That's brilliant. I brought my desktop computer with me because I prefer sitting upright and working on that rather than squinting down at a tiny phone screen. It's a new computer, one my ex has never been near, so it ought to be quite safe to use it.'

'Good. I'm not charging you full rent because I'm not providing full amenities.'

'I can perfectly well pay a reasonable rent, Maggie. I have all the money from the sale of my marital home.'

'You'll need that as a deposit on another house once you're able to settle somewhere and buy a home of your own. But I will ask someone at the estate agent's how much rent would be fair next time I go into the village, only perhaps you can drive me in until this stupid ankle of mine is fully recovered? It would be the right ankle, wouldn't it? If it had been the left one, I could still have driven since my car's an automatic.'

'I can easily take you shopping and that'll be useful as you can show me where everything is.'

'In which case, we'll knock a little more off the rent until I'm driving again.' She gave Lucia a challenging look and said firmly, 'I mean it!'

'Oh, very well.'

'Come to think of it, there's a little bar fridge in the scullery. You could use that for your personal bits and pieces of food. I don't want you to feel tied to my food needs or eating times.'

'I rather like sharing meals, if it's all right with you. I'm not a fussy eater and I don't have any food problems, though I don't like junk food.'

'Do you really not mind sharing meals?'

'Of course I don't.' She'd sounded so wistful Lucia gave her another hug, which was again well received.

'We could go into the village tomorrow, if that's all right with you, and call in at the estate agent's and the employment bureau as well as that little supermarket. It's more than time we bought more fresh fruit and vegetables, too. Tinned and frozen stuff doesn't taste nearly as good, however you fiddle around with it.'

Corin rang up later in the afternoon to see whether Lucia would like to go to the pub for a drink that evening with him and Nate.

'I'd love to.' She looked round but Maggie wasn't within earshot. 'How about we take Maggie too? I think she's going stir crazy. She may be older than us, but she's far too active to sit around all the time and she's really good company.'

'No worries. Happy to do that. I'm not ageist. I like to associate with a wide variety of people, children as well. Shall I come and pick you both up?'

'No need. I can perfectly well drive us there.'

'Then you won't be able to drink alcohol.'

'That doesn't matter. It's the company I enjoy most when I go out.'

Maggie came back soon afterwards and Lucia asked her if she wanted to go out for a drink after tea with Corin and Nate.

'Are you sure you want an old woman hobbling along slowing you down?'

'Certain. Having you along will make us all feel nice and young.'

'Cheek! But thank you. Much as I love my home, I'd absolutely love to get out of it for a while.'

They all enjoyed the evening and while they were out Lucia felt almost carefree. She'd lost most of her friends because of her ex and was loving having people to chat to. Some of Maggie's friends came over too and there were soon eight people sitting at the table, talking, laughing and telling her about the valley.

If only life were always like this.

Chapter Ten

The following morning when Nina went to open up the agency, she found an envelope pushed under the door.

She opened it and scanned the contents, muttering, 'Damn!'

Dear Nina

My grandma is seriously ill and Mum says to go home to Manchester straight away if I want to say a final goodbye to her.

I don't know when I'll be back because I'll need to be there for Mum, plus attending the funeral.

I'm sorry to leave you without help, but I have to see Gran.

Angie

She stared at the note, taking in the implications and noticing a couple of smears which she guessed had been caused by teardrops. How terrible for poor Angie! She'd mentioned her grandma being ill and wept about it a few days ago but hadn't known then how serious it was.

The trouble was, this couldn't have happened at a worse time for Nina. She wouldn't be able to run everything on her own, but didn't intend to ask Don to come back early. She was enjoying doing the work she loved without having him and his sharp remarks nipping at her regularly.

She would have to see if she could get some temporary office help, which he always tried to avoid. He was very mean about staffing levels and would clearly have preferred to be in charge of every detail himself. She was pretty sure she'd now had her suspicions confirmed about the main reason for that. She despised cheats.

Thank goodness his wife had dragged him off on a proper month-long holiday! When he came back, he'd have to put up with whatever Nina had done at the office during his absence. She'd see if she could find some temporary help now and she wasn't going to bring him up to date on anything until he returned.

She didn't want him rushing back to prevent Corin from buying the Marrakin. The more time she spent with this customer, the more she liked him and wished him well, and she didn't want to lose her commission for the sale, either.

Anyway, it didn't matter if Don was grumpy about the changes. She would only be here for a short time after his return, because she'd written her own letter of resignation and had simply filed it with a date stamp, witnessed by Angie.

She smiled. She wasn't staying on a day longer than she had to. And actually, she half hoped he would dismiss her for what she was doing. She hadn't needed a reference from him to get the other job. She knew the people at that office quite well professionally and they were only too aware of what he was like, as was everyone in the same line of work in nearby towns. Not a good team player, Don.

She picked up the phone to ring the local employment bureau.

Lucia drove Maggie into the village in the morning to do some shopping and her friend insisted they visit the employment bureau first because it was close to where they'd parked and it'd be daft to walk past the door, now, wouldn't it?

When they explained why they were there, Jennica stared at them, then got up and plonked loud, smacking kisses on Maggie's cheeks, one after the other.

'You wonderful woman! I've just had an urgent request for a receptionist cum general office person and here you are, bringing me one.'

'You have? Where's this job?'

'Begworth's.'

'The estate agent's here in Essington St Mary? That's convenient.'

'Yes, isn't it?' She turned to Lucia. 'Do you have a résumé?'

'I do.' She fumbled for her phone. 'This is a short summary. I have a full résumé back at Larch House on my desktop.' She'd been working on it only yesterday.

Jennica read it through quickly. 'Can we take a copy of this one? I'm pretty sure it'll be enough, especially as you come recommended by Maggie, so we won't need to do a character check.'

When the résumé had been emailed, she said, 'I'll give

Nina a few minutes to read it then phone and ask her if she'd like to see you – which I'm sure she'll want to do. Is that all right with you?'

Lucia looked at Maggie, who nodded vigorously, so she said, 'Yes, of course.'

Jennica let out a happy sigh. 'You're a gift-wrapped present from Fate today for both Nina and me because I have no one else suitable on my books, only inexperienced youngsters, and her need is urgent.'

'Oh. Right. Good,' Lucia stammered, unable to believe her luck.

'Of course, it's a bit of a junior position for someone with your experience, but I'm sure you won't mind that for a few weeks, will you? They'll pay the usual temping rates, after all, and the duties will be quite light while the owner is away.' She named the amount of pay and Lucia nodded.

Exactly four minutes after the email had been sent, Nina phoned and asked to meet Lucia.

Jennica shared the news and grinned triumphantly at them. 'Didn't I tell you she'd be interested?'

'I'll wait for you in the café round the corner,' Maggie said. 'Go on. Carpe diem.'

Lucia walked with her to the café then left her there and went to the estate agency. There she was interviewed in a casual but thorough way by a charming woman. Within less than quarter of an hour she'd been offered the position and accepted it instantly, delighted to be able to stay in the valley without having to dip into her savings. She might even be able to add to them if she was careful.

Nina beamed at her. 'That's great. Welcome to the agency. I'm afraid I can only guarantee the job till the owner comes back from his holiday abroad in just over a fortnight. After that, who knows? I'm leaving for another job myself in three weeks. But Don will still need help in the office and I doubt Angie will be coming back for a while, if ever, so there's a good chance you'll be asked to stay on.'

Almost as an afterthought, she said softly, 'That poor girl is going to be really broken up about her grandma dying so suddenly. I hope she got back in time to say a proper farewell.'

'Anyone would be upset to lose so close a family member.'

'Yes. Um, back to the job: you couldn't start work this afternoon, could you? Only, I want to show a couple round a house on the far side of the village and I don't like to close the agency while I'm doing it. You never know when someone will walk in off the street and show interest in a property.'

'Yes, I'm happy to start today. I have to take Maggie shopping and run her home first, though, because she's recovering from a sprained ankle, but I can come straight back after I've done that, which will be before lunchtime for sure. Her ankle's a lot better now so it'll be safe to leave her.'

'I can't thank you enough. There's parking behind the shop. Doesn't matter where you put your car till Don gets back, then he has to have the space nearest to the back door.'

From her grimace and eye roll as she said that, she didn't like the owner and Lucia wondered why. Well, she'd no doubt find out.

In the meantime she had a job and somewhere to live. How wonderful was that? She felt like dancing along the street, not walking sedately.

*　*　*

When she rejoined Maggie, she gave her another of those big hugs, saying breathlessly before she even sat down, 'I got the job and Nina wants me to start this afternoon.'

'Congratulations.'

'If you've finished your coffee, we'd better get the shopping done quick as, then I'll run you home.'

That was soon accomplished, with the help of an elderly wheelchair the local supermarket provided for their more infirm customers. When they got back, she put some lunch together for them both, leaving Maggie's in the fridge and taking her own sandwiches with her to eat later.

Things were turning out so well here.

When she got to the estate agent's, Nina showed her where things were and how the computer system worked, then suggested she explore every drawer and cupboard during the afternoon and read some of their contents.

'Is there anything I should, well, avoid looking at? Private stuff, I mean.'

'No. Don's desk is locked, as usual, so you can't help but avoid his private files. Even I'm not allowed in there. And I have nothing in my drawers that I need to hide because I've already cleared out my personal things. It's all business stuff or anonymous things like packets of tissues now.'

She paused, clearly thinking something over, then added, 'I'm in the middle of selling a piece of land up near the top end of Larch Tree Lane – the Marrakin estate. If anyone asks about it, tell them it's sold. And if by any chance Don phones from Spain to ask about sales, tell him you've just started as a temp and don't know any details yet. If he presses the point, tell him the paperwork isn't in the filing cabinet, and as I'm taking it with me, it'll be the absolute truth.'

'All right.'

'Actually, the sale really is about to go through and I don't want anything or anyone to stop it because I think the guy purchasing it will be good for the valley.'

Lucia wondered whether to mention that she was friendly with the buyer but decided not to do that until the following day as Nina now seemed focused on the customers she was meeting soon.

Anyway, why complicate matters at this initial stage? Clearly there was something going on behind the scenes but Nina had such an honest face, she didn't seem the sort to get involved in dodgy deals, so perhaps it was the owner who wasn't to be trusted. What's more, Corin had already said this woman was good to do business with and Lucia instinctively trusted his judgement.

When Nina had left to meet her customers, Lucia found it very interesting to go through the cupboards and files. She learned a lot about local house and land prices, as well as how this sort of business was conducted. That would be helpful when she came to buy a home of her own.

During her time alone she answered three phone calls and dealt with a query from one walk-in guy. Thanks to her investigations of the filing system, she was able to answer two of the phone questions about properties that were for sale but could only promise that Nina would get back to the other person on her return.

When she did come back, Nina beamed at Lucia. 'It's looking good so I'm really glad I had you to hold the fort here! They're following me here.'

A young couple arrived shortly afterwards, looking full of themselves, and Nina took them into her office. She came out shortly afterwards to ask Lucia to make them coffee and whispered, 'I've got a sale here for sure. *And* they've already arranged for finance. I wish all purchases were this straightforward.'

Judging by the broad smiles on the two customers' faces as they walked out hand in hand over an hour later, they were extremely happy about buying their first home.

All in all, Lucia found that the afternoon passed quickly and it seemed a fairly enjoyable way to earn money, far more interesting than most of the temporary office jobs she'd had – or sometimes jobs she'd *endured* would have been a better way of describing them.

Corin spent the afternoon making a rough sketch of the houses' approximate locations on the piece of land. Given the untouched land at the back, there was going to be room for quite a few more dwellings to be built, he reckoned, enough work to occupy him for years, he hoped. He didn't have the 'I want to make a fortune' gene, just loved designing and supervising the building of homes for people.

There were no more phone calls from Nina to interrupt him and he grimaced at how slowly the days were passing till the sale could be legally settled. And this was a rapid settlement, for goodness' sake!

He thought about inviting Lucia and Maggie out for a drink again tonight, but decided it'd be too pushy.

Nate went into the village to get some stationery supplies in the late afternoon and came back with the news that Lucia was temping at the estate agency.

'How did you find that out?'

'I bumped into someone I know and she told me. Apparently, their permanent receptionist has gone home to her parents in the north because of a death in the family and Nina isn't sure she'll ever return.'

'It'll please Lucia to be earning her living again. I think she's been a bit worried about finances because she wants to buy a small place of her own after it's safe to settle down again. I don't blame her. I'm ready for a home of my own now. My wandering years are over.'

'Well, I'm the opposite. I've never wanted to buy. I've rented flats so that I didn't even have a garden to look after. I fiddled around for a couple of years and gradually got into my stride telling stories. Writing should come with a health warning: *Beware! This activity is addictive.*' Nate looked round with a smile. 'This is the first time I've been able to give up my day job. Well, actually, I haven't given it up completely, just taken a year's leave of absence. With a government job, you can sometimes do that. They don't mind too much allowing it, especially if you choose your timing carefully and don't leave in the middle of a project. It also means they can retain skilled staff.'

'Well, it'll all pay off if you get a bestseller and make a fortune.'

'And pigs may fly. Most authors barely earn a living wage. I don't need to live in luxury but I like to eat regularly. Let's not talk about that. I don't even want to think about going back to work in a fiddly, fussy bureaucracy till I have to, even after such a short time. Anyway, I won't find out how much readers like my stories until after my first novel is published and it won't come out for a few months yet. Now, let's change the subject for something more pleasant: food. Do you fancy going to the pub for a meal again tonight?'

'Not really. I can cook for you if you like, which judging by our current store cupboard means opening a tin of soup and making genuine, home-made cheese on toast to go with it.'

'Good idea. My favourite meal.'

'Let's see what's on TV.'

'Can I just ask, so that I don't put my foot into it: does that mean you won't be seeing Lucia again except as a casual friend?'

'No. We're still getting on well but she doesn't want to go steady with anyone till she's settled things once and for all with her ex, which makes sense, I suppose.'

'But you'd rather see more of her.'

'Is it that obvious?'

'It is, rather.'

'Hmm. Well, too bad if it is. I really like her. Haven't *you* ever met anyone special?'

Nate shrugged. 'I thought I had but in the end it didn't work out. The devil's in the detail when you're living with someone and small things they do can be irritating. Even the way someone laughs can make you wince.' He shuddered as if remembering a laugh that had once done that to him.

'That devil and details stuff creeps into a lot of situations.' Corin didn't think that sort of thing would impinge on him and Lucia, though. He hadn't found anything about her to be irritating. *Au contraire.*

So the two men spent a quiet evening in front of the TV and had an early night. And if Corin kept wondering what

Lucia was doing instead of chatting, he hoped he'd hidden his occasional absent-mindedness or Nate had put it down to him watching the programme.

He couldn't actually remember what they'd watched.

In Swindon, Howard Saunders couldn't wait to get home after work so that he could check exactly what his ex-wife was up to. A quick glance at his personal phone during a break between meetings had shown him that her car had left Wiltshire and travelled up to Leicester, which now had him desperate to investigate further.

However, today was Friday and it was the monthly departmental outing to the pub after work so he had to go to that first. He rarely did much chatting, just fixed a smile to his face, nodded occasionally and listened or watched carefully everything that was going on near him. This time the stupid, mindless joviality that surrounded him was even harder to bear than usual.

He checked again when he got home and yes, she was still in Leicester, which was a bit annoying because it was further away from Swindon than that country place she'd first gone to. What the hell was she doing in the Midlands? He knew for certain that she had no relatives or friends in Leicester and her parents were still house-swapping in Australia so she couldn't go to stay with them.

Perhaps that was why she'd gone to Leicester, to get away from everyone she knew. Well, she wouldn't get away from him that easily, and it definitely wouldn't stop him driving there at the weekend to see what she was up to. In the meantime he'd keep track of her financial transactions, which could be very helpful.

He was furious to find that she'd changed her credit card and taken precautions about keeping her accounts secret this time. Someone must have told her how to do that, because she was too stupid about financial matters to work out the various ways to keep that sort of information secret on her own. He sniggered. She never had found out about the small amounts of money he'd filched from her bank account here and there all through their marriage. He always smiled when he thought of that.

The smile faded as he considered the ludicrous legal rules these days about women who left their husbands. Now that the government was infested with higher-level female harridans, they were making it a lot harder to keep track of what ex-wives were doing.

In the meantime, another of his maintenance programs was doing well for the company and the new manager had congratulated him about it, using his first name too, when they passed in the corridor, which showed that he'd been noticed.

He had to keep this job because it gave him good cover for some scams he was setting up on the dark web.

But it was all costing more than he'd expected and he needed more money to do the set-up properly. A half share of Lucia's jewellery would have given his finances a very useful boost.

He'd definitely go up to Leicester tomorrow. He was determined to wear her down about this. He'd done it to her before, after all. You just had to keep going on at her and she caved in.

*   *   *

Nina asked Lucia on the Friday evening if she wanted a day off at the weekend.

'I'd rather work and have the money, if that's all right with you.'

'It's not only fine, it's better for me. You've done really well so far. I've never seen anyone pick things up as quickly.'

'I've worked in a lot of different offices, so I'm used to slotting into new situations quickly. I did temping for several years by choice. Variety of tasks makes life more interesting than doing the same old, same old all the time.'

'You certainly get variety in real estate, though even the best of jobs has its boring patches. I enjoy my work, though.'

'It shows. And you're good at dealing with people.'

Lucia accepted an invitation for her and Maggie to go out for a meal with Corin on Saturday evening, thinking they'd be going as a group again.

But this time they couldn't do that because by late afternoon Nate was deep in writing a key scene and was apparently incapable of rational conversation till he'd got it sorted out, and Maggie had already arranged for one of her friends to come over and bring an Indian takeaway for the two of them to share.

Lucia had been invited to join them but she didn't like to cancel the arrangement with Corin, didn't really want to, either. She worried about them going out as a couple, though. She didn't dare get involved with Corin that way, mustn't, for his sake. She knew what Howard was like when he wanted something.

She'd have liked to get involved with Corin, though, of course she would! He was a delightful person.

Then it occurred to her that she was still reacting to Howard's actions, which meant he was still controlling her activities and relationships. For how long was she going to let his nasty tricks ruin her life?

She really liked Corin and was starting to get angry at herself for letting Howard get away with it again. There had to be a way to stop him once and for all, but she hadn't found it yet.

Look at the time he'd decided to buy a neighbour's old Bentley, taking the money from their joint account, more of it hers than his. He insisted it was to benefit both of them, because customers were impressed by a ride in a beautifully preserved old car, so he'd be earning more money.

At least the value of the car had been taken into account in the mediated divorce settlement, to her advantage, another thing that had made him furious.

Chapter Eleven

Early on the Saturday morning, Howard received a phone call asking him to go into the office and help sort out a digital emergency. By that time he'd been in the car heading north for almost quarter of an hour. But he knew this was another way to help establish himself with the new manager, so felt he had no choice but to do it.

He gave them an estimated time of arrival, then turned round and drove back. He was probably the only one who could sort that particular problem out, anyway. IT needed management input as well as their own technical skills.

It was mid-afternoon before he'd steered what the 'team' was doing onto the right path and could leave them to do the grunt work that would prevent this problem reoccurring. He could barely restrain himself from snapping at the idiots he worked with by that time.

As he set off for Leicester again, he was in a foul mood. Thank goodness for the longer hours of daylight. At least it was still light when he arrived. He parked and settled down with his laptop to work out exactly where in the city her car was located. He was getting closer now but to his surprise it was still where it had been when he started this journey.

He found its location and magnified the map, studying it in puzzlement. What the hell was she doing out there at a car racing stadium? Had she got herself a new guy who was into that sort of thing? She'd better not have done. He wasn't ready to turn her loose yet. He might have failed to train her to be a satisfactory wife but he still had a use for her.

He went out there, paid his entrance money and drove slowly round the huge parking area, looking for red cars. To his surprise there was no sign of her vehicle anywhere and yet the tracer showed it was somewhere close by.

He set out again, driving even more slowly, again checking all the red cars that were parked there.

Suddenly an attendant stepped out in front of his vehicle, one hand held up in a stop sign. Sighing aloud in frustration, Howard braked and forced a smile. 'Something wrong, madam?'

'I was going to ask you that, sir. Do you need some help? I noticed you're driving round for a second time. There are plenty of parking places still left at the lower end, you know. We're never totally full for a demolition derby.'

'I, um, was supposed to meet a friend here, which is why I was driving round.'

'Well, you're more likely to meet him inside now, I should think. I've not seen anyone sitting in a car and the programme is about to start. You don't want to miss the first race, do you?'

'No, definitely not. Thanks for your help. Much appreciated. I'll park and go inside to look for him.' It was another place to check for Lucia anyway. The parking attendant was right. It wasn't likely she'd still be sitting in her car, wherever she'd hidden it.

Inside, he found a place to stand in a less popular area from which he had a good view of a large part of the crowd, not such a good view of the cars when they raced past. Taking out his binoculars, he worked along the rows of people to see whether he could spot his ex. No sign of her, though.

After the first race ended and people began moving about, he ambled round to the other side of the concourse, ready to take a better look at the crowd he'd been standing among. She had to be somewhere.

But once again, there was no sign of her among the crowd. Where the hell was she? She wasn't a drinker, so he doubted she'd be sitting in the bar. Unless her new guy was a drinker. He'd go and check that afterwards, just to be sure.

He lowered the binoculars and glanced up as the cars began screaming round the course. Stupid fools.

Then he noticed a red car among them and lifted up his binoculars again. It was the same make as hers but had a different number plate. When the vehicles came round the course again, he focused on the front left wing of the red car for a moment, not expecting to see the dent she'd never bothered to have made good. But he always checked every detail on principle.

Only, he did see it. You couldn't mistake that dent because it looked like a letter L in Gothic script. He stiffened. There it was. That had to be her car.

It took a moment or two for the information to sink in, then his brain fired up into a sizzling fury. There was only one possible reason: she must have sold the car, damn her! He didn't know why they'd changed the number plate, but it was now being used in a demolition derby. That would destroy it fairly quickly. The vehicles only lasted a few weeks at best, he'd heard.

That was very clever. Who the hell had suggested it to her? She'd never have thought of it herself.

He brought up the tracer on his phone and it was glowing in a dull way, which meant he was within a couple of hundred metres of the vehicle, give or take. Even as he watched, the cars came hurtling round the track and as they roared past him the tracer glowed more brightly then faded again.

Her car might be here but she could be anywhere in the country now, damn her to high hell, because she'd changed her phone so he'd lost that contact point!

He left the stadium straight away, stopping at the first services for a quick meal and then continuing back to Swindon.

How the hell was he to find her now? First her phone then the car put out of action. Who was helping her? Someone must be.

It came to him in the middle of a sleepless night of tossing and turning that there was only one possible lead left for him to follow. The last place he'd found her had been in the country. He'd go back there and see what he could ferret out. It was harder to hide in a small community. Someone might know where she'd gone, or even still be in touch with her, if he was lucky.

In fact, he'd go back the very next day.

Except, he had another of those phone calls from work even before breakfast. The idiots who'd been trying to sort out the details of the problem overnight needed more help.

So he spent his Sunday at the office, finding it hard to appear calm, not working as well as usual because the anger was still simmering – though he was doing better than the rest of his colleagues, of course.

Few people had a brain as sharp as his.

His ex certainly didn't. There had to be a clue of some sort at the place where she'd been staying, at the very least some hint as to where she'd intended to go next or what sort of car she was now using. And he'd find it. Oh, yes.

He'd go back to where he'd last seen her next weekend. No use going there after he finished work during the week. It'd be dark and he'd need to talk to people and they were naturally reluctant to stop and chat after dark.

And when he did eventually find her, he'd maybe allow himself the pleasure of teaching her a hard lesson physically. He'd have to be careful how he did it, mustn't go overboard or let anyone see him doing it, nor must she be able to fight back and damage him.

But still, a real man had a right to behave as the males of the human species had done throughout time, and to make sure their womenfolk were taught, by force if necessary, to do as they were told.

He wasn't the only one who believed that to be what nature had intended. There were some wonderful places with contacts about that on the Internet.

Lucia thoroughly enjoyed spending Saturday evening with just herself and Corin. She always enjoyed his company. So she went ahead and followed Maggie's suggestion to ask his help. It wasn't an excuse to spend time with him and she wasn't going to hold back from encounters any longer.

'Could I ask a favour, Corin?'

'Of course.'

'Could you help me move some of the furniture out of my new bedroom at Larch House and put it in the attic? It's too heavy to manage on my own.'

'My pleasure. I've nothing else planned tomorrow. Will that be a good time?'

'Brilliant, thanks. Aren't there any signs yet of anything else happening with your land purchase?'

'Nina told me not to expect anything much till the end of this week at the soonest, and most likely it'll be finalised on Monday. But I can't help feeling impatient.'

She gave his arm a quick squeeze of sympathy. 'And you're dying to get going.'

'I am indeed. Trouble is, I daren't even arrange for the water to be switched on again till the sale has gone through. I'm going to move in and work from there, so I'll have to buy a small generator for my daily electricity needs. Even the almost habitable of the houses will need rewiring before we can use modern electrical systems.'

'Sounds a good plan.'

'I hope so. Once the contract is signed I thought I'd move into that first house we saw and camp out there with minimal furniture. Maybe Maggie might lend me a few of her old bits and pieces, just the unwanted stuff lying around in the attic? What do you think?'

'I'm sure she would. Are you not comfy living with Nate?'

'He's easy enough to live with because he's mostly inside his own head playing games with his characters, or however storytellers figure it all out. But sadly, the only spare bed is a single, which isn't comfy for a tall person like me. It's OK for one or two nights, but not for weeks.'

She had a sudden idea and had put it into words before she could stop herself. 'Why don't you rent a couple of rooms from Maggie while you're waiting? You couldn't get much closer to your property and there are plenty of double beds available at Larch House. I'm sure she'd let you rent by the week. I think she's shorter of money than she's told anyone.'

He stared at her in surprise. 'You wouldn't mind me doing that? I thought you were trying to keep a distance from any emotional entanglements.' He added in a near whisper, 'Unfortunately.'

'Um, I've decided I wouldn't mind at all. I thought I was trying to be sensible about us, but it's occurred to me since that I'm still letting Howard run my life. Besides—'

'Besides what? Go on.'

'I'm still a bit worried about him. When he finds

out that my old car is in Leicester, which I'm sure he will, he might come back here to check whether I'm still around. I'd feel a lot safer with you in the house as well as Maggie, and she'd be safer too. And my final reason, as if I need one, is that I enjoy your company and I don't see why I should go without it, even though I don't want to rush into anything.'

'I enjoy yours too, Lucia. Greatly. I'll be very happy to see how we get on together.'

They smiled at one another and their silent exchange went on for so long they must have looked rather foolish but she couldn't stop smiling. It seemed so . . . right.

'Let's ask Maggie about a room when you come to help me move stuff,' she managed at last.

'Yes, let's.' He raised his glass of shandy to her. 'Here's hoping.'

He didn't specify exactly what he was hoping for, which was probably just as well.

When Corin turned up the following morning, ready to help her with the furniture, she linked her arm in his and tugged him along towards the library.

'Did you ask Maggie about a room?' he said.

'I waited to do it in case you changed your mind.'

'I haven't done that. Where are you taking me?'

'To ask her now, before we start moving my furniture, then we can move some for you at the same time, if necessary.'

Maggie couldn't hide her delight at the thought of another tenant. And it seemed to Lucia that there had possibly been some relief on her friend's face as well.

'All right if we both remove some of the furniture from our rooms?' she asked.

'Of course it is. I've not tried to do much rearranging of furniture for the past few years because I'm not strong enough, nor are my friends. Just take away anything you don't want. There's plenty of room to store it in the attic, as I already told you, because my father cleared a lot of stuff out of there. In fact, he made that his mission in life at one stage, said it was his gift to the house, spent years on it intermittently.'

She smiled at some image this clearly brought to mind for her, then added, 'If you see anything you prefer up there, don't hesitate to swap it and if you want to borrow anything for your new house, Corin, go right ahead.'

'I thought you said your father had cleared the attic out.'

Maggie chuckled. 'That meant he threw away things that were broken beyond repair and rearranged the rest. He put some things he said would grow in value into the largest bedroom up there, the one used originally by the housekeeper. I haven't a clue whether he was right or not about their value, but perhaps you'd better leave the ones in that room alone. Everything in the main attic space is up for grabs, though, so just take what you like, Corin.'

She sighed and her eyes again focused on something visible only to herself as she whispered, 'He was a lovely man, my father, died too young.'

She waved one hand to dismiss them and they left her dabbing at her eyes.

They had a very satisfying time rearranging their new rooms, then Lucia stayed in hers to sit and read in a comfortable armchair she'd moved into the bay window and Corin went back to the cottage to tell Nate he was leaving and bring his possessions to Larch House.

He also contacted Nina and told her where he'd be if she needed anything signing.

When he got back, the two women were discussing what to make for tea that evening and asked if he'd like to join them for meals. 'I'd love to, except for tonight, because I want to take you both out to dinner to celebrate.'

'Again?' Lucia asked. 'We must be costing you a fortune.'

'I like to celebrate when good things happen and anyway, I think the meals at the pub are very good value.'

Maggie winked at him and said, 'How delightful. I accept and if Lucia doesn't want to join us, she can stay at home on her own.'

Lucia studiously avoided meeting his eyes as she said of course she'd be happy to join them, but she could feel her cheeks growing a little warmer.

So they enjoyed another evening at the pub, met another couple Maggie knew and enjoyed chatting to them. They even had some leftovers from the generous servings to bring home.

When they got back, Maggie said tactfully that she was tired and limped up the stairs, leaving them to say goodnight to one another.

Lucia suddenly felt shy as he took her in his arms

in the kitchen. He did this slowly, giving her plenty of time to move away. She wasn't that stupid and moved willingly forward into his embrace but she appreciated the gesture.

'I desperately need a goodnight kiss, Lucia,' he said softly.

'So do I.'

And the kiss was so brilliant it was hard not to stay in his arms.

But though she wasn't going to stop getting to know him, she didn't intend to leap into his bed, either. 'I don't want to go further yet,' she murmured as she moved back afterwards.

'Whatever you wish.'

'I like to . . . take my time getting to know someone first. I didn't do that last time and I should have done. I've not, you know, had a lot of experience.'

'I've not put myself about a lot, either. Making love has to matter, even if it doesn't turn out to be lasting love. I shall look forward to every step we take along that invisible path, Lucia.'

'In that case, I'd just like to check that the kiss was as good as I thought before I go to bed.'

'How amazing. I was thinking the same thing exactly.'

It was even better and she hugged the pleasure of his kisses to herself as she got ready for sleep. She might not be ready to tumble into his bed yet, but she felt very conscious of him being only a couple of rooms away.

She slept soundly, glad he was there for the best as well as the worst of reasons.

* * *

As the next few days passed, Lucia continued to enjoy Corin's company, and found her new job very pleasant as well. It was rather easy, though, with not enough work to fill her time, so in the end she asked if there were anything else she could do, otherwise she'd like permission to take a novel to read during the quiet times at work.

'Good idea,' Nina said. 'Angie used to read magazines, but I think you'd need more than that to keep your brain occupied. She had a sweet nature, but she wasn't the brightest spark on the planet. And talking of sparks, how are things going with Corin?'

'Really well. Maggie was saying only the other day that he's very easy to live with. I think he's lived in close quarters with a lot of diverse people.'

'He's pleasant to do business with as well.'

On the Wednesday, Angie rang up to say her grandma had died and she'd like to give notice so that she could stay near her family permanently. 'Do you want me to come back and work out my notice, Nina? I'm supposed to give you two weeks.'

'No, dear. I've got a temp doing the job and she can stay on, so there's no problem at all. I'm sorry for your loss.' She waited a minute for the sniffling and nose-blowing to stop before she continued. 'I'll sort out how much holiday pay and so on we owe you and let you know. Do you want anything from your desk at the office sending to you?'

'No need, thanks. I never kept a lot of personal stuff there and you can put my magazines out for customers to look at. My flatmate is sending my clothes and other possessions on to me and finding someone else to share with.' She gave a gulp and said in a shaky voice, 'People have been so kind.'

'That's sorted, then.'

Nina put down the phone and told Lucia what had happened.

'Will you miss her?'

'She was pleasant to work with. I think Don will miss her most. She looked pretty and Don likes to surround himself with good-looking women.'

'You hinted that he was sexist. Is he a groper? Because I won't put up with that.'

'No. He just looks at you. You know the sort of look. Fortunately I wasn't pretty enough to engage his interest.'

'You're elegant rather than merely pretty.' She could feel herself flushing. 'Sorry. I shouldn't have said something so personal.'

Nina chuckled. 'I never mind being complimented. Elegant sounds great to me. You're very attractive, though, and it's harder to counter someone who simply stares at you, so if you don't like working with him, don't hesitate to leave.'

It was Lucia's turn to smile. 'I know one or two tricks to embarrass that sort of man. If he won't stop staring at me, there are bits of him he won't like me staring at in return, especially in public.'

From her amused expression, Nina knew exactly what she was talking about.

'I think you and I get on well enough to be frank with one another, Lucia. Friends?' She held out her right hand and the two of them shook warmly, then Nina became brisk and businesslike again.

'Now, I must phone Mr Drayton and keep him up to date. I'm hoping to sign the contract for that land on Monday, if all goes well.'

'Corin will be so pleased about that. He's absolutely itching to get started. I'll miss him when he moves out of Larch House. The three of us share the cooking and eat together, and we've set the whole world to rights in our discussions in the evenings. We've been out to the pub with Nate a couple of times too, just for a drink.'

'Since we're going to be friends, I'd love to join you at the pub now and then if the others don't mind. I broke up with a guy a couple of months ago and all the friends I'd made round here when I was with him seem to be still in relationships, which means it's a bit uncomfortable at times being the only single in the group.'

'I'm sure Corin and Maggie will welcome your company and I shall definitely enjoy it. In fact, I've met a lot of really nice people since I came here. I do hope I don't have to leave.'

'Because of your ex, you mean?'

'Unfortunately it's a possibility.'

'Has he found out where you are?'

'I don't know. I bet he's found my old car by now, though.'

'Well, that'll be a dead end, won't it, since you didn't have to buy another?'

'With anyone else, perhaps. But I wouldn't be surprised if Howard turns up here to check for clues as to where I went next and to make sure I didn't stay around.'

'Is he really that tenacious?'

'Oh, yes. But I don't want to involve Maggie and Corin in my troubles – or you, come to that – so I might have to make a quick exit if he gets any worse. I sometimes think I'll have to emigrate to Australia or Canada to get completely away from him.'

'You don't need to do that. Once you become friends with someone, they *are* involved. Well, they are if they're real friends. Please don't make a hasty exit. If you need help, you can turn to me as well as to Corin and Maggie.'

Lucia blinked away some incipient tears. Things were going too well, hadn't gone so well since she met Howard and fell into his honey trap. But even though she was fully divorced from him, she still kept worrying about how long he would continue to pester her.

A shiver ran down her spine. She'd read about stalkers, and it described what he was doing. Please let him not find me, she prayed. But she had a heavy, sick feeling that he would, because he'd boasted once how he had gone after someone at a previous place of employment over a year afterwards, when he saw a way to teach her a lesson. He'd even boasted about one or two cruel tricks he'd played on the poor woman.

It had been one of the things that made her start to move back mentally from their marriage. She hadn't believed it at first, then had realised he was actually proud of what he'd done and couldn't resist boasting about it.

Why he had wanted to marry her was still a puzzle, as well as why she'd been so gullible and believed his blandishments. He'd said once that he liked the way she looked, that she did him credit, which seemed a bizarre reason for spending your life together.

She kept coming back to the thought that she didn't want to have to run away again. She loved living here.

That night she lay awake for a long time, going over and over her options, and determination grew in her as the hours of moonlit darkness ticked slowly past: she was going to fight back if he tried to mess her around again. As Nina had said, she had friends here to help her now. And bad as he was, he wasn't a murderer, after all.

Whatever it took, she wasn't going to give up her new life without a fight.

Chapter Twelve

The following Monday, Nina put down the phone in her office and made a triumphant fist in the air to Lucia. 'Yeah! We'll be able to sign the contracts for the Marrakin this afternoon. They're couriering them over straight away, as promised. I'll just phone Corin, then I'll get together every bit of paperwork belonging to the property to hand over to him. He'll be absolutely delighted.'

Half an hour after the contracts arrived, Don Begworth walked into the office, not having given them any notice of his early return to the UK. Fortunately, Nina was crouching down to pick up some papers she'd dropped and though she saw him, he didn't see her, thank goodness. She stayed where she was, hoping she was completely hidden.

He stopped by the reception desk, looking at Lucia appreciatively. 'Who are you? You're very pretty, a big improvement on the last girl, that's for sure.'

Lucia had noticed Nina staying hidden and guessed who this was, so gave him a chill look and started as she meant to continue. 'I'm not hired for my appearance but my skills, thank you very much. I'm only temping here, filling in for Angie, who's had to go home for her grandma's funeral. And you are?'

'I'm Don Begworth and I just happen to own this agency.'

'Oh, sorry. I didn't recognise you.' But she didn't relax her stern expression in the slightest because he was still eyeing her in an offensive way, damn him.

'How's business been going? Anything to report, any contracts pending?'

'I've only just started here, so I'm afraid I have no idea of the business details yet.'

He glanced towards Nina's office and Lucia watched him carefully. No, he definitely hadn't noticed the other woman.

'Is Nina out?'

'She said she was going out this morning.'

'I'll give her a ring and ask her what's happening.' He vanished into his office and closed the blinds and door on the main showroom area.

Lucia relieved her annoyance a little by sticking her tongue out at him, a childish but often comforting gesture. When Nina slipped out of her much smaller office at the rear, still half crouching, she blew a kiss towards the reception desk and scurried out of the back door, closing it quietly behind her.

Lucia had a sudden worry that Don would hear Nina's car start up, so she switched on the radio, selecting a music station and turning up the volume.

A couple of minutes later, Don poked his head out of his office. 'I prefer the girls working in the office to keep quiet.'

'Sorry. I'll keep the noise down. But I'm not a girl. I'm over thirty and that's a woman by any standards, so please don't refer to me as that.'

He scowled at her, hesitated then went back into his office.

Lucia switched the radio off and got out some papers so that she could look busy. Fortunately, it'd be the first of the month in a couple of days, so after she'd dusted every little shelf and corner in the office thoroughly for the second time that day, she could fiddle with the accounts for a while.

She was already quite sure he'd not allow her to read, whether there was any work needing doing or not. She didn't enjoy make-work tasks, which could be tediously boring, but there you were. He'd still be paying for her time even if she sat staring into space for half the day.

He poked his head out of his office again a few minutes later. 'You can make me a cup of coffee since you don't seem all that busy. I take mine black with two spoonfuls of sugar. And are there any biscuits?'

'I'll have a look. If there aren't, do you want me to nip out and buy some?'

'Yes, but after you make my coffee. My coffee pods are in the end cupboard.'

'Yes. Nina showed me and said not to use those.'

'No sign of her yet?'

She pretended to look round. 'No, she's definitely not here.'

'It's not like her to be late and she's not answering her phone. Are you sure she didn't say where she was going?'

'Sorry, but I have no idea where she is. And before you

ask, I've not been here long enough to know where she's likely to be, either. The other receptionist left in such a hurry she didn't have time to leave me any information.'

'She wasn't the most efficient clerk I've ever had working here, but you don't get as much choice of staff in the country. You look like a much more with-it girl – *woman*, I mean.'

She'd obviously made her point so she simply stood staring at him, keeping her face expressionless, just waiting.

He scowled at her, grunted and went back into his office.

She made the cup of coffee as slowly as she could, and couldn't help noticing that he didn't say thank you or even look up when she took it in to him, just pointed to a mat on the desk beside him. She disliked him intensely already and was praying that Nina would manage to stay out of his way until after the contracts had been signed. Corin would be very upset indeed if he lost that property now and she'd be upset for him.

And this nasty man didn't deserve to best Corin, who was going to put the land to good use.

She stayed at the door of his office but had to clear her throat loudly to get his attention. 'I'm just going out to buy some biscuits, Mr Begworth. What sort do you like?'

'Chocolate shortbread. Buy two packets, one for me, one for you gir— for the other staff.'

When she got back, he stared at her breasts again. He must be a slow learner about sexist behaviour. So she stared him down coldly and after a couple of moments he wriggled as if uncomfortable.

'Is something wrong . . . sir?' This time he took the hint about where he looked. She'd outstared better men than him.

He glanced at his watch instead. 'No, nothing's wrong. You can go back to work now, Miss . . . um . . .'

'*Ms* Grey.'

He muttered something under his breath as she went back into the reception area, hiding a smile. She rather thought she'd won that round.

She hoped Nina had got the contracts signed, sealed and delivered. She was glad she was getting back her confidence at dealing with horrible men like this one. Honestly, was he living in the dark ages, behaving like that when he dealt with his staff? Was he as bad with the public?

Come to think of it, this place didn't have the air of a thriving business.

Nina had told Corin to stay within reach of a phone, so when she'd driven a little way up Larch Tree Lane she stopped to text him to say that she was on her way, then drove straight to the big house, going round to the back as he'd said.

He came to the door before she'd even got out of the car, smiling at her. Then the smile faded.

'You look anxious. Is everything all right, Nina?'

'Don just came back.'

'Oh, hell! Has he stopped the sale?'

'Not if we act quickly. I have the contract here already signed by Jeff on behalf of the seller and I put the keys to your new possessions and the other documents about the property in my briefcase earlier, thank goodness, so if we can get this done, I can hand them all over. Is Maggie around? We need a witness to your signature. If she isn't here, we'll have to go and find someone before we can do the deed.'

'It's OK. She's in the kitchen. Come inside.'

He smiled across at Maggie. 'We need you as a witness to a legal document, if that's all right.'

Nina didn't waste time on civilities. 'Will you please sign the contract straight away, Corin, and Maggie, will you please witness it?'

'Of course.'

Nina set everything out on the table. 'After the papers are signed, I'll have to find somewhere in the village to scan them in and email them to Jeff. Once he's got a copy, the sale will be legal. I daren't go into the office till that's done. Afterwards, Don can go to hell for all I care.'

'No need to go into Essington. You can use my fancy new computer to scan them in and send the digital copies to your man. You can courier off a hard copy to him when you go into the village.'

'Oh, great. That'll save me a lot of trouble.'

They did what she asked then she emailed off the scans, holding up one hand to prevent him speaking. 'Jeff said he'd get straight back to me once he got the emailed copy with your signature on it, to acknowledge that the sale has been legally completed. I shan't feel safe until he does that.'

A couple of minutes later, her phone pinged and she answered a message, then flung her arms round Maggie and danced her round the kitchen, before doing the same to Corin.

'Don can't break the contract now.'

'You're sure of that?'

'Utterly certain, though I prepared Jeff for Don trying to do it anyway. Jeff doesn't want it messing around with either because he's going on leave in a couple of days.'

After lunch, Nina walked calmly into the agency and winked at Lucia, giving her a quick thumbs up.

Don came out of his office. 'Where the hell have you been, Nina? Why weren't you answering your phone?'

'How was I to know you'd come back without warning? And anyway, I was out getting the contract for a sale signed. You wouldn't want me to stop doing that to chat on my phone, surely?'

He brightened up. 'Certainly not. Which property was it?'

'That piece of land up near the top of Larch Tree Lane.'

'*What?* I didn't have that shown as for sale in the window. How did a buyer even find it?'

'A guy had seen the land itself and our for sale sign on it.'

'But it had fallen over. I kept meaning to get it erected properly.'

Which she guessed was a lie. 'Well, this guy liked the looks of the place so he walked round the land and decided to buy it. Was I supposed to say no when he walked in off the street and made me a cash offer I couldn't refuse?'

Don made a scornful noise. 'He may have made you an offer, but you haven't had time to get the contract signed, sealed and delivered. I have a better offer, so get back to your buyer and tell him he's been gazumped.'

She'd been going to phone the couriers they used to come and collect the envelope containing the contract, and wished she'd gone into their office instead to send it before coming here.

'No can do, Don. The client wanted it pushing through in a hurry and so did the guy in charge of selling it at the ministry, so it's already been signed, sealed and delivered.'

He looked so stunned, she added slowly, 'It's gone through irrevocably, Don, all fully legal.'

He glared at her then said, 'No, it bloody hasn't. Get your buyer in here and I'll deal with him. He won't know whether it's gone through legally or not.'

'He's a savvy chap.'

'So am I. And you can just do as I say if you want to keep your job.'

She studied him thoughtfully, then went into her office and phoned Corin. 'My boss wants to see you about the contract you just signed.'

'He can't change the sale, though, surely?'

She whispered, 'An attempt will be made, but no, he can't do anything legally.'

'I'll come down to the village straight away. You probably need my support.'

'Best to sort it out once and for all.'

She ended the call and went to smile sweetly at Don from her office doorway. 'He's coming down to the village anyway so he'll pop in to see you while he's here.'

'Show me the contract. And don't you ever go against my wishes again. I told you to leave that plot of land to me.'

'Just a minute.' She picked up the contract and walked

across to the photocopier. By the time he'd realised what she was doing, she'd made two copies. She gave one to Lucia and the other to him, keeping the original herself.

He held out his hand imperatively to Lucia. 'Give me that one. *You* don't need to get involved in this from now on.'

When Lucia made no effort to do this, he tried to snatch it from her. She was too quick for him and made sure she stayed on the other side of the reception desk.

He thumped his clenched fist down on his side of the desk. 'I said, give it me!'

She still didn't move, so he turned to Nina. 'And I want the original from you, as well. Stop messing me around. We're going to do this my way.'

'It's already done.' Nina moved back, also holding her copy out of his reach, worried now about how furiously angry he was looking. 'Don't give him that, though, Lucia.'

'Either you give it to me or you're sacked!' he yelled at her, stabbing one finger a few times to emphasise what he was saying. 'Temps are easy to come by.'

'I'd better leave then, because I'm not going to become involved in doing anything illegal, which is what this sounds like.'

'What do you mean by that? It's not illegal to promise a block of land to a buyer, which I had already done. My guy has a prior right to the land.'

Nina intervened. 'There was no contract or mention of an offer in the file. I checked it carefully. So I'm keeping this to protect my client.'

'Then you're sacked too, you disloyal bitch.' He made

another snatch at the contract but she was too quick for him.

'I've already got a job elsewhere and given my notice, Don, so you can't sack me. I'd better leave straight away, though, because I shan't feel safe on my own with you in this mood. I'll go and pack my things.'

'I'll stay with you till you're ready,' Lucia said.

He glared from one woman to the other, took a hasty step forward then stopped and moved back as the two women glared back, still holding the contracts behind them.

'If you lay one finger on me,' Nina said slowly and emphatically, 'I'll lay a complaint of assault against you, and I have a witness. You'd better stay in my doorway, Lucia, in case he attacks you as well.'

'I've not attacked anyone!' Don roared but kept his distance.

Nina went into her office and began to pack, relieved to be leaving. She'd never seen him so furious and out of control, and she'd forgotten what a nasty feeling he could broadcast if anything upset him.

When the doorbell let out its annoyingly loud two-tone sound, she peeped out of her office and sagged in relief when she saw Corin stroll in.

Don was still standing in the reception area and he turned to the newcomer. 'May I help you, sir?'

'Nina said you wanted to see me. I've just bought one of your properties.'

'Ah. Please come into my office, Mr, um—'

'Drayton. And from the expression on your face, you're angry about something so I'd rather have a witness to our discussion.'

'Well, this woman was just leaving so you can't have her.' Don turned to Lucia and yelled, 'I told you to get out of my business when I fired you! What are you still doing here?'

'You definitely need a witness,' she said to Corin as she moved towards the door. 'He has a very bad temper and I was afraid he'd hit me. He's just sacked both of us.'

She opened the door but didn't go outside.

'He *tried* to sack me,' Nina corrected. 'Only I'd already given my notice so there's nothing to sack.'

'You can't give notice to me when I'm not here,' Don yelled loudly.

'You gave me a signed statement that I could sell houses and make agreements without your approval while you were away, and I didn't have your address or phone number to send my resignation to, so I got it signed and dated and filed it.'

'Of course you had my contact details. My wife said she'd sent them to you!'

'Well, she didn't. She told me not to call except in the direst emergency because she wanted you both to have a real holiday for once.'

His expression said his wife would be another one to feel the brunt of his anger next time he saw her. He gestured to the newcomer. 'Mr Drayton? Let's continue this in my office.'

He managed to shut and lock his office door before Nina could follow Corin inside, but she could see through the window his obvious shock when Corin took him by surprise and moved him gently aside, before unlocking the door and returning to the main area again. His voice was perfectly calm as he said, 'We'll have this discussion out here or not at all, Mr Begworth, and with Ms Perry as a witness.'

Don swelled up in anger, opened and shut his mouth, then strode across to jab his finger at Lucia. 'Out, you, or I'll call the police to eject you.'

'I'll wait for you outside, Nina,' she called.

He slammed and locked the outer door but she stayed in the doorway, from where she could see into the reception area between the two vertical rows of house adverts in the glass door.

Don tried to force a smile, but wasn't very successful. 'Please sit down, Mr Drayton. We can talk out here if you prefer it.'

'I've not got a lot of time to waste so I'll stand, thank you. What did you want to see me about?'

'I'm afraid there has been an error with your alleged purchase of that block of land.'

'What makes you think that?'

'I promised it to a client before I left for Spain. He has a prior right to it.'

'You can't have done or the guy sorting out the sale at the ministry would have known about it.'

'It was a verbal agreement I had with my client.'

'There was no such agreement listed in our files,' Nina said.

'And the guy at the ministry didn't appear to have heard of it either. Therefore I have now bought the block of land fairly and squarely.'

'You're wrong. But we will of course reimburse you for your expenses and inconvenience. Shall we say £10,000?'

Corin continued to smile gently. 'Nope. I've bought the land fair and square, and the sale has gone through. I'm afraid your sloppy ways have lost the land for your customer. It's he who'll need compensating for his trouble, I'd guess.'

'You're wrong, I'm afraid, as my lawyer will make plain.'

'I'm quite sure of my ground because I've been in business long enough to know that the Marrakin is now mine. Now, I don't intend to stand here and debate it all day. I have other things to attend to.'

He turned his back on Begworth and smiled at Nina. 'Go and finish gathering your things, Ms Perry. I think I'd better wait for you and see you out.'

'We'll give you £20,000 in compensation, then, dammit,' Begworth shouted.

Corin gave him a cursory glance and head shake. 'Nothing you say or do will persuade me to change my mind. I want that particular piece of land. It's exactly what I was searching for.'

The expression on Begworth's face suddenly turned dark and threatening. 'I'm sure you'll regret that and change your mind, Mr Drayton, as soon as you think it over. I shall be here from nine o'clock tomorrow morning to deal with it for you.'

'Don't waste your time. I'm quite sure I won't change my mind.'

'And I'm quite sure you will.' Begworth turned to Nina. 'And *you* will regret disobeying my orders if you ever try to get another job near here.'

She turned away and went into her office, not bothering

to tell him where she would be working next.

Begworth locked the back door and removed the key, smiling at Corin. 'Since she's no longer on my staff, Ms Perry can go out the front way with you. Who knows what she'd try to steal if I let her into the private areas of my premises.'

He went into his office and slammed the door, which set the glass partition rattling, then stood behind it, glaring out.

Nina came to her office door. 'He makes me shiver, he's so malevolent.'

'He won't do anything while I'm here, because like most bullies he's basically a coward, but you should take care how you go for a while.'

'I shall be very careful, believe me. I wonder if you'd mind helping me to carry these out? I don't want to leave some of them here and try to come back for them.'

Nina handed him two carrier bags full of bits and pieces, with a desk ornament sticking out of the top of one, then she picked up another bag crammed with papers, a briefcase and her handbag. 'That's it.'

She stared at the back door, which was next to her office. 'Where's the key? Did he just lock that?'

'Yes.'

'How petty can you get? Lucia and I will have to walk right round the block to reach our cars, and I hope he won't be waiting for us at the back.'

'I'll go with you and I won't let him hurt you,' Corin said quietly.

'He's always had a nasty temper but he's never been this bad before. What on earth has got into him?'

'Who knows? Perhaps that piece of land meant more to him personally than anyone realised.'

She stared at Don's office, shaking her head in bafflement, then looked up at the tall man waiting patiently beside her. Unlike her ex-employer, Corin hadn't raised his voice once, but it might have been better if he had. Begworth only seemed to understand shouting and loud emphatic thumps of his fist on the desk when something displeased him.

What if he attacked Corin? Could such a gentle man defend himself?

She looked up at him again. He seemed very fit and strong, unlike Don, who was puffy and had a large paunch. No, Corin would be all right, surely.

Chapter Thirteen

Lucia was waiting for them outside. 'I didn't dare go round the back to pick up my car on my own. Will you come with us to do that, please, Corin?'

'Of course I will. I was intending to anyway. He's well out of order, the way he's been behaving.'

'How did you stay so calm when he was yelling at us?' Nina asked.

'Years of practice at working with excitable people. I soon learned that it didn't pay to lose my temper. Come on, let's get your cars away before he starts throwing things at them.'

Lucia frowned as they walked along the back lane. 'I think I'd better go and report this to the employment bureau afterwards so that they don't send anyone else to work there.'

'We'll all go,' he said. 'It'll be better for you to have witnesses who can confirm your story.'

When they'd retrieved the vehicles, Lucia dropped Corin near his car and they all went to park across at the other side of the village centre near the bureau.

'Don's always had a bad temper, but I've never seen him lose control so completely,' Nina said as she joined them. 'I'm still trying to work out why.'

Corin stopped walking for a moment. 'Maybe he'd lost rather a lot of money he was counting on from that particular deal?'

'Could be, I suppose. But he's had the estate agency for years and this isn't the first lucrative scam he's set up, from what I've noticed. He doesn't have stellar monthly sales, because there aren't enough houses round here for that sort of turnover and he doesn't seem to acquire many listings further afield. But surely he can't be so short of money that one lost deal could make life difficult for him?'

'People don't always handle their money wisely. Is he a gambler?'

It was her turn to stop walking and frown in thought. 'Well, he likes a bet now and then, but I've never seen signs of anything worse than five or ten pounds lost on the horses.'

When they went into the employment bureau and reported what had happened, Jennica stared at them in shock. 'Let me write that down and get you to witness it, then I'll do the accounts for how much he owes me on your behalf, Lucia. You'll be paid for the hours you put in and for the rest of today, I promise you, or I'll take him to court. And I'd just like to say how sorry I am that I placed you somewhere you've been treated so badly.'

'You weren't to know. It was a bit unnerving, though, I must admit.' Especially coming on top of Howard's machinations and threats. 'I'm still available for temping, though.'

'Well, we're all out of Don's orbit now, and I'll not deal with him professionally again if I can help it.' Nina smiled suddenly. 'I wonder how he'll manage to run the office without any staff?'

'With difficulty.'

'I suppose he'll bring his wife in to help out. Linda used to work there when he first started up. I doubt he'd dare threaten her with violence. She's a feisty lady and I've never seen him be anything but ultra-polite with her, whatever he says or does behind her back.'

'I'd better get my stuff home. I think I'll let my new employer know what's happened today as well,' Nina said.

'What exactly do you plan to tell them?'

'The truth. People already know what he's like and the other estate agents don't do business with him unless they have to. Though I've never heard anyone say he threatened them like he just did you, Corin.'

When Nina had driven off, he said, 'I'm going to buy a bottle of good champagne to celebrate my purchase going through. Will you share it with me tonight, Lucia?'

'With pleasure.'

'I'll see you at home, then.'

When he got there, he put the champagne in the fridge to cool, then phoned the water authority to say the sale had gone through and ask them to switch it on again, which he'd prearranged.

By that time, she'd changed into casual clothes and he greeted her with, 'I can't resist going to have a thorough look round my land. Would you like to come too?'

'I'd love to.'

'I want to see if we can find out what's under that big

mound and look inside as many of the houses as we've time for. I'll just change out of these business clothes. Give me jeans any day.'

As they walked outside to his car she said, 'I wonder what the War Ministry used the land for.'

'We'll probably never find out. They can be very secretive and when a place is put up for sale, they usually remove any tell-tale information very carefully first.'

'I suppose so. That Second World War feels to have happened so long ago.'

'Two or three generations now, give or take. I find it fascinating to read about how people lived then. It'll be fun to explore my land together, won't it?'

'I shall enjoy it, Corin. I love historical stuff too, warts and all! Besides, if you don't know what went really wrong in the past and why, how can you avoid making the same mistakes over and over again?'

'True. And if we stand here talking all day, we'll never see anything.'

'I've just had an idea. I'll only be a couple of minutes.'

When he came back carrying a workman's tool bag, his excitement was palpable and made him look younger, she thought. What an attractive man he was!

'Let's go in my car, Lucia.' He brandished the bag at her. 'I've opened one of the removal boxes Maggie let me store in her house and got out a few tools that might come in useful if we can't get into any of the houses. I'm thinking we may have to force one or two locks.'

'What about that bunch of keys Nina gave you?'

'They'll open the doors in theory but locks can stick. Better safe than sorry.'

'Have you brought something to label the keys with?'

He was about to start the car but stopped dead. 'Goodness, that never occurred to me.'

'Well, there was only a jumbled collection of keys on the chain when I saw them in Nina's office so we'd better have some way of labelling them. I have a packet of envelopes in my room. They'll do for starters. You'll have to buy some proper labels.'

She ran up to get the envelopes and rejoined him in the car, feeling excited. 'Have you told your family what you've done?'

'There's only my brother who matters. I'm going to phone Pete tonight. I didn't dare tell him till it was certain, didn't want to jinx it.'

He still didn't set off, was frowning into the distance. 'You know, I can't help wondering whether Begworth will try anything tonight.'

'He did sound rather threatening, didn't he? But why should he do something tonight?'

'He said very specifically that he'd be waiting for me in the office tomorrow morning to cancel the sale. I keep wondering what made him feel so sure of that. Well, he's not getting me to change my mind.'

'Are you worried he might get violent in an attempt to frighten you?'

'Wary, rather than worried. I've had a rather adventurous life for the past decade, so I'm not as helpless as I might look, but I'm good at spotting warning signs of problems to come. And this looks like one to me. In fact, I'd not trust him as far as I could throw him, as the saying goes.'

Instinctively she chanted the words her grandma had always added to that saying, 'And I wouldn't pick him up in the first place.'

He laughed and she said softly, 'My gran always said that. You'd have liked her. You will be careful, though?'

'Of course. I've survived situations that are more dangerous than anything he's likely to do, believe me. But I don't want any of my properties damaged so it's best to be prepared. I shall have to work out how best to safeguard my purchase long term, which will be easier after I've had another look at the place. And I'll never do that unless I start the car.'

As he set off, he said, 'I'm rattling on about my problems. What about yours? Are you still afraid of your ex?'

'Yes. I don't think I've heard the last from Howard, I must admit.'

'I'll help you deal with him if he so much as pops his head over the parapet.'

'Thanks.'

'Ah, here we are. It doesn't take long to drive round from Larch House, does it?'

'The distance is even shorter if you walk through the woods and doesn't take much longer.'

'I'll remember that.'

He took the bunch of keys out of his pocket, shaking them round in his hand until he saw one that looked as if it might fit a padlock, cheering when it unlocked the gate.

As he removed the padlock, he looked at it in distaste. 'I don't like having to use these things. I won't put it back till I leave each day. I don't want to lock you out if you come to see me, as I hope you will.'

'You won't want to lock out the postman, either.'

'Hmm. I think I'll get a freestanding post box to put at the gate, like they have in Australia. I don't want anyone coming into the grounds and trying to poke flyers and advertising material through all the front doors.'

'Note to self: buy and install post box,' she teased. 'Also, buy signs saying *No Junk Mail*.'

He had just driven through the gateway into the Marrakin as she spoke and braked suddenly, looking at her as if he'd never really seen her before. 'What I'm going to put first on my list is to hire a personal assistant. Do you want the job?'

She stared at him, not certain whether he was teasing her or not. 'Seriously?'

'Yes, seriously. Things will be quiet to start off with but the job won't be a sinecure once we get going. You'll be very busy later on, I warn you.'

'I'd love to work with you but I have no experience of the building industry so I'm not quite sure what PAs do for builders.'

'All the better to start with a blank slate, because I like to do things my own way. I'll pay you whatever the going rate is.' He held out his hand and she didn't hesitate to take it and shake on the bargain. Then he got out to close the gate again before she could offer to do it.

She leaned out of the window to call, 'Maybe you'd be better locking the gate while we're looking round today. We'll be out of sight of the entrance for some if not most of the time and we have no idea what Begworth is intending to do.'

Corin stood frowning for a moment, then looked regretfully down at the padlock and clicked it back in place again. 'You're probably right. For the time being, anyway. That means I'll have to get you some keys cut.'

'Surely that'll be one of *my* first jobs?'

'I stand corrected.' He drove the short distance along the overgrown dirt road to the nearest house, which he'd fallen in love with on his first visit, pulling up in front of it. 'I love the potential of this one. I think I'm going to keep it for myself. It'll be pretty once I've set everything to rights again and sorted out the garden. That fence would fall down if it didn't have the overgrown bushes to lean on.'

'The house is pretty even as it is now.'

'Isn't it?'

'I like symmetry in buildings. Those modern houses that are all lumps and bumps and strange angles leave me cold.'

'Me too. And they're often as bad inside as out. I promise you, Lucia, I will never design anything at all like that. I like to build *homes*, not just show houses. Now, let's go inside this house later and look at that mound first. I've been dying to see what's underneath the pile of muck, which looks to me as if it was put in place later than the houses were last worked on. Let's have at it.'

He opened the boot and took out a new shovel and a slender brass measuring pole about six foot long. As he marched round towards the mound, he began whistling the tune from the first ever *Snow White and the Seven Dwarfs* cartoon.

With a smile, she fell in beside him, singing the words

and marching in time to it as well.

He stopped whistling and moving just before they got to the mound, grabbing her arm to stop her going any further. 'Let's test the ground first, see how deep the soft part is. We don't want anything giving way beneath us.'

He stuck the pole into what proved to be fairly soft earth covered by an untidy tangle of grass and wildflowers. The pole went in about three feet before striking something solid and stopping. When Corin moved it along, poking it in a few more times, it went down the same distance.

He stared at it thoughtfully. 'Feels like a continuous solid surface underneath the muck to me. So why make a triangular pile on top of it to make it look like a mound?'

'It doesn't make sense.' She stood back and studied it again. 'You know, if this place was used during the Second World War, maybe this is covering an air raid shelter? It's about the right size.'

'What made you think of that?'

'My grandma told me about the one where she lived in Lancashire as a child and showed me photos. It was a communal shelter at the end of their terrace of houses because the houses didn't have any land apart from small back yards, so they couldn't set up individual shelters. After the war ended, she and the other kids used to play inside the shelter in rainy weather. They played mainly in the outer room where some light shone in through the open entrance, though. She said the darkness further inside frightened them, especially the corridor leading off the back of the second chamber.'

'They could have used a torch, surely?'

'Batteries and even candles were hard to come by at

first after the war ended; at least, they were where she lived, and her parents were saving hard to buy a house so they wouldn't let her spend even a farthing on batteries for torches used only in her games.'

'I never thought about how the people living in terraced housing would have managed for air raid shelters. My relatives lived in a London suburb and they had their own Anderson shelter at the far end of the back garden, with bunk beds in it. They slept there quite often, apparently, especially during the Blitz.'

They were both silent then she added, 'Fancy spending eight months being bombed so often. It must have been dreadful.'

He looked round. 'They were all heroes. But the Blitz was mainly in London, Bristol and . . . was it Merseyside? I wouldn't have thought there was much need for air raid shelters out here in a Wiltshire valley, let alone a big solid shelter like this.'

'Who knows what was going on here? If it really is an old air raid shelter, which we're only guessing about at the moment, they might have thought they might become a target for bombers leaving Bristol. Didn't Nina give you a pile of papers when you signed the contract? Maybe there's some historical information among them.'

'I doubt it. If they kept the place locked away from the public for so long, there must have been a good reason for secrecy, and the information about it wouldn't be handed out afterwards among papers anyone could read.'

He rolled up his sleeves and picked up the shovel.

'Let's see if I can shift enough earth to catch a glimpse of what's underneath at this side of the nearest houses, eh? It doesn't seem to have been compacted so it won't be too hard to dig into.'

Chapter Fourteen

Lucia moved out of his way and watched him for a minute or so, then decided she was wasting time and walked across to look more closely at a nearby cottage. The door was locked and she peered through the front window at a dusty, unfurnished room with cobwebs draped here and there.

She saw Corin stop for a minute to wipe his brow.

'I'm out of practice,' he called. 'What can you see?'

'Nothing much. The windows are filthy.'

'Why don't you see if you can find the key to that house? The bundle of keys is on top of my clothes. We can have a quick peep inside when I need a break.'

From the way he began digging again, he was no stranger to manual toil. If this was how he worked when he was out of practice, what was he like when he was fitter?

She left him to it, went through the keys and soon found one that fitted easily into the old-fashioned lock. But when she tried to turn it, the key stuck and no way could she move it. She'd have to bring some lubricant next time.

She took out her little notebook and scribbled it down under 'Copies of keys' and 'labels' as the third item on her list. She tried to turn the key again, just on principle, wiggling it around. It seemed a little looser, but she still couldn't get it to unlock the door.

Corin stopped digging, put down the shovel and walked across to join her. 'Let me try.' He grinned and pretended to show off his muscles. 'Me heap big macho man.'

She did a mock swoon. 'My hero!'

Taking over, he began fiddling with the key and suddenly it clicked and they both cheered.

'There has to be some advantage to being a big lump of a fellow. We need to bring something to lubricate these old locks next time.'

'Voilà!' She brandished the notebook at him, showing him the embryonic list.

'I knew you'd be efficient. Let's look inside before I go back to my digging.' He let out a happy sigh. 'I'm like a kid in a toyshop. I want to see everything at once. That pile of earth will still be there when we come out, after all.'

This house was disappointing after the first one, with small rooms and windows. There were only two bedrooms upstairs and no visible attic access. It must have been quite a bit older and had no indoor plumbing except for the kitchen tap. It was darker inside than need be because a tree was overhanging the kitchen window at the rear.

There was a rear yard but they didn't seem to have a key to the back door so they could only peer out at what seemed to be two outhouses. The yard had a high wall round it and when they went back outside, Corin levered himself up to look over, but he didn't attempt to climb over.

'I'll wait till we find the other key to see what's in the yard, but I don't think this house will be worth renovating.

Some parts of it are rather crumbly and the roof's sagging at one side.'

He took out a notebook of his own, which had a dirty crumpled cover, as if it had been used a lot, and quickly did a tiny sketch with an arrow to this house's approximate position.

'Let me get back to the digging. That's much more accessible. I was just about to clear what looks like an entrance. Come and see.'

She went across and saw the flat edge of a concrete pad which had been cleared for a couple of yards. As she stepped onto it, the ground started to give way beneath her and she let out an involuntary squeak of shock as she felt herself losing her balance.

Corin grabbed her and yanked her back, then took a big step backwards himself. 'I wasn't expecting that.'

She stood safe in his arms as they watched the soft earth at one side continue to sink slowly downwards, revealing part of a largish hole.

'What the hell is happening here? Let's see if I can scrape more earth away.'

'Be careful.'

'I will. You stay there.' He set her safely to one side, plonked a kiss on her nose and picked up the shovel.

She could feel the warmth of that kiss on her skin even after he moved away. He was a very touchy-feely person. She liked that. Howard had compartmentalised their life, including the rare sexual encounters.

Corin got one corner of the hole clear without anything else giving way, and it was enough to show part of what looked like concrete steps going down, with some planks also showing now. They must have been placed across the third step to hold back the earth, had slipped a bit and were now slanting sideways to reveal the steps that had been behind them leading down into absolute darkness. Trickles of earth were still sifting gently through the gap.

He whistled softly. 'What next? I bet this used to be the main entrance. But it's a rather large staircase for an air raid shelter, don't you think?'

She grabbed his shirt and pulled him back. 'Don't get too close.'

He smiled down at her, one of his lovely gentle smiles. 'It's nice to have someone who cares whether I'm safe or not.' He took her hand and raised it to his lips, then pulled her close and kissed her more thoroughly.

'We're supposed to be exploring,' she said when they came up for air.

'We're free to do what we want when we want, and I need your lovely kisses at regular intervals to keep me going.'

He didn't attempt to start digging again. 'There's a lot of earth been dumped here and more recently than any of the houses were built, by the looks of it. I think it'd be better to use a small earth mover to clear this mess away, so meanwhile I'll see if I can wedge those planks back in place and fill the top steps up again. We don't want anyone falling down it.'

'I'll find a stone and put it at the edge here to mark where they are.'

'See. You're a marvellous PA,' he teased.

When he'd finished, he looked up at the sun, which was moving gradually down towards the horizon. 'We'll explore this place properly another day with better equipment. I reckon we can fit in a quick glance inside another house before we leave, though. It won't get dark for a while yet. I love the long summer twilights, don't you? Is that all right with you?'

'Of course it is.' She looked round as they walked along to the next house to which she had found a key. 'I hope we don't get that horrible estate agent sneaking in tonight and trying to damage these buildings. Some of them are beautiful, even if the interiors have been neglected.'

He turned to stare at the mound again. 'I don't think it was Begworth and Co who covered up that concrete building or cellar or whatever it is. And if not, who did it?'

'Perhaps there are still things down there that someone was intending to come back for.'

'Hmm. I can't think what.'

'We'll have to put up barriers and signs on Larch Tree Lane or else the local lads will be sneaking in to explore and then you might be liable.'

'I agree. I'll set up an electronic surveillance system, too, and maybe hire a caretaker to live in one of the cottages or even move in myself.'

She didn't say it but she'd miss him, was already enjoying having him around at Larch House.

'And I'll go through those papers Nina gave me very carefully indeed. This place is quite a mystery. I wonder if the guy from the ministry who handled the selling knew any details of what it was used for. Perhaps I should get in touch with him?'

'Nina said he was going on holiday for several weeks, so we won't be able to find anything out till after he gets back. Pity. I'm really interested in it now as well.'

Corin picked up his shovel. 'It is fascinating, isn't it? We'll unwrap the mysteries together. Now, just give me a few minutes to toss the rest of the soil back then we'll go and look at another house.'

'While you're playing Mr Muscles, I'll see if I can fit any more keys to doors.' She couldn't stop smiling as she started to walk round the houses. She'd given up pretending she didn't want to get close to him. She did. Wanted it very much. And he seemed to feel the same way.

Ah, to hell with Howard! She'd deal with him if he turned up again – no, *they* would deal with him together. She didn't feel to be facing him on her own any longer and what a difference that made to how she felt!

He'd destroyed her self-confidence, she could see that now, but it was coming back and he'd better watch out.

By the time Corin had finished covering the mound again, so that it'd look untouched from the road, Lucia had found which keys opened three more of the houses, and put them into envelopes with scribbled descriptions of each house. She'd refrained from going inside any of them, because it didn't seem fair to do that until Corin could join her but she was itching to see them.

He put down the shovel and came across looking sweaty, dirty and happy. He marked the houses which had keys on his own map and gave them all numbers.

'Which house do you want to look in?' she asked. 'I doubt we've time for more than one.'

'That one.' He pointed to one of the larger houses. It looked to be in need of some TLC but was a pretty building even so.

'What date do you think it's from originally?'

'1830s or 40s, I should think. Three storeys if you count the attic, which was probably used by the servants. It's rather like the house my family has lived in near the brewery for decades but ours is a bit bigger, I think.'

'Do you miss your old home?'

'Not really. I haven't really lived there since I left university and I never did like the smell of the brewery. Anyway, my mother has the right to live there till she dies or remarries, so I shan't be going back often.'

'Don't you get on with her?'

'No.'

'What about your brother?'

'Pete's great. He'll make a big success of the brewery, I'm sure. He's living in a little flat on the premises.'

'Not with your mother?'

'Hell, no. There would be an explosion if they tried it without intermediaries after the way my father left things.' He took her hand. 'Come on. We can discuss my family another time. Let's go inside while there's enough light to see what it's like.'

He stopped at the front door, shaking his head. 'Actually, I've changed my mind about that. Do you mind locking it up again? I can't get it out of my mind that Begworth said he'd be at the office tomorrow so that I could hand over the land I'd mistakenly bought. He sounded so confident that you have to wonder why. My guess is that he's planning something for tonight to make me back off.'

She stared at him in consternation. 'I'd believe anything of him.'

'I think I need to come here tonight to keep watch and set a few surprises for him if he or someone else turns up to do some damage.'

'Do you really think he'll do that, damage the houses, I mean?'

'Yes. If he's selling the land purely for rezoning to builders who'll be cramming showy but smaller modern houses on small blocks, he won't care whether he damages the present buildings or not. But I'd care. Some people want to destroy the past; I'd rather preserve some of it.'

'Me, too.'

He glanced at his watch. 'We've just got time to nip down to that little hardware store I saw in the village and see if they have anything I could use for security purposes.'

'You'll still be only one man.'

'So? Begworth won't be able to gather a gang together at such short notice, especially not out here in the country. And if he brings in anyone as unfit as himself to help him, I can send them both packing, no worries.'

'Are you really so confident?'

'I've worked in some very dangerous places and I've had to learn to fight dirty at times to save lives.'

He stared into the distance for a few moments, as if remembering something unpleasant, then started collecting his tools.

His expression was no longer bright and excited. The best way to describe it, she thought sadly, was 'grimly determined'.

As they got out of the car in the village, Lucia looked down at her clothing. 'We're a bit mucky to be going shopping.'

'On the contrary, this is perfectly normal for customers of this type of shop. And trust me, since we'll probably be buying a lot of things from them, they won't care what we look like.'

He led the way inside and was soon deep in discussion with the man behind the counter, who turned out to be the owner and was soon taking a keen interest in Corin's dilemma and consequent needs.

They left with a big box of equipment whose uses Corin seemed to understand perfectly, which was more than she did.

By this time Lucia was so worried about his safety, she had to say something. 'Don't you think you need someone with better physical skills than me to act as your personal assistant?'

'Nope. You're delightful to work with – and to be with. And you'll soon learn what I need. The trouble that's upsetting you won't go on for long, believe me.'

'Oh. Well, I like being with you, too, and I enjoy learning new stuff. But I wouldn't be much help in a fight.'

'I don't want you or anyone I employ to be involved in fights on my behalf. I can usually handle that side of things myself. I'd better go and camp out there tonight, though, as I won't be able to get a proper security system set up for a while.'

He seemed to read her mind and gave her a stern look. 'And no, I'm definitely not taking you with me. You'd get in the way. Sadly, we'll have to leave the champagne for another night, but I shan't forget.'

'That's the last thing I care about.'

'What do you really care about?' he asked softly.

'Your safety.' She'd nearly said, 'You' but it was too soon to be so open about her feelings. Not that she didn't trust him; she simply didn't trust herself.

He put one hand on his heart in a mock sentimental gesture. 'In that case I shall have the strength of ten men tonight thinking of you. But I shall need to buy a generator before I move in properly. Can you put it on our shopping list, please?'

She did that and after another pause, he added, 'I have one or two other ideas for the future which will improve safety. I must admit the need for such care has taken me by surprise. I'll share my plans with you when they've had time to ripen. At the moment I have to focus on this initial problem.'

'That means you'll be on your own there tonight, though. What if a group of men turn up to damage things?'

'I'm not going to camp out there with a sign saying *Here I am*, you know. I shall be hiding but ready to pounce. If several men turn up, I shan't do any pouncing. I'll stay hidden, whatever they do, and call the police. But where would Begworth find men so quickly in a village like Essington?'

'Well, I must say I haven't seen anything that looks like unruly groups hanging around the village.'

'And don't forget that I have night vision goggles now. They'll make a big difference.'

But she was still worried and he pulled her close for a moment, rocking her to and fro slightly. 'Stop worrying. I'm going to make long-term security plans that will be rather more sophisticated, but I feel strongly that I have to keep Begworth at bay tonight. I've learned to pay attention when I get a hunch like this.'

He didn't offer her any details of what his security plans would involve and she could see he was eager to get ready so didn't press for further information.

'I'll make you a snack to eat now and a thermos of coffee for later,' she offered.

'That'd be good. And I'd like a nice big snack if you don't mind – something quick, though? The prospect of fighting always makes me feel hungry.'

On the way back to Larch House, they went onto his block of land again, and unloaded the things he'd bought, locking them in the first house. After that they left openly.

'No one will doubt that I've left the place,' he said with a wolfish smile. 'Because that guy further down the road who slid down in his car as we drove past was watching us carefully.'

'I didn't see anyone.'

'You weren't looking. I'm in alert mode now.'

At Larch House, he changed into dark clothes, gobbled down the scrambled eggs on toast that she'd prepared then got ready to leave.

'I'll see you two ladies in the morning. I'm going there on foot so that there isn't a car to betray my presence. Is there any way I can get out of the house without being seen, Maggie?'

'Yes, through the cellar. I'll show you. No one will notice you, I promise.'

'Surely they won't be watching this house as well?' Lucia exclaimed.

'I don't think they will but I'd rather be safe than sorry,' he said quietly.

'You really do think that horrible man will come and try to vandalise your place tonight, don't you?' Lucia asked.

'Highly likely. I'll be there before them, planting a few little surprises and waiting to see what they intend to do. Only, they won't see me. I doubt they'll set out before folk are in bed because they won't want their car to be seen coming here. There might not be a village up at this end, but there are quite a few houses fronting onto Larch Tree Lane close to the top end.'

He pulled her towards him and kissed her cheek, then did the same to Maggie, who was watching him almost as anxiously. 'I'll be all right, I promise you.'

She took him down to the cellar and pointed out the concealed exit.

'Now, just tell me where it's best to enter the woods.'

When she'd watched him vanish into the trees, Maggie went back to Lucia and said quietly, 'I'd back him against that horrible Begworth fellow any day.'

'Would you?'

'Oh, yes. He's a born leader and it shows. I hope he trounces that fellow good and proper. Begworth has tried several times to persuade me to let him sell this house. I considered it briefly the first time, a few years ago, when I was first on my own, but I checked out prices and found he was suggesting a much lower one than its true value. And anyway, I don't really want to leave.'

'That's what he's trying to do with the Marrakin.'

'He's a horrible man, unlike your lovely Corin. I'm off to bed now and I'm taking a poker with me. There are plenty in the house. You should keep one handy as well, just in case your ex comes back while Corin's away. You have only to shout and I'll come running to join in any fun if he does.'

Lucia gave her a hug, then did as she suggested. She wasn't very concerned about Howard turning up during the week but the poker felt good in her hand. She'd be more worried at the weekend if Corin was still sleeping down at the cottages.

But somehow she didn't think her ex would come looking for her mid-week because he was such an eager-beaver at work and really cared about coming top in sales, whatever it took. No, it had always been at weekends that he'd played nasty tricks on her.

She'd rather throw her aunt's jewellery into the sea than give any of it to him, far rather.

She didn't sleep well, though, because she was worried about Corin. She found herself muttering, 'Let him stay safe, please let him stay safe!'

Chapter Fifteen

Corin walked quietly through the woods along the almost invisible path that Maggie had pointed out as leading towards the boundary between her domain and his new property. He stopped for a moment to heft his rucksack into a more comfortable position on his back, enjoying the dappled moonlit beauty of the woods. The moon was only half full but it provided enough light for him to find his way easily across this unknown territory.

When he came to the place Lucia had told him about, where the post and wire fence changed to drystone wall between the front parts of their properties, he stopped to put on the night vision goggles and some fuzzy overshoes that would blur any footprints he might leave. He'd picked up a few useful tricks like that when working in dangerous areas overseas.

As he clambered over the wall onto his own land, he was careful to make as little noise as possible, especially when he got closer to the group of buildings, even though he didn't think any intruders would be there this early. He walked round the area checking, just to be sure, and saw no sign of anyone.

Some of the houses looked almost normal in the dim light, though one showed its sad, ruined status all too clearly. He was sure one of the better houses would be the focus of any damage intruders might cause, because there wouldn't be nearly as much benefit to be gained by vandalising the less attractive ones.

He decided to keep watch near the first house, guessing that if anyone did come to cause trouble they'd take the easy route and hit on the first building they reached so that they could get away quickly.

In the meantime, he set a few little surprises to greet any intruders, then sat on a low wall and sent out an email to a group of people he'd worked with on and off in various developing countries. They were closer than most friends, felt almost like family and they kept in touch, meeting up in person when they could. If any of them was available to help him during the next week or two, he was sure they'd come here, just as he'd go to their help if they asked for it.

Some of them had admitted that they'd reached the same stage in life as he had and were preparing to settle down permanently in the UK. He'd discussed it at length with a few of them the last time they'd had a get-together. James Dugall had said frankly that he'd done his bit for humanity and wasn't taking on another project overseas, however worthy the cause.

Only to these friends had Corin admitted that his coming project would be his last and then, even before that job was completed, his father's death had speeded up his permanent return to the UK by a few weeks. He wondered how far along the others were with their plans now and where exactly in the world they all were.

He asked if anyone was free to help him 'repel boarders', the codeword they'd chosen long ago for an urgent situation.

He didn't expect any replies that night, but to his surprise one arrived almost immediately from James, who said he was finding it altogether too peaceful living in the wilds of Northumberland near his farmer son and wouldn't mind having a bit of a romp.

James was considerably older than Corin, though by how much no one knew exactly. Corin reckoned his friend must be two or three decades older, for all he was fit and strong still. He'd once mentioned that he'd lost his much-loved wife a decade ago and as they got to know one another better, he'd shared photos of his grown-up children. Quite recently those present at a get-together in the UK had drunk the health of James's first grandchild and smiled at another photo.

Corin replied immediately, thanking James, giving him directions to Larch House and saying he'd not only be welcome to join in the fun, but there was a job managing a big building project that he might like to think about taking on later. He'd love to get James on board as site manager. The man was a miracle at organising anything and everything.

He ended with *Got to go into quiet mode now*, and shut down his phone. As he did that, he remembered that he hadn't phoned his brother, but he couldn't risk making any more noises now so he'd try to catch up with Pete the following day.

He donned his night goggles, then he put on surgical gloves and made sure his special camera was easily available, before walking to the area nearest to the gate. By now he knew every detail of this part of the terrain and earlier he'd found a couple of potential hiding places among the long grass and deep shadows. He finished off his preparations, which involved siting a trip cord across the ground at the gateway to the garden of the first house, then settled into hiding a short distance from it with an extension to the trip cord convenient for use.

Since half the fence was damaged, there was no need for anyone to use the gateway at all to get into the overgrown garden but in his experience, where there was a path people usually stuck to it whatever the condition of the nearby fences.

He blew a kiss at his potential trap. If someone turned up to cause mischief tonight, it'd be ideally placed to upset them. It was a bit risky keeping watch on his own but he'd take great care not to get trapped. James would probably turn up here the next day and if his friend got delayed, he'd hire some short-term security officers.

The fact that he'd spotted a watcher in a car parked on the nearby street earlier had suggested very strongly that something was being planned. Well, any of Begworth's playmates who showed up tonight were in for a shock or two. If the estate agent thought that by vandalising Corin's properties he could persuade him simply to give back the land he'd just bought, he was about to learn differently.

An hour later, the sound of a car engine alerted him to the arrival of a vehicle, which stopped further down the street. To his surprise it had come with its headlights blazing and the two men who got out strolled openly up the gentle slope, clambering clumsily over the padlocked gate. One of them tripped and cursed as he flailed around and almost fell.

Not fit or agile, then.

They seemed unaware that even low voices carried a long way on a still night and were chatting about what they were about to do. Definitely amateurs.

Some liquid was sloshing about in a container. They lowered their voices but when he heard the word 'petrol', Corin tensed, suddenly becoming far more concerned about what was intended. Were they really planning to set fire to one of his properties?

And what was the one who'd spoken carrying the petrol in? Something much smaller than the usual container, that was sure, and it had glinted in the moonlight. Surely that wasn't a glass bottle swinging to and fro in the fellow's hand?

It was!

What idiots carried petrol in something so easily broken and not designed for the job?

'Which house shall we set alight?' the second one asked.

As they began discussing how to do it, Corin edged backwards and dialled 999 from behind the house on a spare pre-paid phone. He reported an arson attempt in progress but refused to give his name, saying he didn't want to be targeted by anyone later. Then he put the phone away.

He went back to keeping an eye on them, surprised that they'd stopped to chat about what they were going to do with the money they'd earn even before they reached their target.

'Begworth thinks burning one house will be enough to show that fellow he means business about getting this property back,' one said. 'Pity. It's such easy money. I told him we'd be happy to come back and torch another one if tonight doesn't do the trick.'

'Well, this one is nearest to the road, so we'll be able to make a quick getaway before anyone spots the fire. Couldn't be better placed.'

'Really easy money.'

No, Corin thought, *not going to be as easy as you think, my lad. I'll make sure of that.*

As they approached the garden, he tugged the strong but thin cord he'd tied to one gatepost. It lay hidden among tall grass and weeds and he'd hooked it to the other side. He could pull the trailing end to bring it to just above ankle height just as they started to walk into the garden and he intended to fix it firmly in place at that height.

What had once been a crazy paved path was nice and uneven just there, which would also help throw them off balance. He moved back into the shadows, keeping hold of the trailing cord, waiting for the inevitable to happen.

He hadn't wanted to injure anyone, but when he heard them discussing how well the house might burn, he changed his mind abruptly. They were happily contemplating destroying someone's house. He hoped they did injure themselves, damn them!

As the leading man approached the gateway, swinging the bottle containing petrol carelessly to and fro by his side, Corin tossed a small stone to one side, then another one and let out a faint mewing sound.

They both stopped to stare. 'What was that?'

'Sounded like a cat. Ignore it.'

With their attention diverted, Corin pulled the cord tight, quickly slipping the loop at the end in place on a jagged part of a nearby post. The man carrying the petrol didn't notice the obstacle and fell headlong over it, yelling in shock. When he started to fall, he grabbed his friend and as a consequence he dragged the other man down with him.

Thank you, very helpful, Corin thought.

The bottle fell and smashed on the stones of the path with enough force to send petrol splashing upwards onto them. As they fell helplessly in a tangle of arms and legs, they soaked up more petrol from where the bottle had broken on the paving.

Job done.

Crouching, Corin moved back along the line of shadow near the hedge till he reached the larger patch of darkness near the house. *Try torching it now, you idiots!* he thought.

'What the hell happened?' one asked loudly.

'There's a cord stretched across the path, hidden in the long grass. Someone must have pulled it tight.'

'Well, thanks to you grabbing my arm, the damned petrol's gone all over me as well!'

'I'm absolutely covered in it and I've cut myself on the glass too.'

They both looked round for their assailant but by then Corin was well out of sight. He'd probably accomplished his main purpose and stopped them getting to the beautiful old house but he waited to be sure of that.

'I can't see anyone. He must have run off.'

'Never mind that. Will you move off my legs? I can't get up.'

They stood up, one yelping that he'd cut his hand on the glass again and it was bleeding. The other was trying in vain to shake the petrol off his clothes.

It didn't seem to occur to either of them to flee or even to keep more than a cursory watch for another attack. *Wonderful response to an emergency*, Corin thought. He moved on towards the drystone wall at the side of the property, but stopped again there to watch what was happening from a safe distance.

'This petrol stinks! I don't know what my wife will say.'

'Never mind your wife. The petrol's stinging like hell where it's on my skin. I didn't think there was that much in the bottle. If whoever did this throws a match at us, we'll go up in flames.'

'Oh, hell! You're right. I never thought of that! I'm not risking it. I'm taking my clothes off, in case he's still nearby.' He began to strip and groaned loudly. 'It's soaked through to my underpants, even.'

'Get them off, then.'

'I can't walk down the street naked!'

'Better that than going up in flames. Anyway, no one's out and about at this hour and our car's only just down the hill.'

Corin grinned. He'd been taking photos with his night-view camera as they stripped and by the time they were both stark naked, he was having difficulty holding back his laughter. They were not the most lovely specimens of manhood and one was distinctly chubby.

They undressed completely, leaving the clothes where they fell, and started hobbling along towards the road barefoot.

Then one let out a yip of pain. 'I've trodden on some more damned glass. I need my shoes.' They both returned to put them back on before continuing.

Corin couldn't believe that they had left the pile of petrol-soaked clothes behind them as they headed towards the big outer gate.

They moved slowly, moaning as taller plants scratched delicate parts of their bodies. Once there was a muffled shriek from the leader, who had stumbled sideways and scraped against a shrub.

He clutched his bare backside. 'Whoever the hell planted spiky bushes all over this garden wants shoving into them naked!'

The other one shushed him and they stopped for a moment to argue about the prospect of walking down the street without clothes and whether anyone would recognise their old gardening clothes. That led them to wonder how they could get the petrol off their skin before they got home, not to mention the difficulty of explaining their complete lack of clothes to their wives.

By that time Corin was aching with held-back laughter and rocking to and fro. He was praying that the photos would be as amusing as the live event because he was definitely going to put them online.

There were more yelps and moans as the men overcame their modesty and climbed over the gate, scraping certain usually well-protected parts of their bodies on the top. Then they hobbled off down Larch Tree Lane, arguing now about who was going to drive.

They hadn't reached their vehicle, however, when a police car suddenly revealed its presence by switching on its blue roof light, and using its headlights to illuminate the two men in all their glory.

They separated and tried to flee, but the police officers were younger and far more agile.

Their early amusement at the sight of two middle-aged, naked men limping down the hill changed abruptly at the smell of petrol on their captives' bodies, instead of the booze they'd expected.

'It wasn't a nuisance call, then. They're arsonists,' one of them said and shook the man he was holding. 'Shut up, you!'

They handcuffed the men and radioed in for a fire crew to investigate what had happened and make sure the area was now safe from going up in flames.

'Gotcha!' Corin whispered, then shook his head at his own comment. No, wrong! The two intruders had 'got' themselves by their careless behaviour. Who the hell were they? Refugees from a Mr Stupid contest?

Pity it wasn't Begworth himself, though.

He had decided not to reveal his own part in the farcical events but he might send one or two photos of the naked villains to the police via a rather special website he knew from which he couldn't be traced. He'd show them to Maggie as well, to see if she recognised the idiots.

He was pleased with how things had turned out, but suddenly felt exhausted. It had been a long and busy day.

He left for Larch House when the fire team turned up and he'd overheard enough to be sure his houses would be safe. By now police tapes were tied across the gateway and spotlights connected to batteries had been put in place and switched on.

He'd keep a very careful watch on his property from now on. And on Begworth. By hell he would!

The incident might have had its funny side but underneath it was deadly serious, and with a more skilled team of villains, it might have had dire consequences.

Setting an empty building on fire could still kill someone. What if there had been a rough sleeper in the abandoned house and the men had succeeded in setting it alight?

He hoped the law would deal very severely with those two.

He let himself back into Larch House by the cellar door, though he felt pretty sure no one would be watching this house. When there was a sound from the kitchen, he tensed and spun round quickly but relaxed almost immediately. There was still enough moonlight shining through the windows to see Lucia standing in the doorway, a poker in her hand and her hair streaming over her shoulders.

'It's only me,' he said quietly. 'Don't put the lights on. We don't want to show any sign of being awake.'

'Why? What's happened?'

He explained and chuckled again. 'I'll show you the photos in the morning. They're going to cause a sensation online. I'll probably front up at my houses tomorrow, bump into the police and be appropriately shocked about what has happened.

She flung herself into his arms. 'They might have *killed* you, though.'

He hugged her close. 'Not those two birdbrains. They were in more danger of killing themselves.'

'You're sure you didn't leave any signs of being there?'

'I was wearing special shoe covers. Trust me. I was really careful. And even if there are any signs of footprints from my other visits there, no one will think it strange. It's my property, after all. And it's staying mine!'

'Do you think this will stop Begworth trying anything else?'

'I don't know. Depends how desperate he is, I suppose. But I phoned my friend James and he's coming to help out. He'll be arriving later today so I shall have a very experienced man by my side then.'

'Good.' She yawned suddenly.

'You look exhausted.'

'Yes. But I didn't want to go to bed till I was sure you'd got back safely, Corin, and I've not calmed down yet.'

'Then since I'm feeling the same, let's cuddle down on the sofa in the library for a few minutes and have a quiet chat. I need to wind down before I'll be able to sleep, I must admit.'

'I'd like that. Cuddles run in my family.'

She fell asleep almost immediately, so they didn't get much chatting done, but he loved holding her in his arms. He was awake for a little longer, still geared up for action. He knew he didn't smell of petrol, but somehow he felt as if he could smell it in the air still.

He was looking forward to taking their relationship further. But before they got truly serious, he and Lucia not only had to sort out any further problems with Begworth but deal with her ex and make it plain to him that it was in his own best interest to stay away from her.

Who'd have thought that life in the tame old UK could be so eventful after what he'd experienced overseas? He'd thought he was coming back to a more peaceful existence. Ha! He was now estranged from his mother and had made an enemy in Essing Valley.

He yawned again and closed his eyes, just for a minute or two.

And woke to smell coffee. He blinked and saw Maggie standing nearby with a mug in each hand, smiling down at them in a fond, motherly way. That made him feel an extra layer of happiness. She was such a nice woman.

Chapter Sixteen

As they sat eating breakfast in the kitchen, Corin found a message on his phone from James sent yesterday evening saying he'd drive through the night and probably arrive mid-morning. Good.

While he had his phone out, he showed the two women the photos of the intruders from last night and they all chuckled at the unlovely sight.

'Did you recognise them, Maggie? Are they locals?'

'Yes. They're the Molson brothers, a pair of ne'er-do-wells from down Pedding End, which is as near a slum as we get in the valley.'

He whipped out his notebook and wrote that down. 'The police won't have had any difficulty identifying them last night, then?'

'No. They're already well acquainted with them for minor offences. Though the two of them have mostly settled down since they married and started families.'

He put his notebook away and turned to Lucia. 'Can you go into the village to buy some sort of camping stove and sleeping bags for James and me? I don't like to leave the place unguarded, even in the daytime, not till Begworth's been dealt with.'

'No need.' Maggie hastily swallowed her mouthful of toast. 'There's some old camping equipment piled in one corner of the attic. Why don't you check that out first? You could borrow it and save your money.'

'You're sure that would be all right?'

'Of course it would. It's just sitting there rotting quietly. I don't guarantee the condition it's in, mind. You'll need to give it a good airing.'

They went straight up to find out what was available and Corin paused in the attic doorway, marvelling at the huge, cluttered space lit by a couple of dormer windows and skylights.

Maggie gave him a gentle push so that she could get past and went across to one of the nearby corners. 'There's a little paraffin stove over here too. It might be old-fashioned but it still works. I even have some paraffin in one of the outhouses because I've had to use it during one or two serious winter power outages over the years, so I keep a small supply handy.'

She smiled as she added, 'And I store my flammable liquid in a proper container, unlike your friends of last night.'

'Thanks. This is going to be very useful.'

'There are all sorts of other oddments: crockery, cutlery and battered cooking equipment. Would those be of any use as well?'

He already felt comfortable enough with her to grab hold of her and plonk a kiss on her nearest cheek. 'You're an angel.'

She went a bit pink but seemed to like the attention.

After she'd helped him and Lucia sort out and put into a big box all kinds of household bits and pieces, she also found two stained and crumpled sleeping bags and some flattened old pillows stored in a rubbish-bin liner. 'You may as well take these with you as well.'

'Are you sure?'

'Yes, of course I am. I'm well past the age of camping out, believe me, and I'm old-fashioned enough to prefer matching crockery for my own use, only I don't like to throw away things that might come in useful one day. My generation don't go as much for disposable stuff as the current one. It doesn't matter if you break or lose anything, by the way, Corin. Don't even think of replacing such rubbishy stuff.'

'I can't thank you enough.' He surprised her by pressing another kiss on her cheek, which made her give him a shy smile. 'I'll fill my thermos as well, if that's all right with you, because the mains power won't be on for a long time down there, I'm guessing.'

He turned to Lucia. 'Till we get a generator set up, we'll have to depend on nearly instant food. Can you please go to the local minimart this morning and stock up with tins and packets that can be prepared easily, or heated on the Primus?'

'Of course.' She got out her notebook. 'Anything else?'

'A couple of plastic buckets and a washing-up bowl, also a pack of bottled water for drinking. And will you get a pack of beer and a couple of bottles of white wine as well. James is a beer drinker and I'm not.'

'Why don't you like beer? I thought your family owned a brewery.'

'I've never liked the taste or the smell.' He shuddered involuntarily.

'Goodness. Your parents must have liked that.'

'They made their displeasure all too plain.'

He stared blindly into space for a moment, looking a bit upset, so she patted his arm and he clasped her hand for a moment, smiling again. 'And anything else you think might come in useful.' He fumbled in his pocket and took out his wallet. 'Use this credit card.'

'All right. I'll see what I can find for you,' she said softly.

After breakfast, they both set off. He saw her slow down at the entrance to the Marrakin, staring at it, then drive past.

He turned into it himself but though the gates were now wide open, there was police tape everywhere so he had to park on the outer drive. It looked very showy but there were only two young constables on guard duty with their car parked nearby and they looked chilled through, poor things. When he introduced himself as the owner, they asked for proof, then talked more openly to him about the plans for today.

As it wasn't considered an urgent case, the investigation team hadn't come out yet. It was hoped they'd be there around lunchtime at the latest.

He felt so sorry for them that he sacrificed his thermos and gave them each a coffee. He had to maintain a solemn expression as they chatted but the memory of last night's shenanigans was still sharp in his mind and made him want to smile.

It was clear from the lack of the intruders' footprints

anywhere near the closest house that they hadn't got that far, let alone entered it, so the officers didn't try to prevent him from unloading his car and taking the stuff into the house, as long as he avoided the area where the intruders had clearly been.

The two of them even helped him to take the things inside and seemed to enjoy seeing what it was like. They did that one at a time in order to keep watch on the area still.

'It could be a lovely house,' one of them said wistfully. 'Good-sized rooms.'

'I hope it will be lovely again once I've modernised it.'

After the officers had both been round, he walked through the house again much more slowly on his own, studying the details. He was delighted to find that the water had been turned on, though when he tried the kitchen taps, rusty-looking liquid gushed out in uneven spurts. He hoped it'd settle down after he'd run it for a while to clear the pipes but he didn't fancy drinking it till it'd been tested for purity.

He turned on the stop taps and water began running jerkily into the antiquated bathroom fittings. He waited for the cistern to fill and tried flushing the toilet. Thank goodness it worked OK, even if it was discoloured and rusty where the original water had dried up in it long ago.

He and James could sleep in the house for a day or two but he was dying to get a generator fixed up and start working on it. He enjoyed doing jobs himself from time to time, to keep his hand in. He'd slept in far worse places overseas and so had James.

And then at last he remembered that he needed to phone his brother, so went downstairs, poured out the last of the coffee from the thermos and settled down on one of the broad window seats, hoping Pete would be available for a chat.

He was lucky. Pete was just taking a break. So Corin started by telling him about the purchase and the eventful evening. Eventually he felt duty-bound to ask about their mother.

'She's been very quiet. Goes out a lot with Lionel Pethick, but from what I've seen, he doesn't seem to make her all that happy.'

'I don't think anything ever makes her truly happy.'

Pete's tone became sharper. 'Tell me about it. She's always complained bitterly about her lot in life, heaven knows why. You avoided that by staying away, but I had to live with it. I can't understand why she felt like that, either. Father didn't treat her unkindly and there was always enough money to live comfortably, plus what she inherited from her side of the family. And she still has plenty left, whatever she tells you.'

There was a moment's silence, then Corin said, 'Well, never mind her. Tell me how the brewery is going?'

That led to a long description of the new drinks and Pete emailed copies of the labels from his personal account while they were chatting. He hadn't wasted time since he took over, had now settled on the details of the labels for use on the drinks, with a happy face in one corner to indicate it was alcohol-free.

Corin was mildly interested but after a while he

pretended the detectives wanted to speak to him about the would-be arsonists and ended the call.

When he went outside again, he found that two detectives really had arrived and did want to speak to him.

He knew what he suspected but asked them anyway, 'What made these men do it? I've only just bought the property so I'm not aware of its background. Perhaps Mr Begworth knows something. Have you got any information out of the men?'

'They refuse to say. But someone had used a trip wire to stop them so trouble must have been expected.'

'Goodness!'

Unfortunately, Corin couldn't report what he'd overheard the men saying about Begworth hiring them without giving away his presence here last night. He still thought it best to keep that secret from the police, more because of a feeling that the estate agent might not stop his efforts to get the land back and he wanted the fellow to be unsure about who exactly was protecting it. He intended to look into Begworth's background very carefully indeed.

The senior of the two detectives stared thoughtfully at Corin as if slightly suspicious, but he merely gazed calmly back.

'How did you get on with Begworth, Mr Drayton?'

'I only met him the once, so it wasn't a question of getting on with him. He was away on holiday at the time I saw this property and made an offer. It was another agent who sold it to me, Nina Perry. I was surprised to find that he was unhappy about me buying it and he offered to buy it back and give me a sweetener of £20,000.'

'That is strange. You'd think he'd be pleased. It would have been a substantial sale, I should think.'

Corin gained the detectives' goodwill by telling them exactly how much he'd paid and that the money came from years of careful investments while he'd been working abroad, not from any hidden partners.

'You should ask Nina about Begworth's reaction,' he added. 'He apparently flew into a rage and said it had been promised to someone else. But she told me she'd checked the office records and found no sign of any prior agreement after I made my offer. Nor did the guy at the ministry find anything about another offer in the paperwork at their end.'

The senior officer frowned. 'Have you had anything further to do with Begworth since?'

From his tone of voice, the estate agent wasn't one of their favourite people.

'No. I only met him that once, as I said. I didn't believe what Begworth claimed and I have no intention whatsoever of cancelling the sale. I'm very happy indeed with this piece of land. It's perfect for my purposes. I'm an architect and I'm going to build some very pretty houses here.'

'Ones that'll fit in with our local area, I hope?' the younger detective asked.

'Definitely. And I shan't shoehorn them onto the land, either. They build modern houses too close together for my liking.'

'That's good to know. I live in the valley and I know everyone would like more people living round here, but not the sort who live cheek-by-jowl in dormitory developments and do their shopping elsewhere.'

Corin nodded but when he didn't comment, the senior detective said, 'You've been very frank and helpful, and I thank you for that, sir. Is there anything else you think we ought to know?'

'Well, you may find it of interest that Begworth sacked both Ms Perry and the temporary receptionist, a Ms Lucia Grey, at the same time as he and I had our meeting and disagreement. That surprised me as they both seemed very pleasant and efficient.'

'Sacked them both?'

'Yes. I was there and saw it.'

'We shall definitely talk to him and to the two ladies concerned. Will you be staying near here, sir?'

'I'm staying at Larch House at present.'

They both smiled. 'Ms Hatherall is a well-liked member of our local community.'

'She's been very kind to me.'

'She's kind to everyone. We'll leave you to get on with your day, then, sir.'

When the detectives had walked off to talk to the young constables again, Corin heard a noise behind him and turned to see James standing nearby, looking thoughtful.

He went across to shake hands and clap his friend on the shoulder. 'You made good time getting here from Northumberland. Great to see you again. Sorry I didn't notice you arrive.'

His friend shrugged. 'Doesn't matter. I've been here for a while, listening. Interesting situation.'

'Let's move away before we discuss some other aspects.' He saw one of the detectives look round so raised his voice. 'I'll show you this house first, James. I thought we could camp in it for a few days – if you don't mind putting up with the lack of modern conveniences, that is.'

James grinned at him. 'We've both lived in much worse conditions than this. At least we'll have a roof over our heads.'

They waited till they were well out of earshot, then James asked, 'What's all this really about? When you were talking to those detectives, you had that cagey expression you get when you're not being entirely truthful. I've known you long enough to recognise it.'

'I didn't want them to know I was here last night, helping two idiots make fools of themselves instead of letting them burn down one of my houses. They were targeting this one, in fact, but they didn't get near it, thank goodness.'

'You were taking a bit of a risk, confronting two intruders on your own. Couldn't you have hired some help?'

'I hadn't realised what their intentions were when I came to keep watch. I didn't expect arson here in peaceful Wiltshire, just a few smashed windows and so on. Fortunately for me, they were incompetent fools.'

'We won't either of us take any more risks like that, my lad, not if I'm going to get involved. I have never wanted to be a dead hero. And by the way, congratulations on your award.'

Corin shrugged and tugged an imaginary forelock. 'I

won't take any more risks, your lordship. Anyway, I'm sure things will go well now you're here keeping your eagle eye on the situation.'

'I hope so. Tell me more about this Lucia. Your voice softens when you talk about her. Anyone would think you're rather taken with her.'

And heaven help him, Corin couldn't stop himself smiling and confiding, 'I am. Very taken.'

Then he felt the smile fade. 'Trouble is, she's being stalked by her ex. So I have to help her sort that out as well as dealing with my own problems before the two of us can move on to pleasanter pastures. She and I are a right old pair, aren't we? Can you face helping me deal with double complications?'

'I can if you'll keep the serious side of romancing until after we've sorted everything out. I don't want you to be too distracted.'

'Lucia and I have both more or less agreed about that and are tiptoeing carefully around commitment.'

James nodded approval. 'Glad to hear you're being sensible. Still, it's good that you've found someone you can care for. It's about time you put your genes back into the pool of humanity. I've done that nicely now. My Jen has another sprog cooking. And my son hasn't even started, though I hope he will have children before too long.'

'But it's great that you'll be a double grandfather from Jen now.'

'I think so. And actually, my son has just met someone promising. Nice lass, she is. It's only recent but I'm starting to hope.'

Corin felt suddenly jealous of James. He had Pete, but his brother was a long way from romance and marriage, with such an intense commitment needed to save the brewery. And the two of them had no other close relatives at all. Corin would love a real family of his own. James was right: it was more than time.

He could only pray that things would work out for him and Lucia. It wouldn't be his fault if they didn't.

Chapter Seventeen

Don Begworth didn't ask his wife to come in and help out the first day he was on his own, because he wanted to find out how the two men he'd paid to set light to the house had got on, men he'd played with when they were all lads. He definitely didn't want Linda poking her nose into that. She was too honest for her own good or they could have made a lot more money.

He waited for the news to come to him, not wanting to look too eager to find out. The trouble was, business had been a bit quiet lately and no one had come into the agency. If he didn't manage to find anything out, he'd drive up the hill after lunch to see for himself how bad it was. Serve that sod who'd bought it right if he lost a fixer-upper and the value of the whole property went down.

As the morning ticked past slowly and there was no sign of the two brothers, Don grew increasingly worried. He'd been expecting Drayton to come in and sell him the house.

He picked up the phone and put it down again. No,

what was he thinking of? He mustn't phone the Molsons directly, mustn't betray any connection with them.

For the second time he wondered whether he should drive up the hill and look for himself. No, better not do that either. How galling it was not to know what had happened.

Something must have gone wrong or they would have been here for their money before now. They were always short of money and had done little vandalising jobs for him before to lower the value of a property, but nothing as big and permanent as this job. What could possibly have gone wrong, though? How difficult could it be to set fire to a deserted property with no neighbours close enough to see you do it or to stop it going up in flames till it was too late to save anything?

Then his wife turned up uninvited late in the morning and from the expression on her face, she was full of news. He crossed his fingers behind his back.

'Have you heard?' Linda asked before she'd even got through the door.

'Heard what?' He tried to sound casual but hope rose again that the lads had succeeded as he waited impatiently for her to tell him about the fire. She did that sometimes, damn her, got you interested then kept you waiting till you had to almost beg for an explanation.

'Last night someone tried to burn down one of those cottages at the top end of Larch Tree Lane.'

'Nooo, surely not? They didn't succeed, I hope?'

'No. The police nabbed them before they'd even touched it.'

His heart sank. His secret partner would *not* be pleased.

'Guess who it was? Those Molson brothers you used to hang around with. I never liked them. Born losers, they are. The best of it is, some young guy was out for a walk to clear his head after attending a party and saw them so he stopped to take photos. You know what people are like these days with their smartphones. The two men were stark naked, apparently.'

'Naked?'

'Yes. I saw the photos online.' She giggled then pulled out her own phone. 'Look. They're hilarious. What idiots! Look at the belly on that one. Apparently, the young guy heard them yelling in panic because they'd broken the bottle and splashed the petrol all over themselves instead of using it on the house. That's why they took their clothes off, afraid of being set alight. The photos have gone viral all over the Internet already.'

He stared at her in horror, terrified that those two fools might implicate him. 'Wow. Can't believe it. Nice of you to let me know.'

'I'm not here for that. I just heard about it on the way here. I'm here because I've decided that if you've sacked Nina *and* a temp receptionist – and both on the same day, how stupid can you get? – you're going to need help in the office. You never were any good at paperwork. And I still remember how to sell a house though I shall want commission paying to me personally if I do sell one, not putting into our joint account.'

'No need to trouble you. I can easily hire another temp. You've got your own business to run these days, my dear. I don't want to take you away from that.'

'Things have been a bit slow lately. I don't have any bookings to run dinner or cocktail parties for the next couple of weeks and I won't take any until we have this place running smoothly again. It's about time I checked how my investment in it is going. We might not enjoy working together but we both like making money and I might be able to tweak your methods and smarten this place up a bit.' She waved one arm to include their surroundings.

'That's . . . um, really kind of you.'

The way she looked at him said she was somewhat suspicious about the sackings and he guessed that'd be part of the reason she'd come here. She intended to find out exactly what was going on. Linda was altogether too sharp for his liking and it annoyed the hell out of him how willing she was to pay the so-called correct amount of tax. He didn't let himself smile, but he and his friend didn't do that.

She grew even more suspicious when two police officers came into the agency soon afterwards and asked to speak to him privately.

'You can say whatever it is in front of me. I'm not only his wife but his business partner.'

They looked at him questioningly.

He didn't dare do anything except agree. 'It's all right for her to be present.' The two of them might no longer share a bed, and he was planning how to get out of the relationship with his money intact, but no one else knew that.

As usual, Linda took over. She gestured to the

customer seating and jerked her head at him. 'Perhaps you could lock the outer door, Don *dear*, and we'll all sit down. We may as well make ourselves comfortable. I'm sure these officers do more than enough standing around.'

She didn't say much as the policemen told him what had happened and asked questions about the recent sale of the Marrakin property, but the thoughtful looks she shot in his direction at one or two of his answers made him shiver.

He'd been really happy when she decided to leave the real estate business to his care because it didn't bring in a good enough income for them both. That had left him free to make extra money tax-free by co-operating with a very savvy guy he knew.

It was worrying him big time that she was poking her nose in again suddenly. What had made her decide to do that? Had she heard something?

If she had, she didn't say anything after the police had left except, 'I'll continue going through the books.'

Oh hell! He watched her take the recent hard copies of files and photos out of the drawer of his desk, the ones that hadn't been doctored, and bring up the recent accounts on the computer. All the time he was praying his secret partner had been right when he said she'd never realise what was going on as long as Don kept his share of the profits somewhere out of her reach.

She flapped her hand at him. 'Go and check that all the listings adverts in the window are up to date, and for heaven's sake tidy up the reception area. It's looking very run-down. You should be doing the dusting every single day unless you want to look as if you're about to go out of business.'

When she'd finished going through the paperwork, she didn't comment, just said, 'I'll hire new staff and make sure they know their job. Firing two people on the same day sounds more as if there's something wrong with you than with them. Make sure you don't alienate the new ones.'

'I've been away on holiday, remember? Your choice. The staff got slack without supervision.'

'The point of the holiday was that we were supposed to be getting together again, and all you did was prove you weren't interested – or capable of much, either.'

'You didn't show real interest either,' he shot back at her

'I never did like sleeping with a drunk. And you were on edge the whole time, then you insisted we come back early. I'm still wondering exactly why.'

'I don't like sitting around doing nothing.'

'You could have fooled me, looking at the state of this place. Well, we've agreed to continue to work together till we've built up a bigger nest egg before we get an amicable divorce, so you need to get more house listings for a start. Now, set out that reception area properly. The furniture's all jumbled up.'

He watched her go through the rest of the books, frowning at him from time to time, then leave. When she'd gone, he kicked the chair she'd been sitting in right across the room. Not time for a full break-up yet, but she was going to get a shock when it happened. A big shock when she found that he'd taken most of the money with him.

And serve the bitch right!

That night, Corin would have liked to take James out to the pub for a meal and also to invite the two women from Larch House to join them. Unfortunately, he didn't like to leave his property unguarded, so in the end he phoned Lucia and suggested she and Maggie come round for a meal and he'd get a take-away delivered from the Indian restaurant in the village. He'd glanced at the menu in the window and it had looked tempting.

She hesitated, then said, 'I'd have loved to come, and I'm sure Maggie would have too, but we have the same problem as you, Corin. At the moment I don't like to leave this house unoccupied after dark, let alone go out and about in the village.'

'You're still worried about Howard turning up? Even after him tracing your car to Leicester? Surely he'll be searching in that area now, not round here.'

'He boasts that he never leaves a detail or a possibility unchecked. It's my guess he'll come back when he doesn't find anything there, to check the last place he saw me. But if I don't go out in the daytime at weekends and stay out of sight at home as much as possible, there may be just a chance that he'll think he's checked everything. It's my only hope for a safe outcome.'

'No, it isn't. I'm here too. If he comes after you in earnest again, promise you'll turn to me for help.'

'Only if I have to. He really is a nasty person who holds grudges and will wait years to get his revenge on someone who's upset him. I don't want you becoming a target as well.'

'Not many people are that persistent.'

'He has nothing better to do with his time after work. He isn't into what he thinks of as meaningless socialising and he's scornful about time-wasting hobbies.'

'You must have had a terrible time with him.'

'Yes. He hid his real feelings till after we were married very cleverly, I must admit. Since then, well, I've never met anyone else in my whole life like him. He feels he's always in the right, always entitled to win, always superior to others. That need to sort out every detail before he'll stop pursuing something makes him an excellent salesperson.'

'It must have been very hard for you.'

He heard the muffled gulp at the other end and guessed she was close to tears. He wished he could take her in his arms and— It was at that moment he realised she was definitely the one he wanted to be with permanently and that he wasn't going to let anyone hurt her, whatever it took.

'We'll have to leave it for tonight, then, Lucia, but we'll work out some way of dealing with it all. If you think I'm going to stop seeing you, you're wrong – unless you tell me you never want to see me again.'

A few seconds' silence, then, 'I can't tell you a big fat lie like that.'

'Good. Don't even tell me a small thin lie, either.'

He heard her chuckle. He loved the soft gurgle of laughter that was so particularly hers. Hearing it warmed something inside him every single time.

'I shan't *want* to stop seeing you, but—' She broke off abruptly as if worried that she'd given her feelings away, as if she didn't quite dare trust in love again.

'I'm determined to keep seeing you, Lucia. And if you run away to save me, I'll be running after you too.'

'Oh, Corin—'

She'd been going to say something and had stopped herself. He didn't want to discuss their feelings over the phone, dammit, so he didn't pursue the matter for the time being. There were some things you couldn't really do on the phone. He wanted to feel her in his arms as he told her how much he loved her.

He had a sudden thought. 'What if I found someone we could trust to keep watch over Larch House or this place, and then either pair of us could go to the other house for the evening, even if we think it wiser not to go out in public? Just as a temporary measure, mind.'

'Let me ask Maggie what she thinks.'

Lucia explained the situation quickly and Maggie frowned, then said slowly, 'Young Eddie at the garage has just got engaged and is saving up to get married. Maybe he and Scarlett would like to spend the odd evening here keeping an eye on the house and getting paid for doing it.'

'Are they saving for a fancy wedding?'

'Heavens, no! Ted's grandson wouldn't be so stupid as to waste that much money on one day's grandstanding. They're saving up to put down a deposit on a house. Much more important than a fancy party. Trouble is, house prices keep rising, so it's hard for them to build up a big enough sum for the deposit. Let me speak to Corin.'

Maggie explained the situation and agreed to talk to Eddie about it the following day and see how much he would charge for keeping watch, then she handed the phone back to Lucia and went to watch TV in the library.

It was a full half hour before her young friend ended the call and rejoined her, a full hour since the call had begun but she didn't mention that.

As they were eating their meal, Lucia asked suddenly, 'Am I being too cautious about dealing with Howard, Maggie?'

'No, I think you're being very sensible. You read about such dreadful things happening with men who stalk their former partners. But I'd not mind if you joined Corin and James in the evening and left me here. You'd be safe going to and fro in a car, or letting Corin pick you up and bring you back, and I'm used to being here on my own. I'd keep the windows and doors locked. There would be no reason for your ex to come after me, would there?'

'As long as I'm staying here, I'll not leave you on your own until I know for sure that Howard has stopped stalking me. His temper can be very chancy and I'd be worried that he'd hit out at you in some way if he couldn't get hold of me.'

The older woman shook her head, sighing. 'This feels as if we've strayed into an old-fashioned B-grade whodunit movie. There has to be a way to stop your ex and I'd put money on you and Corin finding it.'

Lucia sighed. If there was a way, she hadn't worked it out. And for all her determination not to let Howard ruin her life, she still felt afraid of him and the fact that he was so much stronger than her physically didn't help.

She didn't want Corin getting hurt, either. He might be a tall, strong man, but Howard was the master of dirty tricks in all aspects of life.

Chapter Eighteen

Howard left the office building on Friday afternoon, pasted a smile on his face and went into a nearby bar to attend the regular 'drinkies' session with his work colleagues. He didn't ingest anything alcoholic because it didn't agree with him and he didn't even like the taste. Besides, he wanted to leave very early in the morning feeling fully alert.

He usually raised his glass of white wine to his lips a couple of times without drinking any, then held it for the rest of the evening. He frequently ditched the contents of his glass into a plant pot, especially if the manager was buying an extra round to celebrate some big sale and it'd look better to seem to be enjoying the man's generosity.

The event seemed to drag on for even longer this time, but he never allowed himself to be the first to leave.

He had everything ready so was in bed within five minutes of getting back to his flat.

Just over eight hours later, he set off and arrived in the scruffy little village he'd visited previously around the time of day that people were doing their weekend shopping. There was a small farmers' market in the open space near the church with all sorts of pitiful offerings. Who knew where the misshapen fruit and vegetables had been and how hygienic the stallholders who'd picked them were? He preferred to buy his food from big supermarkets, which were at least checked every now and then for their mandatory level of hygiene. He and his ex had never agreed about that.

He found a shabby café where he could sit near the window, half-concealed by a large plant, and watch people with nothing better to do stroll past and stop to waste their time gossiping. He bought a mug of coffee and made it last, ignoring the dirty looks from the waitress.

Though he stayed for nearly an hour and kept a careful eye on the stalls outside, he saw no sign of Lucia or that old hag whose house she'd been staying in last time he was here. Hmm. Better check the house next, just in case she was still hanging around.

He went back to his car and drove slowly up Larch Tree Lane. What sort of place had only one main road that led to a dead end where hikers dressed like shabby scarecrows hung out? A nowhere place, that's what. People even moved about more slowly here, presumably because their brains were firing so sluggishly, for lack of stimulation.

He stopped in the car park at the top of the road, slowing down to study the state of the two entrances to Larch House as he passed them. It had been very convenient to use these last time he'd needed to get in and out of its grounds. Talk about inviting intruders, leaving gates open all the time like that!

The second drive, which came out higher up than the first, was still not being used by many vehicles, judging by the long grass covering it. The lower drive looked as if it was used, though not often. Even that, when studied in broad daylight, betrayed how run-down and in need of maintenance work everything was.

If he'd inherited a large house with grounds as big as this, he'd have kept them immaculate and sold them during an upmarket period. Well, one day he'd have the money to buy a bigger than average house, by hell he would, but not one in an out-of-the-way dump like this. He deserved a beautiful home because he worked hard and was intelligent.

When he was settled again, he'd find a more suitable wife, one with good old-fashioned values about her role in the relationship. Tried and tested, those gender-based roles were. It was what nature itself had intended.

He scowled as he thought of the person who owned Larch House. What had that old woman ever done to deserve it? His guess was nothing apart from being the child of a previous owner. She hadn't married and provided the next heir, the stupid bitch – or maybe no one had been able to face marrying her.

As for his ex-wife, she didn't even know the true value of her family jewels, she was so stupid financially. The mediator had been wrong: as her ex-husband, he *deserved* half their value for putting up with her.

He sniggered as he remembered how Lucia had never guessed that he'd been bleeding small amounts of money from their household account the whole time they were together. It had given him a good deal of pleasure to do that.

When he got out of the car, he put on a worn old anorak

he'd brought specially today. He only normally used it for doing gardening jobs in winter. He also pulled a beanie down to his eyebrows so that he'd not stand out among the hikers. When he started walking, he nodded to anyone he passed, simply because they all nodded to him first, but he didn't stop to chat, only continued to amble slowly up the trail.

Not until there were no people nearby to see him did he leave the main track, veering off into the woods and making his way quickly down the slight slope till he came to the wire-and-pole fence that separated the grounds of Larch House from public land.

He found a place where the fence had been knocked down and passed through the gap before continuing down the hill. He stopped when he came within sight of the big house, pleased to find a faint track that seemed to lead right round it. He could have walked in either direction but chose to turn right. When he came to a conveniently placed fallen log, he sat on the end of it, mostly hidden behind a tree, and kept watch on the rear of the house, which had seemed to be used as the main entrance last time he'd been here because it was where they'd parked all the cars.

His luck was in today because only an hour afterwards a small car drew up and Lucia got out.

Well, well! He'd guessed correctly. She was still here and seemed to have a new vehicle. He'd checked regularly online – so easy for a man of his skills to hack in – but had seen no signs of that purchase. Had she not registered the vehicle properly? He noted down the car's reggo, wondering how long she was intending to stay in this godforsaken hole.

Another car drew up and parked next to hers. A guy got out, smiling at her, and they started moving towards one another. When he held out his arms, she ran into them and they kissed. And it was no casual embrace, either.

Howard stiffened and couldn't hold back an angry growl. What the hell was going on here? The house was owned by an old woman. Was this guy a relative of hers or just someone having it off with his ex?

He got his phone out and took a couple of shots, frowning at them. The guy looked familiar. Why? He hadn't seen him in the flesh before, he was sure. Maybe on TV or in the newspapers. But why?

It'd come back to him. It always did eventually.

Lucia looked the same as last time he'd seen her, not making the most of herself. Which was a good thing at the moment because any guy would quickly tire of her sloppy appearance and ways. This one still looked quite enthusiastic, though.

Well, he'd better not stay enthusiastic. Howard hadn't finished with his ex yet, not till he got his share of that money, so if necessary he'd intervene and do something to make them quarrel. He wasn't having her shacking up permanently with any other guy till he got what he wanted from her financially, then she could do what she wanted.

He took a photo of the guy's car as well, just in case, then made his way back up the hill. He'd come back during the night and ferret around, see if both cars were still there.

He might even be able to get into the house if he waited till they were all asleep. He was rather good at picking locks, had learned to do that as a teenager so that he could find out what his parents were keeping in a locked filing cabinet. What a disappointment that had been, though, like most things about them.

In fact, they were a couple of no-hopers and he was glad they'd emigrated. He'd kept in touch vaguely for a while, but hadn't bothered to contact them for years because he was quite sure they'd leave everything to his father's nephew whom they'd gone out to join. Not that they had much to leave.

After Corin had left, Lucia couldn't settle to watching TV so went to bed early. But she couldn't settle to sleep because the feeling of anxiety had returned and intensified. When she felt like this, she had to wonder if she could somehow sense Howard nearby, because bad things had quite often happened after any brief encounter with him.

No, that was ridiculous. Whatever was causing her insomnia, it couldn't be that sort of thing. She wasn't a believer in woo-woo, never had been. And she couldn't blame every mischance on Howard.

But there had been enough of them to make life uncomfortable and she still worried about what he might do.

If she were living with a man like Corin she'd feel safe, she was sure. He had such quiet strength. But he hadn't tried to seduce her so perhaps he wasn't ready for a permanent relationship and intimacy, or wasn't sure enough of her. It took a while to get to know someone properly.

The trouble was she wasn't sure she could commit to a man long-term either, not quite yet. Though her attitude to that had changed a lot since she'd met Corin.

And there was also the fact that she didn't want to leave

Maggie on her own. She really liked the older woman. It was as if Maggie was a previously undiscovered aunt, the sort of older relative she could enjoy. Perhaps you had to be without oldies in your life to appreciate their value.

Oh, what did she know? She'd made such a mess of things, falling for Howard's blandishments. What she couldn't understand was why she'd been so easily fooled by him and was worried she'd be fooled again by another man.

No, not Corin. She smiled even to think of him.

In the end she got up and prowled round the downstairs rooms, seeing her way quite well without switching on the lights because the moon was nearing full and she'd always had good night vision.

When she went back upstairs, she had to pass Maggie's room and she hesitated outside it, wondering whether to wake her friend up. No, she was being ridiculous, acting like a frightened child. She had to pull herself together.

She seemed to have been on an emotional rollercoaster ever since she broke up with Howard: now angry, now afraid, now defiant.

In her own bedroom, she hesitated, but couldn't settle, so went for another prowl round the house. There was something very soothing about moving from one quiet shadowy room to another and finding only peaceful silence.

Then the silence was suddenly broken by the sound of a car engine somewhere close by and she stiffened, listening carefully. It sounded to be coming from the nearby public car park. Who would be there at this time of the night? A pair of lovers? A birdwatcher?

Or her ex?

It was a while before she got to sleep and she managed only an uneasy, broken sleep, because she kept wondering who had been in that car.

It wasn't possible to shake the feeling that something unpleasant was brewing. She'd never felt it as strongly as she did tonight.

James was a night owl, rarely going to bed before midnight and needing six hours' sleep at most, while his friend Corin was a lark, greeting the dawn with a happy smile but not enjoying late nights. That should work out well with only the two of them to keep watch, they decided.

It was such a lovely night, with a three-quarters-full moon riding serenely across a nearly cloudless sky. James stood at the back door breathing in the cool fresh air, was tempted and went to tell his friend he was going out for a prowl round the woods.

'I know those two idiots are in custody and I'm sure they won't be coming back here any time soon, but while there's a lull, I'd like to get to know the feel of the grounds at night. Anyway, I enjoy walking through moonlit woods and missed that badly on some of my postings.'

'Do you want some night-vision goggles? There's a pair on the boot shelf near the back door.'

'That'll be great, especially tonight when I'm in new territory.'

'You might find it easiest to go straight up to the top of the hill – there's a path that starts near the ruined house – and start your explorations there. My grounds and Maggie's are really part of the same terrain geographically speaking and, in fact, there's only a half-ruined wire-and-post fence nominally separating our territories at the top end. A little lower down you'll see an old cart track which circles Larch House and touches the edge of my terrain as well. It's still faintly visible nowadays because of the centuries local carts used it.'

'Sounds a very pleasant walk.'

'It is. My land is much bigger than Maggie's nowadays, because part of hers was sequestered decades ago during World War Two by the Ministry of Defence and combined with this area. Most of the buildings were occupied by them, I think, and they created that building under the mound, but no one is quite sure what the government was doing here, even now. They were not only very secretive about it then but they still are. I'm going to try to find out what they were doing but I'm not feeling hopeful.'

'I thought the MOD gave the confiscated areas back after the war.'

'Not all of them were returned and they've kept a few even now. They did compensate Maggie's family financially in the end, she told me, though her grimace as she said that suggested they weren't exactly generous. Lucia and I suspect she's rather short of money these days.'

'You seem to have got to know your immediate neighbours fairly quickly.'

Corin nodded and smiled as if thinking of something or someone pleasant. He didn't volunteer any more comments, though.

James left him to sleep and strolled up the gentle slope, using a pair of the best night goggles he'd ever used. He'd have to buy some of these recently produced ones for himself. He went straight towards the top end as Corin had suggested, following the side fence on the far side from Larch House. A couple of hours' reconnoitring should teach him quite a lot.

He enjoyed the outing greatly. Such a beautiful country, England. He loved being back in a temperate climate. And this part of the country was softer than Northumberland, the vegetation more lush. He'd already realised that he preferred that.

Good thing he'd only rented a unit just outside Newcastle upon Tyne for the time being, because he still wasn't sure where to settle permanently, or even whether he would be able to settle down in one place. He'd been trying to make a permanent home near his son, but it wasn't working out as well as he'd hoped. They had very different ideas about farming and use of land, not to mention politics, movies, music. You name it! That hadn't changed since his son was a teenager.

Let's face it, he'd been glad when Corin asked for his help and gave him a valid excuse for leaving.

As he began to make his way down the other side of Corin's land, he heard something that made him stop dead in his tracks, frowning. That wasn't an animal. He had very acute hearing, even now, in his late sixties, and usually found it easy to recognise even the faintest sounds. This one had definitely been made by a human being.

He'd never have made that much noise. Was this someone not bothering about being heard or was the person simply not used to the countryside?

He moved to crouch behind a bush and waited, peering through the sparser top foliage. The person was moving away from him towards Larch House. He could see the outline of it and its outbuildings through the trees. What was this guy – well, the figure looked masculine – doing out at this hour of the night on someone else's property?

He soon realised that the person was keeping to the faint former cart track Corin had told him about.

When the man stopped in the middle of a clearing about fifty metres ahead and stood looking round, James stayed where he was, watching. The man was also wearing night-vision goggles. As the other man began moving again, James waited till he was far enough ahead not to notice any inadvertent sounds before following him. However good you were, you sometimes couldn't help making a slight noise, especially on previously unexplored territory.

Hmm. Why was someone moving around the outside of Larch House at this late hour? This couldn't be a casual stroll through the woods, because you'd have to cross a fence to get in here.

Lucia had mentioned that her ex was stalking her and Corin had asked James to keep an eye open for the fellow and if he saw even the slightest sign of someone prowling around to let them know.

Was this her ex? It seemed likely.

Tomorrow he'd ask Lucia if she had any photos and make sure he memorised her ex's appearance. Unfortunately, this guy was rather bundled up in clothes and had a beanie pulled right down, so his features and even his body build weren't easy to make out. That beanie must be deliberate camouflage because it wasn't a cold night.

James kept his distance, following the man round the rear of house and across to the far side where there was a public car park. He was able to get close enough to see and memorise the stranger's number plate, then watched him take off his outer clothes and toss them into the back of the vehicle. This time he got a good view of the face.

The stranger rubbed his forehead as if it was aching before settling into the driving seat and starting the engine. The sound made James wince. It seemed like an insult to Mother Nature, a rude intrusion into the peace of the night. He'd never have parked there. Sounds carried further on still nights like this.

The vehicle moved out of the car park and the sound of it gradually throbbed away into the distance. James smiled. He now had a fairly accurate view of the fellow's face and body. Quite tall with thinning hair on top and rather large ears. He had been scowling the whole time, as if it was his natural expression. There wouldn't be much difficulty recognising him again.

James continued his own perambulations. There was no sign of any other human beings out on the prowl, no lights showing in Larch House and not even a distant sound of other car engines from anywhere further down the main road. He'd have heard them on such a still night.

Only this one stranger, prowling round the house, definitely prowling, not merely out for a walk.

By the time he got back he was nicely tired, his mind full of moonlight and beauty.

There were no sounds from the room where Corin had laid his sleeping bag, so his friend was most likely fast asleep by now. No use waking him. James went straight to sleep as well. Time enough in the morning to mention the man he'd seen to Corin and Lucia.

It looked like being an interesting visit. What else was going on in this rather quiet corner of Wiltshire?

James joined Corin for a simple breakfast, vowing to buy something more substantial to eat the next day. Bacon didn't need much cooking and would last a day or two outside a fridge. He'd checked the old Primus stove Maggie had given Corin and found it in good working order, so they could eat fry-ups of all sorts, even a Chinese meal if they bought ready-cooked rice.

As Corin put some cheese and crispbreads out, he asked, 'How did it go last night? See anything interesting?'

'Yes. I saw a guy prowling round Larch House. Do you have a photo of Lucia's ex?'

'I don't but I should think she will have. I'll text her and suggest we meet ASAP to check that out.'

'Is there much of a rush to catch him?'

'There is if he's found her. He sounds to be the sort who might turn violent if thwarted for too long and she's actually heard him boast about physically hurting people who've upset him. Damn the fellow! Any sensible person would have gone his own way after his marriage broke up.'

James frowned. 'Stalkers aren't sensible people, are they? Or even sane? Sounds like she chose a really bad 'un. I must admit, I took a dislike to this one's scowling face even seen only by moonlight. You do sometimes, don't you? And for no immediately obvious reason.'

'I've known it happen. But I have an excellent reason to dislike this guy. He's really upset her, and that upsets me.'

After they'd finished eating, James asked, 'What about your problems? We need to check that estate agent guy out as well as Lucia's ex.' He smiled at Corin. 'Plenty to keep us busy. I'm so glad I came, not just to help you, but because I reckon life is going to be much more interesting round here than living in a village near Newcastle and helping my son with a flock of sheep and a few cows.'

'I could never see you as a farmer, I must admit. What's your daughter doing with herself?'

'She was managing a café in Bristol but she's stopped because of the second pregnancy and is reconsidering her future. She's into a very mumsy phase, I think. There's also a young cousin living near them who was a bright spark. I might fund her for something if she finds a worthwhile project. She's managing a small café at the moment. She doesn't have qualifications but she's always enjoyed cooking and from what I've tasted, she's really good at it.'

'Is she on her own or with someone?'

'She's with someone but unless I'm much mistaken, her feelings for him are on the wane. He's a nice guy but quiet. She says she's not looking for a quiet life yet and he is.'

'She's a bit like you, then. I was a bit surprised when I heard your retirement plans.'

'Well, I thought it'd be good to be near my family, but I've now proved there's not enough going on around my son to fill my days. And I'm not ready to sit around doing nothing. I'm not going back to volunteer overseas again, though. I really am enjoying being in the UK again.'

Corin's phone buzzed and he picked it up. 'Lucia says to go over for coffee as soon as we like. I think we'll be safe to leave this place in the daytime. This isn't the Wild West, after all. When we get back, I'm wondering whether to hire someone to uncover whatever's under that mound. It's got a concrete structure underneath and I have to wonder what the MOD had been doing there.'

'I should leave it till you've sorted the other problems out. You've enough on your plate and though all your friends are proud of what you did last year, even you can't kill all the scorpions at once.'

'I did what had to be done and I wish people would stop going on about it.'

'OK. But you well and truly deserved that award, you know.'

Corin heaved a sigh and changed the subject. 'Let's walk across to Larch House. It's almost as quick as taking the car.'

'Good idea. It'd be good to see some of your land by daylight. It's a decent-sized chunk of territory. I'm still fitting the details of it together in a mental map.'

'So am I. The countryside is lovely round here, isn't it?'

James smiled. 'And I bet your Lucia's lovely as well.'

Chapter Nineteen

As closing time approached, Linda gave her husband another of those basilisk stares.

'Coming home for tea, Don?'

'Probably not. I've arranged to meet someone for a drink.'

'Is she pretty?'

'I'm meeting a business acquaintance, a guy not a woman.'

She shrugged and started to clear her desk and get her things together. 'If I hear you've been seen with a woman in Essington, you're out of the house on your ear *tout de suite*. I'm not having my friends and neighbours pitying me.'

'I know, I know! We've been over that a few times and the lines are drawn. I get the message.'

He sighed in relief after she'd left and he no longer had to be careful what he said. The first thing to do was phone his friend and turn a lie into a truth.

'Linda's left for the day. Fancy going out for a meal?'

'Why not? We'll try that country pub again. They

know how to cook a nice, rare steak and it's not likely many people from Essington will be there. I'm a bit fed up of my wife, too. I wonder why we bother to marry them at all.'

'I've been wondering that for a few years, Gustav. Only it's expensive getting rid of them once you've tied the knot and they do have a few uses.'

When he'd put the phone down, Don looked round and scowled. Linda was right. It did look a bit dingy. Maybe he could nudge her into revamping the decor. That should keep her busy for a while and hopefully give her less time to poke her nose too deeply in his affairs and cause mischief.

It took quarter of an hour to get to the pub when there was a perfectly good pub in Essington. He was fed up to the teeth of all this cloak-and-dagger stuff, but there you were. Linda was such an annoyingly savvy woman. You had to take care if you wanted to swindle a wife like her out of her share of the business.

He let out a snort of laughter at the mere thought of that. Not long to go now. Then the smile faded, because two or three years seemed like a long time to wait. But he'd need enough to live off in comfort for the rest of his life, so he couldn't do anything till he and Gustav had amassed more money.

His friend was crunching the numbers, had assured him that their plans were foolproof and that he was stacking their extra money in an overseas bank account. Don had made sure it required input from both of them to draw money out. That should be all right, surely?

Only, was any plan ever foolproof? Who knew? But

his friend had done all he'd promised so far, which was as good as it got. In fact, he was a pleasant fellow in every way, unlike Don's snarling misery of a wife. He should never have agreed to that holiday. Look at the setback it'd caused.

He walked into the pub and nodded to the man behind the bar, then ambled across to what had become their usual table in the far corner, smiling at his friend and sitting down. 'Good evening.'

Soon afterwards, a couple of women came in and Don looked them over automatically. Too old and not dressy enough for his taste. He turned back to Gustav, pointing his thumb down in a dismissive gesture.

That brought a faint smile to his companion's face, but as usual, Gustav didn't miss a thing and as soon as Don's drink order had been taken, he said, 'You look a bit down in the dumps. Wife getting you down?'

'No more than usual. I just can't wait to get out of that bloody valley and start a more enjoyable life.'

'The end is in sight now.'

The women went to sit by the rear window, closer than Don would have liked but why would complete strangers be trying to eavesdrop on him and his friend? There wouldn't be much that they'd understand even if they did hear anything. He'd never seen them before in his life and probably never would again.

He forgot about them and settled down to discuss what to do about the fiasco with the land sale.

Gustav lost his smile. 'I told you to wait and sort it out properly. Instead you hired two idiots who made a total mess of it, and that will have put the purchaser on his guard. I told you: I have connections who can handle this for you. If they put the frighteners on this Drayton fellow, he'll be selling it back to you in a month.'

'That'll be good.'

'Cost you, though.'

'Doesn't it always when you arrange anything?'

'If you want a job doing properly . . .'

'Yeah, yeah!'

The waitress came up with their drinks so they waited till she'd taken their food order then began to discuss a timeline for making their final financial strike and getting out of the business and the country. It cheered Don up considerably even to think of that.

He was about to order another drink when Gustav put one hand over the menu. 'You've had enough booze. It'd really muck things up for you to get breathalysed and lose your licence. You can't sell houses or land without driving around.'

It took Don a minute or two to get his desire for a drink under control. 'Yeah, I suppose you're right. I'll have a nice little nightcap when I get home.' Or even a nice big nightcap.

'Have you thought any more about what I said about getting hold of that Larch House to sell? It'd bring in a nice big sum and it's right next to the Marrakin, so they'll fit nicely together and it'll probably increase the current value of the property by thirty per cent if we play it carefully with a big developer.'

Don stared at him. 'I wish. I tried to tempt her to sell a few years ago, and then again last year, but she's a stubborn bitch and refuses point blank to do it.'

'If we can't change her mind, perhaps my friends and I can remove the obstacle permanently for you?'

Don stared in shock, then shook his head vigorously. 'No way. I'm not getting involved in that sort of thing.'

'Oh well, if she's old, she might help us by dropping off her perch anyway.'

The two women finished their drinks and nibbles, then got up to leave. Don watched them morosely. Pity they hadn't been younger and prettier. He was in the mood for a bit on the side.

As he drove home, depression settled in again. It was all taking so damned long. He wanted out of this boring life ASAP, was itching to sail off into the sunset and start enjoying life to the full. Gustav had already begun looking for a new home for him, had shown him a couple of photos of the sort of property they could find, living close to one another. That had made him even more eager to sell up and decamp.

To his relief, Linda wasn't around when he got back though he heard the sound of a TV coming from her bedroom.

He got out the whisky and poured himself a good big shot. It didn't last long, so he poured another. Good stuff, that.

Early in the morning, Linda heard the ping of her phone and debated whether to bother answering it. She was feeling unhappy about her personal situation, sick to death of Don, and she didn't want any more of his clumsy mess-ups to deal with. She checked to see who'd called and changed her mind about answering when an old friend's name showed.

'Kathy here. Long time no see.'

'Too long. What are you doing back in this neck of the woods?'

'Visiting a friend. Look, never mind the small talk. This friend and I went out for a drink last night and your husband happened to be sitting nearby with another guy, a shifty-looking chap if ever I saw one. I don't think your Don realises how good the acoustics are in that pub. To cut a long story short, my friend is a private investigator and she'd been testing out a new gadget to help with eavesdropping on targeted people so when I heard part of what they were talking about, I asked her to switch it on fully. After that, we caught everything your husband was saying.'

'Oh, drat. I wish I'd been there to hear it.'

'I asked her to record it.'

'Really?'

'Yes. Why don't you come over for breakfast, or if you've already eaten, my friend makes great coffee. You can have a listen but I warn you, you'll be shocked at what your Don is planning.'

Linda could feel her spirits rising in spite of the fact that in one sense Kathy was a bringer of bad news. She'd known for a year or two that Don was up to something, and had made sure he couldn't touch the finances of her own business or sell this jointly owned house without her permission. If she could find out the details of what he was planning for their estate agency and a couple of rental properties they owned, maybe she could better protect her own interest in them as well.

She couldn't wait to get him completely out of her life. He'd changed over the past few years and there was something distinctly nasty about him these days.

It was only a ten-minute drive to the home of Kathy's friend, thank goodness. Linda walked eagerly up the path to the front door and raised her hand to use the old-fashioned knocker, but the door opened before she could touch it. Kathy gave her a quick hug, then held her at arm's length and ran a searching look over her as only Kathy could.

'Am I right in guessing that your marriage is over, Linda? I don't want to break up a relationship that still has a chance.'

'It's been over for several years, in any real sense. And what do you mean by "break up"?'

'Come and meet Hillary then we'll tell you.'

Her friend was waiting for them in what looked like a normal living room, except for the array of sound equipment instead of books in the tall bookcase to one side. Its glass-fronted doors were wide open and lights were winking inside it here and there.

Linda suddenly felt impatient. 'Never mind the coffee. Let me listen to what you recorded.'

'All right. Afterwards we'll discuss what to do about it. Do sit down.'

She took the seat on the sofa that Hillary indicated and was glad when Kathy came to sit next to her.

What she heard took away any doubts Linda had had about the need for watching Don carefully. She had trouble pulling herself together afterwards. When Kathy took her hand and gave it a squeeze, that helped, but only a bit.

'This is far worse than I'd expected. I never thought he'd get involved in . . .'

Her friend finished for her, 'In major fraud.'

'Yes. He mustn't get away with stealing from me but I don't quite know what to do.'

Hillary took over. 'I was in the police force till I took early retirement, dealing with financial fraud towards the end. I still have contacts in that area. I don't think we should do anything except pass this information on to the authorities. It's on too big a scale.'

She felt numb, unable to focus, was still in shock. 'I'll go with whatever you say.'

Kathy patted her hand. 'I'm sure official involvement will give you the best chance of getting out of it with your money intact.'

'I hope so. I've worked hard for it, harder than him, that's for sure.'

'I'll phone a friend of mine and have a quiet word. He specialises in money crimes and will probably know this Gustav guy.' She smiled gently. 'I just happened to take a quick photo of the two men on my way back from the ladies'. Look.' She held it out.

Linda stared at it. She didn't recognise the other man, but she did recognise that look of utter greed on her husband's face. 'Should I say something to Maggie, who owns the other piece of land? I don't know her very well, but she's liked and respected in the valley. I don't care to think of her being swindled.'

'Leave that to Hillary's friend,' Kathy advised.

'He'll do it quickly?'

'I'm sure he'll handle it with due care and diligence.'

As she was driving home, the nastiness of it all hit Linda again and she pulled over into a lay-by and burst into tears. The man she'd once loved enough to marry was not only trying to steal her retirement money but was dealing with people who were prepared to commit murder. It made her feel literally sick.

She wept helplessly for a few moments but gradually forced herself to stop. It would do no good. The best she could hope for was to keep her money – and see that filthy rat in jail.

After the tears had stopped and she'd wiped her eyes, she took several deep breaths and put her guard up again. Don wasn't worth the tears and she'd been fooling herself that they could do something about their marriage when she'd insisted on them taking a holiday together.

It was her youthful self she was weeping for now as much as anything, the young woman who'd been filled with so much hope for her life and marriage.

And she hadn't even come out of it with children. It wasn't till she'd suggested getting medical help at conceiving a baby that he'd admitted he'd secretly had a vasectomy. That had shaken their marriage to the core but she'd agreed to stay together until the business took off.

Only it had never taken off as he'd promised and she was now in her mid-forties, too late for her to do anything about having a family, even if she met another guy straight away.

Chapter Twenty

When Corin asked Lucia to come and have coffee with them, he spoke casually, but at the end of the call he added quietly, 'It's rather important.' She guessed then that he had found something out and probably about Howard.

But what?

'Why don't you take them a small gift.' Maggie cut off half of the cake she'd baked yesterday. 'I'm sure they'll welcome this, whatever the news. Oh, wait! I'll find a container for it. They won't have anything suitable down there.'

Lucia drove to the Marrakin, going a bit too fast but who was likely to see her in this lonely spot?

She found the main gate open so drove straight inside and parked outside the first house next to the cars belonging to the two men.

Corin came to the door, looking rather solemn. 'Thanks for coming so quickly.'

She held out the cake. 'I'm the bearer of a gift from Maggie.'

He peeped into the tin, sniffed and gave her a little nod

of approval. 'Smells yummy. Tell her thanks. We'll enjoy some later.'

When they told her about the man James had seen in the woods last night, she got out her phone and showed them a photo of Howard.

James nodded. 'That's definitely the man who was prowling round Larch House. Can you email me a copy of it?' He paused to let that sink in, then asked, 'What do you want us to do about it?'

Such a surge of anger roiled through her that she had to take several deep breaths before she could answer. 'I'd rather do something myself, much rather.'

The men exchanged worried glances.

'Such as?' Corin asked.

'Give me a minute. I need to think. A cup of tea wouldn't hurt.'

By the time the kettle had boiled on the little paraffin stove, an idea had come to her.

'What Howard cares about most is his job. He seems to be making good money from it, enough to run two cars still.'

They looked at her in surprise.

'Why two?' James asked.

'He has a cheap little runabout for everyday getting around and a rather luxurious old Bentley. It's one of the few things in the world that he seems to love. He says he only keeps it to impress customers and I'm sure they do enjoy riding in it, but really it's for his own pleasure. He bought it with our joint savings without asking me and we had a big row about that. The price was taken into account by the mediator, it was such a large sum. That money is another thing that upsets Howard. He blames me for taking from him.'

'Is there anything you can do that you think may stop him harassing you once and for all?'

'You don't easily stop Howard. But I can make a start by threatening to complain to his boss, who is a decent, happily married guy. I'll go and tell my ex I intend to do that if he doesn't stop and try to make him understand that I mean it. I doubt it'll stop him completely but *he* cares so much about his job, it may make him hold off and I'll try to think of some follow-up to ram my point home.'

The two men exchanged glances. 'I don't think you should confront him on your own,' Corin said. 'Will you let me come with you?'

'As long as you leave it to me to do the actual threatening. I need to learn to be more proactive.'

'All right. When do you want to go?'

'Tomorrow. If we leave really early, I can confront him as he's arriving at work.'

'All right.'

She smiled at him a little sadly. 'I hate confrontations and arguments so I've been a coward, letting him bully me. I won't chicken out this time, though.'

'I do understand. I've studied bullies. I've had to, because in some of the places I've worked they were ruling the roost till we started projects there. If bullies sense any hesitation or tendency to give in, they push more but if there's a fight back from the intended victim, even if it's clearly hopeless, they're much less likely to pursue their threats.'

She stared at him, then nodded slowly. 'You're right. So tomorrow morning it is, then, for my first volley?'

'Yes. But we'll go in my car if you don't mind.' He patted his own thigh. 'It's a lot more comfortable for someone with long legs than your smaller one. Now, let's spend some time today sorting out the accounts for my new business.'

'Yes, let's. I've plenty of experience of office systems but you'll have to tell me what you need for a building company.'

'A very small building company.'

'Start as you mean to go on with good office systems. Your staff will thank you one day.'

They set off as agreed and once they were on the way in the lighter early morning traffic, she said, 'I'm still determined to confront him but I'm dreading it. Am I an utter coward?'

'I think you're a gentle, civilised person, not the sort to get into fights of any sort if you can avoid it.'

'Have you been involved in many fights?'

'Unfortunately, I've had to be. I don't start fights for no reason, believe me, but if you're a guy who's taller than average you run into people from childhood onwards who deliberately pick fights to prove themselves against you. I studied self-defence tactics out of necessity. Later on, in some of the places where I've worked, I've been very thankful for the skills that gave me, for the sake of those we were trying to help.'

They didn't chat much after that. Lucia was bracing herself for the coming confrontation and Corin, though keeping an eye on her, was giving her the mental space to do that. From the dark circles under her eyes, she hadn't slept very well, but he approved of her determination to confront her ex because it meant she'd be making a start on confronting her own fear of him as well.

Once they got to Bristol, she showed him where to park and said quietly, 'We'll wait a little while before I go there. He arrives at work almost to the minute each day and we gave ourselves plenty of time to get here. Um, I'd rather face him on my own, if you don't mind.'

'Whatever suits you. I shall stay nearby where I can keep an eye on you, though.'

She nodded acceptance of that and shortly afterwards glanced at her watch. 'It's almost time.' She went to wait at the front of the building.

He followed but didn't think she even noticed him, she was so focused on this effort.

Sure enough, a couple of minutes later Howard walked briskly along the street from the staff car park, stopping in surprise at the sight of her.

'Have you a minute?' she asked.

He didn't speak, just shrugged and waited, looking her body up and down in that horrible, knowing way he was only too aware annoyed her greatly.

'Better get on with it, Lulu. I can only spare you five minutes.'

His response made her even angrier. 'It won't take five minutes. I'm here to tell you that if you don't stop harassing me, I shall make a formal complaint to your senior manager.'

He scowled at her. 'Don't you dare go near my employers! They have nothing to do with our relationship.'

'That's easy to ensure. Stop harassing me and I'll stay away completely.'

'I haven't been harassing you. I don't know what gives you that idea.'

'I've seen you in some CCTV images and have been able to download a few.'

'I don't believe you. You aren't good enough at tech stuff.' He took a step forward, standing too close now, looming over her, making her feel ill at ease.

Someone moved to join them and she guessed it was Corin before she even glanced sideways.

His voice was calm. 'You're wasting your time, darling. I don't think this person is capable of listening to you or has the decency to stop the harassment.'

Howard stared at Corin, seeming surprised by his presence.

'I'll just leave you with one promise from me, Saunders: I'm going to give you a surprise later today. I hope it'll emphasise that you should stay away from us both from now on if you value your own comforts.'

As Corin put his arm round her, Lucia watched Howard do that little bouncy movement of his head and shoulders that only happened when he was seething with fury about something.

'Who the hell are you to threaten me?'

'I'm not threatening you. Why would I need to do that? I'm merely promising to give you a little surprise.' He turned away from Howard. 'Come along now, darling. We don't want to be late for our meeting.'

She let Corin tug her away because the sight of Howard's twisted, furious expression made her feel literally sick. She didn't speak till they got back to the car, then she said, 'Thank you. I was glad you joined me because he seems to be less in control of his anger. He made me shiver, he looked so malevolent.'

'He's a sicko.' Corin tapped the side of his forehead in an age-old gesture. 'You can tell from his body language as well as from what he says. I'm not influenced by what you've told me about him; it stands out a mile that he's a wrong 'un. Now, tell me where he keeps that fancy car of his. I'm presuming it's somewhere safer than outside his house.'

It was the last thing she'd expected to hear. 'Why?'

When he told her, she stared at him, then chuckled. 'I can't imagine anything that will upset him more. Especially if no one has a clue about how it happened.'

Howard watched them walk away, feeling furious at the sight of that arm protectively round her shoulders. He was tall but this man was taller. And he looked familiar. Where had he seen that face before? In the newspapers? On TV? He snapped his fingers, trying to bring the information to mind, because he knew he wasn't mistaken. But he couldn't bring the name to mind.

It would come to him. Oh, yes. The information would fall in place sooner or later. It always did.

All day he had trouble focusing on his work, because the stranger's face kept appearing in his mind, not to mention the sight of him hugging Lucia. Who the hell was he?

As for her, she was disgusting, was clearly putting herself out to anyone willing to help her. Well, it wouldn't get her off the hook. She wasn't keeping all that money, whatever it took for him to winkle his share out of her.

By the end of the day, his work colleagues were

avoiding him openly. He knew he had been much sharper with them than was polite and was glad the manager was out all afternoon because somehow he couldn't hold back his anger as well as usual.

That was definitely her fault and he'd make her pay for it as well before he was done.

When he went out to his car at the end of the day, Howard sat scowling round and thumped his clenched fist down on his steering wheel a few times before he set off. He still hadn't remembered who that fellow was, dammit!

He hesitated then decided to go for a ride in his Bentley instead of going home. It was one of his special treats, a reward for a particularly good sale, or a way of raising his spirits when others had been utterly stupid about something.

He drove straight to the special garage which he paid to look after his Bentley. They kept a whole raft of expensive cars there for people, such beautiful old vehicles he sometimes just sat in his own and stared round at them. He parked his everyday car in the street outside and strolled into the foyer, feeling more relaxed just to be here.

The guard on duty at the entrance frowned at him. 'Back again, Mr Saunders? We don't often see you twice in one day.'

'Back again? I haven't been here for a few days.'

'Jim said you were here earlier when he was on duty. You don't often come here in the mornings, so he noticed it particularly.'

'He was mistaken.'

Howard didn't stop to argue but continued on his way up to the top floor, eager to see his car, if only to sit in it.

He loved to smell the real leather upholstery and liked to run his fingers over the immaculate paintwork.

Only his car wasn't in its usual place.

He stared round in surprise, wondering if they'd been shuffling the cars about. They'd done that once or twice when he first brought his here, until he'd made it plain that he didn't want it leaving anywhere else but here in the corner, out of the direct sunlight.

He hurried up and down the double row of expensive vehicles but there was no sign of his. *Where was it?* A loud growl of anger escaped him and he ran to open the door to the emergency staircase, pounding down it to the ground floor, too impatient to wait for the lift.

'Where is it? What have you done with my car?' he yelled, thumping his hand down on the guard's desk.

'We haven't done anything with your car, sir.'

'Someone has. It's not there.'

The man stared at him, then studied the record book. 'It says here that you took it out this morning and there is no note about it being brought back, so it's still out.'

If someone had told him he had suddenly been transported to the moon, Howard could not have been more astonished. This time he couldn't help believing what he was told because this guy was so calmly certain. 'I haven't been here at all today until now. Someone must have stolen it. Did you have someone temporary on duty?'

'No. The duty guard today was a regular. He recognised you and logged your arrival in the book. You must have been here.'

'I – *was* – *not* – *here!*' He thumped the desk, then

thumped it again. What he wanted to do was punch this idiot in the face.

'I'd better call the manager.'

The manager arrived within a few minutes and he too studied the record book, looking baffled.

'We'd better go through the CCTV footage,' he said abruptly.

And they found an image that could indeed have been Howard, except that he didn't own an overcoat like that or ever wear a cap. The person kept away from the camera and hurried through with a quick wave to the guard.

He managed not to shout but his voice came out louder than usual. 'That was *not* me.'

'It looks like you.'

So they went through some CCTV footage from another camera, which showed a man getting quickly into the lift, and a third camera on the upper floor showed him driving out and down the exit ramp in the Bentley not long afterwards.

Howard was shocked rigid. What was going on? The man he'd seen on the screen could have been mistaken for him if only glanced at, he supposed. 'I want the police calling in. My car's been stolen and it's a valuable vehicle.'

Luckily there was a police station nearby but it took nearly an hour for two officers to arrive. They also went through the CCTV footage, shook their heads and said it looked like him. Then they studied him again suspiciously as if they thought he was pulling some trick.

In the end he didn't get home till ten o'clock at night because he had to go down to the police station and raise merry hell to get them to check everything they could.

Eventually they said their shift was ending and he should go home and sleep on it. The case didn't have priority as no one had been harmed. Maybe he'd think of some new avenue of inquiry by the morning.

That was a put-off if he'd ever heard one but he bit back an angry response because by then he was utterly exhausted, not to mention ravenously hungry, so he went back to his unit. He was about to drive into his designated parking place at the rear of his unit when he realised his Bentley was there. He had to slam on his brakes to avoid running into it.

He sat in the car, gaping, finding it hard to believe what he was seeing. It was difficult even to breathe for a moment or two. Then he parked his runabout nearby and got out.

His first thought was to check whether the person who'd broken into the car had damaged it. He switched on the outdoor lights and went all round it, letting out a shuddering sigh of relief when he saw no sign of anything wrong with the lock or, indeed, with any part of the car that he could see. How on earth had the thief broken into it and got it to drive?

He leaned against the front wall of the unit for a moment or two, rubbing his aching forehead, then took out his key to unlock the car.

No, he'd better not touch it yet. Who the hell had done this? And why?

As he went inside to call the police from the privacy of his home, he suddenly remembered the parting words of the guy with Lucia, who had promised him a surprise. Was it possible they'd done this?

It was more than possible; it was the only explanation that made any sense. But how could they have done it all without a key to his car?

He felt sick with fury but felt obliged to phone the police and explain that someone had played a practical joke on him and his Bentley was here.

The police told him not to touch the car and especially not to get into it.

He had to wait nearly an hour before another bored-looking pair of officers turned up and examined the Bentley in a cursory manner.

'Do you have a key, sir?'

He held it out. 'I'm sorry you've been inconvenienced and I thank you for your help. But if you could just check everything out before you go, I'd be grateful.'

They checked various things, then shrugged. 'It's been thoroughly cleaned and there's no sign of fingerprints or other marks. Thankfully there doesn't appear to be any damage. Do you want to pursue this matter further or are you going to ignore the, um, practical joke?'

'I think I know who did it so I'll deal with him myself.' By hell he would!

After they'd gone, he went inside, picked up a vase and hurled it into the sink, then realised he'd picked up a valuable piece instead of the cheap one standing next to it and let out an angry moan before smashing up the cheap one as well.

In the middle of the night, he woke and couldn't get back to sleep again.

Lucia and her lover weren't going to get away with this. He'd find a way to pay them both back. But he had to do it without incriminating himself, so he'd better not rush into it.

Damn! He had a busy week ahead of him at work. He'd not be able to do anything till next weekend. But that would give him time to plan carefully.

And who the hell was that man with Lucia? He still hadn't been able to remember.

Chapter Twenty-One

James phoned Corin to ask him to be sure to get back by dusk, so sadly he and Lucia couldn't stay to watch the effect on Howard of finding the Bentley parked outside his unit.

They found the gates of the Marrakin open and James came to the door to greet them. 'Glad you could get back on time. We're expecting visitors, only they'll be coming across both sides of the neighbouring land on foot and keeping out of sight.'

'Who are they?'

James gave them a smug look. 'Members of a major fraud squad. I happen to know someone there.'

'You certainly know some useful people.'

'So do you, Corin. You know one of these at least. Rani Mahato is in charge there now, and she was delighted with the information we shared. It apparently connected with something they were already investigating and was a big help.'

'Good to hear. And we couldn't have a better person working on this. She's a bit senior now to be making personal calls, though, isn't she?'

James shrugged. 'Who knows? Depends how important this project of hers is to the authorities. She and a guy called Liam should be here shortly to discuss the situation and what to do next. Have you eaten?'

'Yes, we grabbed some takeaway when we stopped for petrol. Not healthy but fills the gap.' He patted his stomach.

'Good. I said we'd leave the back door unlocked so that they didn't have to wait in view of anyone for us to open it. Oh, and I rang Maggie earlier and warned her that you'd be late, Lucia. Did you know she's into opera? We had a great chat.'

'She has quite a collection of records, rare vinyls as well as CDs.'

'So she said. I'm going across to listen to some of them once we've sorted things out about this property of yours, Corin.'

Ten minutes later, the back door opened and two people slipped inside.

James went across to greet the woman and clasp her hand in both his. 'Rani, my dear friend. Great to see you again.'

'It's been a while. Nice to see you too, Corin. Can we do our catching up another time, though, and get straight down to making plans? We need to act quickly on this.'

Lucia studied her with interest. She was of medium height, dwarfed by the three men, had short, iron-grey hair and was smartly dressed, though in clothes suitable for forays into moonlit woods. A pair of night goggles was now hanging from a cord round her neck. There was an air of authority about her that wasn't due to the expensive clothes, however; it came from inside and she was obviously a natural leader.

Lucia silenced her thoughts and paid full attention as Rani took charge.

'You haven't discussed anything with your friends yet, James?'

'No, not yet. Well, I didn't have the full picture.'

'Liam is going to keep watch outside with another guy while I explain, electronically as well as literally.'

Her companion nodded and went out, moving quietly and making no sound as he opened and closed the door.

'We have identified a group of criminals dealing mainly in financial matters at a major international level. They're quite prepared to kill to get rid of any opposition so we have to take care how we go.'

This was greeted with dead silence, then Lucia asked, 'How does this concern us?'

'Your local estate agent is working with them and they're targeting Corin's land and perhaps considering the land next door, expecting the combination to be much more lucrative to developers. This is one of their minor projects but is connected to something else they're targeting. They're about to put more serious pressure on you to sell it back to Begworth, Corin.'

'I've already refused to sell and I shan't change my mind about that.'

'Be very careful from now on. These people don't necessarily accept refusals.'

'Excuse me, but is this worth the involvement of someone at your level, Rani? This land can't be a major project.'

'As I said, it has certain connections that make it particularly attractive.'

'Can I ask what?'

'I'll explain in a minute.'

Lucia clutched Corin's arm, couldn't help it.

Rani turned to Lucia. 'Your stalker is getting in the way of our operation, Ms Grey, so we need to deal with him quickly. Can I ask what happened in Bristol today?'

They explained and she frowned. 'Do you think what you've done will stop him?'

'No. But it'll make him hesitate and he usually waits till the weekend to act anyway. He's had no absences from work for years and is quite obsessive about that.'

Another pause, then Rani said, 'Hmm. We'll leave him out of it for the moment, then. Would you three be prepared to assist us?'

Corin took over. 'I'm still wondering why you're putting this much effort into my problem.'

Rani looked at James as if asking him something.

He said quietly, 'We've both known Corin for years and he hasn't changed. I trust him absolutely.'

She considered this for a moment then said, 'Important as your land problem is, Corin, there's a major worry here on site that could affect national security. We don't want these people poking their noses into what's been left inside your mound, Corin.'

All three of them stared at her in surprise.

After a slight hesitation, she continued, 'Due to a sudden death at the MOD a few years ago, the air raid shelter wasn't cleared out properly when the last group stopped working here. Certain items should have been removed from it before the land was put on the market.'

Corin asked what his friends were thinking. 'That's important even all these years since the war?'

'Yes. Very important scientifically because one project was continued there, which is why we kept the place for so long. I can't give you any more details than that. You'll have to take my word about its importance. We're hoping you'll pretend to employ some agents from our team as security guards for a while, Mr Drayton. They can keep an eye on the situation and act as necessary.'

'I'm happy to oblige in any way.'

'Good. We'll post concealed guards on your property as well as the visible ones, but we don't want anyone seeing them arrive and we can't give them camping gear, so I hope you'll let them into your houses.'

Lucia intervened. 'I think Maggie would be happy to put some of them up, if that's any help. She has plenty of rooms.'

'We'll be keeping an eye on her house as well. And you should stay at Larch House while this is going on, Lucia. And it's a kind offer, but the hidden guards are more likely to be needed here. But we'll still leave a couple of our people at Larch House. The whole thing could be very dangerous.'

She explained the general plans, then she and Liam left.

Corin turned to Lucia. 'I'll take you home straight away. You will do as she asks and stay there till we've sorted this out, won't you?'

Lucia nodded. She knew her limitations.

By the time he got back, two men had turned up 'to keep an eye on things', though Rani had said she didn't expect anything to happen that night.

To his relief it didn't. He wished he could get Lucia right away from here, but even if she'd agree, she didn't seem to have anywhere else to go.

Surely she and Maggie would be safe at Larch House with two guards looking after them from tomorrow onwards?

The trouble was, this was major crime, not break-ins and burglary.

In the morning, Maggie insisted on sending food down for the others' breakfast so Lucia took it there.

'Do you want me to go and stock up on food at that little supermarket?' she asked Corin.

'Good idea. And bring plenty of bottled water for our guests. The tap water isn't clear yet.'

He paused, then shook his head. 'Don't shop locally this time, much as I'd like to support those shops. If anyone sees you, they'll be surprised at how much you're buying for just yourself and Maggie. Can you go to that big shopping centre just outside the valley and do your buying there, perhaps even in two lots? Take some blankets to cover things with.'

'Of course.'

'We won't unload most of the stuff from your car till after dark, however, except for a box of bottled water and one of food.'

Soon after she'd left, a man in the security uniform of a big national company arrived, coming in openly by car.

'The rest of the crew will be here after dark, coming cross country on foot,' he told them. 'Rani thought it'd look strange not to have someone on duty near the entrance and the others will need some sleep, so I'm it. I don't guarantee to repel an invading army, though.' He laughed at his own joke, looking like a benevolent uncle, though his eyes were shrewd and watchful.

'Do you have any idea of what to expect when they come?' James asked.

'No, but the boss is guessing it'll be skilled personnel to deal with what's in that mound of yours.'

Which showed, Corin thought, that this chap was more senior than his uniform implied.

Later in the day, a young couple who looked very much in love knocked on Maggie's back door quite openly and asked if she had a room to rent.

When she hesitated, they identified themselves in a whisper as hired to keep watch on her house, so she let them in and found them a room.

'It's feeling very strange,' she whispered to Lucia when her friend returned from shopping.

'I agree. And I don't like it at all.'

'Me neither.'

'I worry about Corin.'

'If anyone knows how to look after himself, it's your Corin.'

'Do you think he is?'

'Is what?'

'My Corin.' She could feel herself blushing slightly.

'I've no doubt whatsoever about that.'

'I don't know how I got so lucky.'

That afternoon, Don received a text from Gustav suggesting he eat dinner at the Essington pub and stay there till closing time. And he was not to get drunk.

His heart clenched and he wondered what they were planning to do, couldn't help worrying about it. Somehow he didn't dare ask his so-called friend for details, because you could only go so far with Gustav. By now Don was more than a little afraid of what he'd got himself into.

Don's wife saw him come into the pub on his own, but when he looked across at her and hesitated, as if wondering whether to join them, she turned her back on him.

He sagged visibly, as if upset, and went to sit alone.

Linda turned to her friend Kathy, who was dining there with her. 'Try not even to catch Don's eye. I'm not having him joining us.'

'Things that bad between you now?'

'Yes. He just gets worse with keeping and I don't trust him at all these days. He's got something going on and I don't know what. I'm going to the ladies'. Won't be long.'

When she was on her own in a cubicle, she phoned Nina and asked her to let Lucia or Corin know that she thought something was going on that night from the nervousness Don was showing. 'I don't have their personal phone numbers and I think this might be urgent.'

'I'll do it but tell me more about why you say that?'

'Don rarely uses this pub and he's just about twitching with nerves. What's more, he only bought a shandy. He normally likes to get well sozzled when he does come here because he can walk, or rather stagger home afterwards.'

'OK. I'll pass it on.'

'Do it straight away, will you, please?'

'Yes, of course. Is there a reason you can't ring them yourself if I give you the number?'

'I'm worried Don might be keeping tabs on who I call. Please. Do it quickly.'

It was the best she could do. She had to leave it to the officials now.

When she got back to her seat, she saw Don finish ordering a meal at the counter then look her way again. She scowled and he went back to the far side of the room and sat by himself at a small corner table, watching the people around him. People from the village nodded to him but they didn't join him or invite him to join them.

After a while, he got out his phone and began to fiddle with it.

She sneaked glances across the room at regular intervals and saw him pick at his food and push half of it aside to be cleared away. That wasn't like him, either. He was normally a very hearty eater and was getting quite a belly on him.

Don made two pints of shandy last him all evening. That was so unlike him, she felt even more worried. She could only pray that Nina had got through to Lucia and the nice guy she had hooked up with.

Corin called in at Larch house briefly because he thought if anyone was watching what he was doing, they'd expect him to do that. And anyway, he needed a kiss and a big hug.

Lucia didn't seem to mind providing them at all.

When Nina rang just then and passed the message on to Lucia, she suggested Nina speak to Corin directly and passed her phone to him.

He listened, asked a couple of questions then ended the call.

'It only confirms what Rani said: there is something being planned for tonight. I'm going to go back to my house now.'

'I wish I could come with you.'

'Not wise. You aren't trained in combat and I won't be able to protect myself properly if I'm taking care of you as well.'

She hated to agree with him about that, but he was right. 'Very well. At least Howard isn't likely to turn up tonight, it being mid-week, so I'll be all right here at Larch House.'

'With Rani's two young officers posted there, you should be safe even if he does turn up.'

After he left, she felt quite sick with apprehension for his safety but she knew he was right about her staying here being the best course.

'We'll come through this,' Maggie said quietly after she'd locked the back door behind him.

At intervals, one of the young guards went out to patrol the grounds near Larch House; the other stayed with Maggie and Lucia.

They were both very alert at all times.

Chapter Twenty-Two

Howard sat fretting in his office the day after the fiasco, unable to settle to work. His fury at Lucia and her lover for stealing his beloved Bentley simply wouldn't subside. No one drove it without his permission, no one at all!

Did they think that would stop him acting against her? If so, they were as stupid as the rest of the world.

In the end he went to his manager and claimed a sudden onset of a headache and flu-like symptoms. 'I'm sorry and I hate to let you down, but I can't seem to concentrate, so I think I'd better go home.'

'You don't look yourself, I must admit. There's a bad virus going round. My cousin's had it, was off work for a week. You're quite right to go home. We don't want to spread it round the office. Don't come back until you're sure you're fully recovered. Heaven knows you've never taken a day's sick leave before, so you must be feeling bad.'

That remark added another layer of anger. Lucia would regret spoiling his record of never missing a day at work as well.

He went home and packed some special little tools that

would help him get into that big house without making a noise. It had such clumsy old locks it'd be easy. Then he fretted to and fro in his unit until it was time to get ready to leave.

Feeling a sense of relief that he could now do something else to pay her back and make her realise she wouldn't get away without giving him the rest of the money he was entitled to, he changed into his dark clothes and set off in time to arrive at Essington well after night had fallen.

He parked his car on the upper part of Larch Tree Lane, not in the car park, facing downwards, ready for a quick escape if necessary. Then he smiled and set off up the hill towards the drive that wasn't used. He was delighted to see the car belonging to that tall chap parked outside the house closest to the road on the block of land next to the old hag's estate. Good. That fellow wouldn't be able to interfere this time.

When he reached the upper drive, he relaxed a little and stopped to listen in case anyone was prowling around. He'd do that every few minutes from now on. You couldn't be too careful. As he walked along it, he kept to the shadows, of which there were plenty.

If he managed to reach her without being spotted, he might take her outside and allow himself to slap her around a bit. She richly deserved it and if he left her tied up, he'd be long gone and safely in bed before daylight and people started to look for her.

Just before eleven o'clock, four men slipped through the woods from the patch of untended shrubs and trees on the far side of the Marrakin from Larch House.

They were good at moving through the woods, but not one of them noticed the two people following them, who were even better at it.

The followers sounded the warning buzzers in their pockets to alert James and Corin to the new arrivals, and did the same to the rest of their own group, who were in locations between the various old houses.

'It's begun,' James said quietly when he heard his phone buzz. 'Let's hope everyone on our side stays safe.' Corin and the guard who'd stayed inside with them nodded.

Five minutes later, two buzzes in quick succession signalled that the intruders were getting close and would shortly be taken out by the men waiting for them.

As he waited, Corin felt that inner silence settle on him that always came before a fight and listened calmly to the yells of shock and anger that suddenly erupted outside.

He and James had been warned not to join in and to leave it to the professionals but had insisted on making a few preparations of their own inside. Their in-house guard had made them wear stab-proof vests, which they didn't mind, but they liked to be better prepared than that.

The guard had simply shrugged at what they were doing, clearly not believing their efforts would be needed. He looked rather scornful of their primitive, old-fashioned tactics too.

Suddenly James said, 'I heard a sound from the front of the house.'

All three of them froze.

'They're probably making a two-pronged attack,' James whispered. 'Are they after us as well or just diverting attention from the mound?'

Their guard was looking anxious. 'I don't think even Rani expected them to put so many people into an attack on this place. Why is that mound so important?'

Corin shot a quick glance at James. Their guard mustn't know what was concealed there either.

Then a small explosion blew open the front door and debris rained down inside the house. James dived for the stairs.

Their in-house guard was already speaking on the phone and fumbling for his gun when Corin said, 'Upstairs, now!' and took him by surprise, dragging him up after James as the debris began to settle.

Corin and James got to the top of the stairs and peered down, then retreated to the main bedroom, again dragging their guard with them. The two of them weren't armed with guns of any sort and they were worried that their attackers might be.

'I have to stay here on the landing,' the guard protested in a low voice.

'Not yet.'

They waited behind the slightly open bedroom door as an intruder appeared and began to creep up the stairs, followed by another. At a suitable moment, James triggered the booby trap they'd prepared and some heavy old lawn bowls he'd found in the cellar cascaded from a net overhead at the top. It was a childish trick but enough to take the intruders by surprise and make them struggle to keep their footing.

One of their attackers, crouching low, was taken by surprise because while he was avoiding one heavy ball, another one hit him on the head as it bounced sideways off the wall. It was heavy enough to send him tumbling down the stairs and he let out an involuntary cry of pain as he landed at the bottom.

James and Corin threw a blanket with weighted corners over the remaining attacker before he'd had time to recover his full balance. 'We've got him. Get the other!' Corin yelled at their guard.

He was already moving swiftly and clicked some handcuffs on the man now groaning in agony at the bottom of the stairs. It was obvious why he was making no attempt to get away because his leg was twisted to one side at an unnatural angle.

'Bit of luck, that,' James said.

'Boy's Own stuff, but it still works sometimes.' Corin smiled in satisfaction.

No one else attempted to come into the house and the yells from outside grew fainter and faded into the distance. It was a while, however, before the captain in charge came to join them.

'We've rounded most of them up. A few of the sods got away, but we won't be long catching them.'

Then he saw the two men handcuffed to the bannisters and beamed at his subordinate. 'Well done, Bill.'

'These two did it, not me,' the guard said. 'You wouldn't believe how well a simple, old-fashioned trap can work. I've never seen the like.'

James grinned. 'I've had a lot of years in primitive places to practise my skills and have worked with Corin here before.'

The leader stared at him. 'Corin? Not Corin Drayton?'

'I'm afraid so.'

'I didn't realise it was you we were trying to defend.'

'I'd rather not publicise my name or past activities, if you don't mind, because I want to settle permanently in the valley and lead a quieter life from now on.'

'OK. But it's great to meet you. I very much admired the way you saved those people.'

Corin shrugged helplessly. He never knew what to say to that sort of admiring comment.

'Well, let's take these guys to join the others. We'll have to carry that one.'

Corin voiced some doubts. 'Look, I'm wondering if this attack was more of a diversion. Did any of them get through to the mound?'

'Don't worry. We had more people hidden there.'

'Must be important.'

'Oh, it is, believe me.'

'I reckon they'll have a back-up plan to save some of their financial investments in this mess. Their effort was a bit disappointing, really,' James said. 'I'd have thought they'd employ people more skilled than this.'

'From what I heard in our briefing, they haven't usually been reduced to physical means of attack. It's probably their weak spot. They must have been desperate even to try it.'

'The rewards would have been huge if they'd got inside the mound and found what's stored there. It'd fetch a lot of money.'

James let out a loud, aggrieved sigh. 'Is anyone ever going to tell us what's hidden there? We're good guys too, remember.'

'Sorry. It's so highly classified I doubt it. The stuff was

thought to have been cleared out years ago.'

Corin exchanged frustrated glances with James.

Then he thought of Lucia and said, 'I need to check that my lass is all right.'

'Don't go on your own.'

'No, mama!' Corin mocked.

Howard approached Larch House carefully, seeing no sign of lights inside it. He went round to the library, which he'd noted when reconnoitring and planned to use as his entry point. There was no sign of anyone moving around inside. Well, there wasn't likely to be at this late hour.

He used his special set of adaptable keys to unlock the door and crept inside, pausing for a moment to make sure there was still no movement on the ground floor and leaving the door slightly ajar.

As he made his way through the darkened rooms, he memorised their pattern carefully. If he had to run for it, he wanted to get out quick smart.

He found a kitchen and other rooms at the back, then decided he'd risk going upstairs.

As he got halfway up, he heard a faint sound and turned to see someone standing at the bottom of the stairs. Oh, hell!

Something hit the back of his head just as he started to move and ironically the missile was what saved him, because it bounced off into the face of the guy coming up towards him. That gave him time to leap over the handrail and down to the hall floor, only to cannon into another person, who began to yell for someone to help her.

Again, luck was with him and after a very brief struggle he managed to tear himself free and run across to the library and out of the door.

Outside, he saw another figure approaching so veered to one side and managed to run into the woods, intending to exit via the path he'd used on a previous visit.

His heart was pounding madly. They were chasing after him, he could hear them, and he didn't know if he could continue to outrun them, but he had to get away, had to.

Suddenly, as he was nearly at the spot where the stone wall between the two pieces of land began, a man came out of nowhere.

He tried to avoid him but suddenly there was a sharp pain in his head and the world blurred around him as he started falling helplessly.

'That sod must have broken away from the main pack,' the man said. 'Lock him up with the others.'

Howard felt dizzy, couldn't seem to think straight. He tried to protest but was told to shut up or they'd gag him and was so terrified he did that, they looked so fierce.

Don's phone rang as he was leaving the pub at closing time. He tugged it quickly out of his pocket. A voice he recognised said, 'Sit in your car till we give you the all-clear.'

It seemed a long time before the phone rang again and Gustav said, 'You can go home now.' His tone was icy, quite unlike the way he normally chatted, and the sharp edge of command it now carried made Don shiver, for some weird reason.

'What happened?'

'Never mind that. Just listen carefully. Do not try to touch your secondary investments tonight. I need to move them to safety. Just go straight to bed and stay there till morning.'

The connection was cut and he was left staring at his phone.

He stole a quick glance across the car park and to his horror saw that his wife was sitting in her car with some other female and was watching him like a raptor with prey in view. Why hadn't he noticed them before?

He shivered again. When she was angry, Linda could be vicious and persistent. To hell with Gustav's instructions. He needed to get out of the country for a while, and away from *her*. For that he definitely needed to take out some of his emergency savings, because he'd had a bit of bad luck with the horses lately.

Decision taken, he started the car and headed for home. She'd better keep to her bedroom when she got back. He had no time to bother with her now.

Linda watched him drive away, then turned to Kathy. 'I don't want to go home to him. I've never seen him look quite so . . . vicious.'

'Why don't we go back to my flat? My spare bedroom is at your disposal for as long as you feel you need it.'

'Thanks. I think I'll take you up on that for a couple of nights.'

'I'll even lend you a nightie and—' Kathy began, hesitated then admitted, 'I didn't like the look on his face either. Scrub using my flat. There's no one else living in the nearby units at the moment. Let's go to my cousin's house.

She'll not mind and she's surrounded by people who'll come running if we have to shout for help.'

'He won't be able to follow us there. Thank you.'

She had never before been physically afraid of Don, but she was tonight.

Chapter Twenty-Three

At head office, Rani sat at her computer and followed the reports coming in about what was going on. Something wasn't right about this raid on the Marrakin.

She hadn't expected the intruders to be so easily defeated, not when you considered that her opponents' skill had enabled them to elude capture by her people for two whole years.

She told those watching the mound to be double careful. They were a good team and like her they were puzzled at how poorly the raid on the houses had been executed and now, all of a sudden, their computer program wasn't working as expected.

She didn't often follow an impulse but she did tonight, ordering the IT squad to execute their back-up plan ahead of time. Heaven help her if she was wrong. This was undeniably risking discovery.

Then the locally based crim logged into an account, something they hadn't expected but which was good news.

She looked across the room and didn't let herself smile at the excitement on her newest recruit's face. That lass was highly promising, had several times surprised them by a maverick approach that worked.

'I think your instructions are being diverted and tampered with, ma'am,' the young officer said. 'We may have a traitor among us. But luckily for us, they seem to have an outlier who isn't following the others' pattern of behaviour. I think I can—' She broke off to work furiously.

'*What?*' Rani couldn't think straight for a moment, this was so astonishing.

'I know a manoeuvre that will circumvent this intervention and track down this outlier, ma'am. Shall I apply it?'

So Rani took a second chance that day and said, 'Yes. Quick as you can.'

Don went home and switched on his computer, glad now that he hadn't been drinking tonight. He counted two pints of shandy consumed over the course of a whole evening as going teetotal.

He logged in then took a deep breath and opened his special account. He couldn't take much out but the way the program was set allowed him to take some in an emergency.

The account seemed to take a long time to come up and when he looked at it, he blinked his eyes. Something was wrong. There was nothing in the account, except for a measly $100 US. What was going on?

He picked up the phone to ring his friend but when he pressed the pre-set button, he got a message which said that this phone account had been discontinued.

He went through each procedure all over again, unwilling to believe what the messages were telling him.

No wonder Gustav had told him not to touch that account. They must have hacked into it to clear it out completely.

As he sat back, a sick chill ran through him. He'd been robbed. And he couldn't complain to the police because the account had contained the results of illicit procedures and he'd wind up in jail if he brought it to the attention of the authorities.

He stood up and began to walk round the house, moaning and cursing, then he went out and got into his car, unable to bear being shut up indoors with his useless regrets.

He set off, driving into the countryside, going anywhere at all, unable to escape his unhappy thoughts and the knowledge that he was a ruined man.

He couldn't even touch the accounts he shared with Linda, because he needed her with him at the local bank to do that and he knew without telling that she'd not allow him to take anything out of their operating capital. And you couldn't quickly access the value of a rental property. You had to sell it first.

Without thinking, he yelled aloud in mental agony and pressed down on the accelerator. He didn't even see the lorry that was driving along the main road as he turned onto it without looking.

He didn't see the wall into which the big vehicle tossed his car, either. After that, he was beyond seeing anything again.

Cars stopped, the lorry driver got out of his cab, but

before anyone could get to Don's car, it exploded into a mass of flame and the spectators moved quickly back from it.

'I've called the police,' someone called.

'Poor sod,' a woman muttered.

'Stupid sod,' a man said scornfully. 'He must have been drunk to drive like that. Good thing he didn't take anyone else out with him.'

When Howard regained consciousness, he was lying on a bed in what looked like a hospital room. He tried to sit up and discovered that his arm was clamped to a rail at the side of the bed by a pair of handcuffs.

'What happened?' he muttered, trying to find his way through the fog in his brain.

'You were seen breaking into a house,' a voice said. 'Then you were caught running away from it.'

He turned to see a very young police officer sitting beside the bed.

When a sound made him look the other way, he saw a nurse come in and study a flickering monitor next to the bed.

'I'll get the doctor to check him first, but he seems to be recovering fast.' She cast a disapproving look in Howard's direction. 'He's lucky he escaped with only light concussion. I can't abide thieves.'

'I'm not a thief!' he protested.

'Only because you were chased away before you could steal anything,' the young officer said. 'The rest of your gang is in the lock-up, which is where you're going to join them as soon as the doctor releases you.'

'Someone was chasing me,' Howard protested. 'I was trying to get away from them. I'm *not* a thief. And I'm not a member of any gang, either.'

'Shut up.'

Half an hour later, he was wheeled out to a police vehicle and locked in the back of it.

'I want a lawyer!' he'd pleaded several times but in vain. What was going on? Surely you were entitled to a lawyer?

Things got even worse after that. To his horror, he was shut in a large cell which only had seats round the edges. Four other men were in it already.

'Here's another of your friends,' the sergeant who'd brought him in said.

'He's not one of ours,' one of the seated figures protested. 'Never seen him before in my life.'

'He was caught in the same raid, in the grounds of the same house. Why would anyone else be there at that time of night but your lot?' He gave Howard a poke in the back with a very hard fingertip. 'Go on! Get out of the wheelchair and sit down over there.'

'I'm not sitting down with criminals,' Howard protested.

'Stand up, then.' He left the cell with the wheelchair and locked the door behind him, then pushed it away along the corridor and banged another door shut behind him at the far end of it.

Howard stared at the four hostile faces in panic.

'Be careful who you're calling criminals,' one of them said in a low voice.

Howard shivered and pressed himself back against the bars of the cell door.

It was at exactly that moment that he remembered where

he'd seen that guy's face and what he was called. Drayton. Corin Drayton. Hailed as a hero for saving the lives of a group of women and children in some tiny godforsaken country no one had ever heard of before. Given an award by the queen herself.

Oh, hell. The man was famous for his self-defence skills. If he ever got out of here, Howard wasn't going near that bitch again. She'd certainly found herself a good protector, damn her to high hell.

He *would* get out of here. He wasn't a criminal, as would surely be proved. This was just a glitch.

He fainted at the hearing when it was ordered that he be detained in custody in a special high-security holding house, couldn't believe what was happening to him.

Which caused his new companions to mock him when they were back in custody.

He had never been as frightened of anything in his life as he was of being shut up in close quarters with them.

If he got out of here, no, *when* he got out of here, he was retiring. The world had gone crazy and swept him along with it.

Lucia knew perfectly well who it was they'd chased away from her house but pretended to the woman who interviewed her in the small hours of the morning that she hadn't been able to see him clearly. The last thing she intended to do was identify her ex. Let him stew in custody. She smiled at the mere thought of finicky, fussy Howard going through all those indignities. Serve him right.

She was wondering whether to follow Maggie's example and go to bed when there was the sound of a car outside.

When she peeped out of the window, she saw Corin get out of the passenger seat and her heart gave a little leap of happiness.

'It's my partner,' she told the man guarding her.

She didn't wait for his answer, but flung open the back door. When Corin stopped and held out his arms, she ran towards him and into his embrace, which was turning into one of her favourite ways of saying hello.

'Are you all right? They said you'd had an intruder up here.'

She whispered, 'It was Howard but I pretended I hadn't recognised him and he ran off through the woods. Apparently the police arrested him and took him away with some other intruders.'

He let out a splutter of laughter which turned into a great big belly laugh. 'He'll be put in jail with them, then. Poor man. I almost feel so sorry for him. Almost, but not quite.' He gave a dismissive wave towards the car and James waved back and drove off.

Then Corin wrapped one arm round her and they walked into the kitchen. He stopped to smile at the guard. 'Do you need us for anything or can we go to bed?'

'I don't need you. They've used drones and heat sensors to check the woods and there's no one else wandering round. Didn't you hear the helicopter flying over them?'

'No. I was too busy chatting to the leader of your team. He wants to see me when it's daylight, so I need to get some sleep after I've finished explaining to my fiancée what happened.'

'You can relax all you like. I'll still be keeping watch but there won't be any other intruders. They've just caught the last one.' He walked away into the hall.

Lucia looked at Corin. 'That's the most unromantic proposal of marriage that I've ever heard of. But I accept.'

'Good. Let's go up to your bedroom and I'll propose again on one knee with my right hand pressed against my heart, if you want.'

'Come upstairs. This I have to see.'

She saw the guard giving them a sentimental smile from the hall doorway and she felt herself smile too.

'Did you mean it?' she asked as she closed the bedroom door.

'Very much. It just came out. Seemed right.'

'It seems right to me too, Corin. Especially now.'

He laughed abruptly. 'I wish I could see Howard in jail. They won't easily let him out if he was caught in that sweep of the grounds.'

'Good riddance.' She sat down on the bed and a yawn escaped her. 'Sorry. I'm the one being unromantic now but I'm exhausted.'

'I'm not surprised. We'll seal our bargain in the usual way when we have a bit more privacy. Apart from anything else, Rani wants to see me, James and you about that mound early tomorrow morning.'

'Let's lie down and cuddle. That'll seal our bargain well enough for the moment.'

He was so big and warm, she nestled against him – and woke because he was shaking her gently.

'What? I thought we were going to sleep.'

'We did sleep. Good thing I set my watch to wake me, sleepyhead. It's morning. Grab a quick shower and we'll go and see Rani. No one willingly keeps that lady waiting.'

Maggie joined them. 'I've got some breakfast ready but we'll take it down to James, shall we?' She didn't wait for their answer but lifted a huge basket into the back of the car and got in beside it.

They found James at the house, also looking weary. 'I needn't have driven back here after I left you. I didn't get much sleep.' He yawned. 'I have to grab a quick cup of coffee before we leave or I'll fall asleep again standing up.'

Maggie joined them. 'I'll make the coffee while you three gobble down a scone or two. I made a few yesterday.'

They all beamed at her.

'Actually, I'm ravenous,' Lucia said in surprise.

'Well, we didn't get much chance to eat yesterday, did we?' Corin replied.

Maggie paused for a moment to stare at Lucia and Corin. 'Is it my imagination or is there a glow to you two?'

'We got engaged last night,' Corin said. 'After the most unromantic proposal you've ever heard of. I'm ashamed of myself for doing it so badly.'

But he didn't look ashamed as he beamed at his fiancée.

'It's what you said that matters, not how you said it,' Lucia told him softly.

'I know you're wanting to talk lovey-dovey, but you'd better hurry up and eat something,' James said. 'Rani rarely parts with information unless it's prised out of her but I'm determined to find something out about that mound of yours.'

They had to park on the verge and walk up to the first house, threading their way past several large dark vehicles with tinted windows parked close to it.

A young man who was clearly an aide didn't bother to greet them as they walked up to the front door, just opened the door and said, 'The boss is waiting for you.'

They found Rani in what had been the bare living room area, but which now contained a few office chairs and two modern desks.

Lucia blinked in surprise at the sight of them. This had all been done during the last part of the night while they were sleeping.

Rani stood up to greet them, smiling. 'How are you? I hope you got some refreshing sleep. I certainly didn't.'

There was the grumbling roar of large machinery and she gestured to the rear of the house. 'We're digging out the entrance to the old air raid shelter. I took your permission for granted, I'm afraid, Corin, though I can make it official if necessary.'

'Feel free to do whatever it takes.'

'Thank you. We'll make good any damage before we leave.' She hesitated. 'I suppose you deserve some sort of an explanation. I can only offer you the condensed version, though.' She cocked her head on one side.

They waited.

'The Marrakin was used as a rather special research and development station during World War Two, as you may have guessed, and some of the work was carried on afterwards, it was so important. It wasn't the sort of thing anyone wanted to fall into hostile hands, so when it was decided to move everything to a more modern facility and close the place down, it was all done very quietly.'

'Must have been rather a delicate operation.'

'Chemical weapons have to be guarded very carefully indeed.'

That made them both stare at her.

'I can't give you any further details, you'll understand why. When the officer in charge died suddenly, everyone thought from his paperwork that the necessary work had already been carried out and there was only the tidying-up to do, so the mound was closed and covered over. Turns out there was a further room at the rear containing rather important material.'

She stared into space for a moment or two, then said, 'It's only recently come to light that not everything was brought out, but the new officer in charge went on holiday and the property was sold rather suddenly. A chapter of errors which will *not* be repeated when dealing with that sort of material again if I have my way.'

Her voice and expression were suddenly so steely that she could have been a different person, then she gradually relaxed a little.

'The place will have to be completely cleared out and checked before it can be returned to you, Corin.'

'Do what you have to. I'm hoping you won't cover the mound up again though. It'll save me some money if you don't.'

'You can discuss details with the site foreman after it's all been cleared. Tell him what you want. And that, I'm afraid, is all I can tell you.'

'It's enough. I find it amazing how the ramifications of World War Two are still having an effect all these decades later,' James said.

'Let's pray we never have another war on such a scale again.'

They all murmured agreement.

Rani's tone changed to conversational. 'Just satisfy my curiosity before I let you go, would you, Corin? What are you going to do with this land?'

'Build some houses for people with money and a desire for a peaceful life in the country. I'll make it as eco-friendly as possible, but also as attractive as I can make the dwellings. That'll definitely be for the richer type of person. However, I plan to build a few smaller units for deserving people who are poor financially but rich in skills, artists and such. I can afford that.'

'Lucky you. And the original air raid shelter? What happens to that building? It's a bit of a lump to remove.'

'I have a few ideas but nothing concrete. Maybe a café or a small museum to give people an experience of wartime conditions. This is a tourist area, after all. I'm definitely not going to demolish it. The younger generations need to know what things were like, what people put up with in an all-out war. And I know a young woman who is itching to run a café and try out some of her special healthy recipes. I'll get in touch with her when everything settles down.'

Rani slowly nodded her head. 'Good idea. I'll let you know when we've finished with it. Please don't try to get into the mound until then.'

When the three of them walked outside, they moved slowly.

'I need a few nights' proper sleep and I might start after I've fed my face,' James said.

The other two nodded and smiled at one another.

He rolled his eyes. 'I'm going back to Larch House in my own car. You two lovebirds need some time on your own now, I think.'

'I think we need a good sleep more than anything.' Corin took Lucia's hand and raised it to his lips. 'I'm exhausted.'

'So am I. But happy.' In her turn, she raised his hand to her lips. 'We'll go back to Larch House as well. I think I can manage to stay upright till I crawl into that wonderful bed again.'

He pretended to be upset. 'Now who's being romantic?'

'I had fancy romantic gestures once. Now I want sincerity and normal life.'

'I can promise you that, my love.'

Epilogue

The bride was so nervous, she wiped off her crooked lipstick and gave up the effort to wear any. 'I can't keep my hand steady.'

Maggie smiled at her. 'You have good colour in your lips anyway and he'll love you just as much without lipstick. Come down and join your parents. They seem to have got over their jetlag now.'

'Fancy them flying back from Australia just for the wedding.'

'They were worried you were making another mistake.'

Lucia turned a glowing smile on her. 'I'm not. Corin is wonderful. And they get on really well with him.'

'That's great, then, so calm down.'

'When the fuss is all over.'

After a quick glance in the mirror, the groom said, 'Hurry up! I don't want to keep her waiting.'

James took him by the shoulders and gave him a little shake. 'She won't run away, you know that, and we've got plenty of time to get to the wedding venue. Now, let me redo your tie for you and stop worrying! You're looking great.'

'I don't know why I agreed to all this fancy stuff.'

'Because your friends weren't going to let you get away with a hurried wedding and wanted to celebrate with you.'

Corin took a deep breath. 'I'd still rather have sneaked away and got married in peace, then had a party afterwards.'

When he walked out into the lobby of the fancy hotel where they were staying, Corin managed – most of the time – to talk sense to his friends and family. But he kept looking round.

James grabbed his arm. 'She's meeting you there, remember. It's bad luck to see her before the ceremony. Ah! Your limo is here. Thank goodness.'

When they got to the wedding venue, Corin strode inside, looking round for Lucia.

James whispered something to one of their friends, who grinned and hurried off.

'Come on, Corin. We need to get into our places.' James took the groom's arm and didn't let go till he had him standing in position.

And then Lucia came into the room and Corin's tension vanished. His face lit up with joy and he held out his hand as she moved towards him.

James gave a happy nod and stepped back. It was delightful to see their love shining so brightly.

'You look beautiful, my darling,' Corin said.

'And you are the most adorable man in this room.' She

took the hand he was holding out and they stood smiling at one another.

'If you're ready?'

'What? Oh, sorry.' But Corin kept hold of her hand.

They turned to face the celebrant and when it was all over and they were married, they walked out in such a glow of happiness that people murmured, 'Aww!' as they passed.

The wedding meal was excellent but neither of them ate much or noticed what they were putting into their mouths.

They didn't pay much attention to the speeches either, kept smiling at one another, or squeezing hands.

As soon as they could do it politely, they slipped away from the fuss to start the rest of their lives together.

It might be a union forged in fire, as Rani had said once, but they were both utterly certain they would be happy together – utterly, gloriously certain.

ANNA JACOBS was born in Lancashire at the beginning of the Second World War. She has lived in different parts of England as well as Australia, and has enjoyed setting her modern and historical novels in both countries. She is addicted to telling stories and celebrated the publication of her 100th novel (A Valley Wedding) in 2022 and 60 years of marriage to her very best friend and husband in the same year.